A TIMELY DEATH

Janet Neel is the *nom de plume* of Janet Cohen. She lives in north London with her husband and three children. After reading law at Cambridge, she qualified as a solicitor. She spent some time in the USA designing war games, and then returned to London, where she worked first in industrial relations in the construction industry and then, for thirteen years, as an administrator in the Department of Trade and Industry. As well as being a director of Charterhouse Bank, the Yorkshire Building Society, Waddington plc and BPP Holdings plc, she is also a Governor of the BBC.

Janet Neel is the author of *Death's Bright Angel*, which won the 1988 John Creasey Award for the best first crime novel; *Death on Site*; *Death of a Partner*, which was shortlisted for the 1991 Crime Writers' Association Gold Dagger Award; *Death Among the Dons*, which was shortlisted for the 1993 Crime Writers' Association Gold Dagger Award; and *A Timely Death*. As Janet Cohen she has written two highly acclaimed novels, *The Highest Bidder* and *Children of a Harsh Winter*. All of her books are published by Penguin.

A TIMELY DEATH

Janet Neel

PENGUIN BOOKS

PENGUIN BOOKS

Published by the Penguin Group
Penguin Books Ltd, 27 Wrights Lane, London W8 5TZ, England
Penguin Putnam Inc., 375 Hudson Street, New York, New York 10014, USA
Penguin Books Australia Ltd, Ringwood, Victoria, Australia
Penguin Books Canada Ltd, 10 Alcorn Avenue, Toronto, Ontario, Canada M4V 3B2
Penguin Books (NZ) Ltd, 182–190 Wairau Road, Auckland 10, New Zealand

Penguin Books Ltd, Registered Offices: Harmondsworth, Middlesex, England

First published by Constable & Company Ltd 1996
Published in Penguin Books 1997
3 5 7 9 10 8 6 4 2

Printed in England by Clays Ltd, St Ives plc

For my mother and loyal supporter
Mary Neel

1

Thursday, 31 March

Annabelle Brewster sat on a small, uncomfortable high-backed chair and hated everything around her. The high-ceilinged room which must once have been elegant, was now dishevelled and dirty, with ill-drawn children's pictures thumb-tacked up at random, yellow, scarred paint and raw plaster pockmarked with holes. A square of carpet, the design so obscured by dirt and age as to be unintelligible, lay unevenly across dusty, greying floorboards. The room was crowded with humanity and smelled, faintly but distinctly, of feet. Opposite her a small Indian woman in a sari was failing to control three racketing small boys in jeans and anoraks; next to her a large woman in her thirties, feet in slippers, hair hanging lankly, was smoking non-stop and talking at the same time to a patient, weary Jamaican woman.

Annabelle stared straight ahead, reminding herself that if she walked out of this awful place she had nowhere else to go. She straightened her back against the inadequate, creaking chair. The door opened, for the fifth time since she had arrived, revealing a tiny office, occupied by a small, rickety desk, and a woman of the sort she resented: the Young Superwoman type. This was a prime example of the genus: tall and slim in an expensive yellow jacket, good shoes, short, efficient, dark hair, neat gold ear-rings and a pricey black leather briefcase, casually resting on the floor beside her. She looked like the headmistress of Annabelle's expensive boarding-school and she was using the same casual competence to deal with the variety of demands being made of her.

By the time Annabelle was called to the tiny office she was in an incoherent rage with her surroundings and everything about her situation. She got up stiffly and stalked across the room, trying to rise above the bruise which was slowly closing her right eye, the nagging pain in her right shoulder and the chilly sensation of having nothing on her feet but an old down-at-heel pair of court shoes half a size too small for her.

'You're Annabelle?' Superwoman had risen to greet her; as she had feared the woman topped her by a couple of inches and smelt, prosperously, of lily of the valley. 'You've just arrived?'

'I've been here an hour and a half.'

'I'm sorry about that. I'm new, so I'm slow.'

She had a ladder in her tights and the leather heels of her smart shoes were scratched, Annabelle noticed, in a moment of vicious pleasure. The small room was as scruffy and as decorated with pictures by untalented infants as the big room, but a gas fire flared and popped on the wall, and it was warm.

'May I take your coat?'

'I'll keep it on.' Annabelle knew she was sounding churlish and did not care. Superwoman poured her a cup of coffee without asking if she wanted it and she decided to take it rather than throw it down the woman's good jacket.

'Oh dear, I'm afraid you need to see a doctor and I should have done that first. That bump on your head needs looking at.'

'No, it doesn't.'

'Perhaps later.'

'It doesn't anyway.' She put the coffee cup to her lips, drawn by the smell, and tasted it cautiously. It was thick with sugar, which she normally detested, but she gulped it down and waited, dumb with anger.

'Would you like another coffee? No? My name's Francesca. I'm the duty officer tonight. You need a bed for the night.' It was a statement not a question and Annabelle nodded reluctantly. 'And a bath, and some night clothes?'

'Yes.' It was all she could manage without weeping or screaming.

'There's a small single room as an emergency room, apparently. I mean for people who . . . well . . . who . . .'

'Come in off the street.'

'Indeed. Yes.' Superwoman consulted a piece of paper. 'Is there someone we can ring, or that you would like to ring?'

'If there was I wouldn't be here.'

'No. Quite. Sorry.'

Annabelle, relaxed by seeing that this Francesca was satisfactorily rattled, considered her covertly. Tired and pale with dark circles under the blue eyes, and younger than she had seemed at first too, perhaps only in her early thirties.

'The thing is it's my first night,' Francesca was saying anxiously. 'I'm substituting for a much more experienced person – well, for my Mum, actually. I knew what to do with the people who are already here but I don't seem to have done the right things in the right order for you. Look, shall we just get you to bed and you can explain to someone competent in the morning, or would you like to talk to me and I'll write it down and leave it for the next day's duty officer?'

Annabelle was sufficiently disarmed by this anxious chatter to put her cup out for a refill, and the other woman smiled in relief.

'Mum's a regular, you see. She's been here ever since this refuge opened. But she's got flu and they're short-handed, so I'm doing two of her shifts this week. It turned out to be me or no one.'

'You're a social worker?'

'No. Mum is. I work for a women's college.' She held up the coffee jug enquiringly. 'Yes? What do you do, Annabelle? Blast. Yes, Margaret?'

The large woman who had been in the waiting-room put her head round the door, lank hair dull under the lighting. 'I'm sorry, miss, but de kids in Room J, dere all crying and dey've all got spots.'

'What sort of spots?' Francesca put her coffee cup down unevenly.

'Here, Patrick.' She produced from behind her back a flushed and weeping small boy, aged about six, dressed in faded pyjamas made for an older child. 'Show de lady.'

Annabelle watched as Francesca squatted beside the child Patrick, laddering her tights further, coaxing him to show her the spots then, there's a good lad. Nice with him but useless. She watched as long as she could bear it, then when Patrick started to weep again, got to her feet wincing as the too-small shoes caught the blister they had rubbed. She scooped the child up and sat him on the desk under the only half-way decent light in the room and tilted his head to look as his neck, then felt his forehead. 'Do you have a headache, Patrick?' she asked, as one grown-up to another, and the child stopped grizzling to consider the point.

'A little.'

'Where? Which part of the head?' She flicked his pyjama top up

9

while he was giving the question his best attention and received with due gravity the answer that it was sort of everywhere, miss.

'I want to look at your throat now, please.' She reached round for her coffee spoon and reversed it, holding his tongue down with the shaft. She straightened up, feeling the pain in her ribs, and met Superwoman's interested and respectful regard. 'Patrick has measles, I'm afraid.'

The lank-haired Margaret clasped the child to her so that he started crying again. 'Oh, never say dat, miss. Dey'll *all* have it.'

'I suppose there can be no doubt, Annabelle?'

'No. The spots inside the mouth are definitive for diagnosis.' Francesca rose from the floor, removed the elegant jacket and dispatched Margaret and Patrick back to their room with a promise of attendance and extra blankets.

'Well, what a good thing you were here,' she said briskly, and checked, coffee pot in hand. 'That really *does* come under the heading of things which might have been better put, doesn't it? I *am* sorry, for the third time tonight. Just before I work out what to do about measles – we have over twenty children under this inadequate and leaking roof tonight – let me install you in a bedroom.'

'It's these bloody shoes,' Annabelle heard herself say. 'If I could get something different on my feet, I'd give you a hand.'

'We have a clothing cupboard. It was the second thing they showed me.'

By two in the morning Annabelle was eating egg and bacon in the huge kitchen, cooked by Francesca on one of the five gas stoves arranged in a row along one wall. She pushed her plate away and reached for her mug of tea, narrowly avoiding slopping it over the navy tracksuit, a size too large, somewhat out of shape, and bearing the insignia of a local sports club, in which she was now dressed. Her feet were wreathed in two layers of thick cotton socks and some aged trainers. Her head still ached, but Francesca had given her three Anadins with the tracksuit and the pain had receded.

'I didn't ask. Have you had measles, Francesca?'

'Badly, when I was a child, as I had everything. My own little William has not yet had the injection though.' Francesca was drinking her tea almost solid with sugar, living on borrowed energy, hands dirty, and hair flattened, but retaining her air of competence and command. Of the twenty-three children and sixteen adult women crammed into every corner of the Acton Refuge that night, five children definitely had measles and a further ten had ominous symptoms. Only five of the total child population had been vaccinated so the rest would probably suffer the full rigours of the disease. This was bad enough but, as Annabelle had immediately seen, the worse problem might lie with the adult female population. All the women were here because they had fled, after unbelievably many years of serious ill-treatment at the hands of their men. All, by definition, had lost self-respect, all had neglected themselves and their physical health, and seven of them had lived their childhood abroad, in countries where they had not been exposed to measles. Adult measles was rare in the normal UK population, but serious at any time; in this suffering, uprooted, crowded community it could be devastating.

'Any of the women who get it will have to go to hospital,' Francesca said wearily. 'But it's January. We aren't going to be very welcome in the modern NHS. Still, come the dawn I'll get on to the practice that looks after this place. They're good, but I was under instructions – that was the first thing they told me even before the clothing cupboard – not to call them out unless we had to. They always come at night if someone comes in wounded, and we want to keep it that way. With you here, I was sure we could manage until surgery hours, or that you would tell me if we couldn't.' She poured Annabelle another cup of tea which she gulped thirstily along with the thumping compliment so casually implied.

She sat, quiet, listening to the noises of the house and reflecting on the last few hours, the feverish children, the women in every corner in the house, and the sheer ugly untidiness of the place, with its dirty battered paint, and faded curtains that did not quite fit. The room in which they sat was a case in point; five clean but ancient gas stoves, linoleum, the colour faded beyond recognition, chipped cupboards, piles of mismatched plates and rickety uneven chairs. She took mental refuge in the bright, sparsely furnished bedroom which she and Antony had shared, with the cool, narrow-striped blue duvet cover, and the blue towels in the white and silver bathroom.

'So what brought you here, Annabelle?'

That was what annoyed her so much about Superwomen, she thought, returning reluctantly to the acid yellow walls and

11

chipped plastic table tops of the present reality, they didn't go with the flow, they pushed on, destroying the mood and other people's escapist fantasies. She cast round for a rebuff, but Francesca was apparently concentrating on getting five spoonfuls of sugar into a small mug of tea. Well, she could do that too, so she cut a small slice of bread and proceeded very slowly to wipe up the last morsel of egg from her plate.

'Where did you train?' Francesca asked, as if she had never started on the previous question.

'St Mary's. After Bristol, that was.'

'Are you still there?'

'No. I'm half-way through the GP training. I wanted at first to be a consultant, but . . .' She hesitated. 'The hours were too long and Antony – the person I live with – well . . . it was too difficult.' She gripped the table, daring Francesca to ask why or what was difficult.

'What sort of consultant did you want to be?'

'Oh, a paediatrician. A children's specialist.'

'Why? I mean, do you like children?'

'Not particularly.' She let go of the table in sheer surprise. 'I've never quite said that to myself. But it's not necessary. You can be rather bored by children and still be a good specialist.'

'Indeed. I don't myself like children in the sense that people mean, but I don't think I'm a bad mother. So do you regret giving up?'

Annabelle let herself think, as she had not for over a year, of the ward at St Mary's, and the way that the chronically ill children looked at you, carefully, weighing you up, against their experience of smiling adults bent on carrying out yet another incomprehensible and painful procedure. And when you actually managed to deal with the disease or the defect, how the children forgot instantly that they had ever been ill, and rushed off to their families with joy untouched by any adult perception that the future might hold the same again. She found she could not answer and looked down, feeling tears at the back of her eyes and in her swelling throat.

'Tell me about Antony.'

Still overwhelmed by the realisation of what she had given up, so casually, she talked as if she was by herself, barely noticing Francesca getting up to light one of the ovens so as to get warmth into the kitchen, chilling now in the dead cold before dawn.

'Antony's a doctor too. He was just qualified when I met him. I was in my second year at Bristol and he came down to recruit for the medical school. The university department's got a good name. He's terribly good-looking, and he was so nice; everyone – well, all the girls – wanted to go to St Mary's. Six of us went up to see it and at the end of the tour Antony got me by myself and asked me out.' She stopped to remember that heart-stopping moment. All through the afternoon of visits to clinics and pep talks with harried consultants she had reminded herself that Antony was being nice to everyone in the group, unwilling to let herself hope that such a dazzler was attracted specifically to her. She thought herself not plain exactly, but nondescript; medium-sized, light brown curly hair, ordinary round face. And she had no opinion of her ability to attract wonderful men like Antony. Her admirers had been confined to serious young men typically coming from Yorkshire like herself, having to work hard to hold their place in the department and equally hard to manage on their grants. Antony had seemed like a golden star from another world with his aura of easy success and casual riches and, of course, the looks that drew all eyes.

'What does he look like?' Francesca, elbows on the table, watching her, was as rapt as a child being told a story.

'He's tall. He has dark straight hair and very blue eyes.' She fumbled for a handkerchief, remembering how she had sat, the other side of a small table in San Lorenzo's, entranced by the whole look of him, the vitality, the sheer beauty of the dark hair above the very blue eyes. He had taken his jacket off, asking her permission first as none of the students she knew at Bristol would have done. She had watched the line of his collar against his neck and wanted him as she had never wanted anyone before. He had seen it – well, of course he had – and had called for the bill after their main course and taken her back to his flat. She drew breath sharply, remembering how lovely it had been, totally unlike the brief encounters in cold student bedrooms with young men whose experience was as limited as hers. This was grown-up passion and although she had not then reached orgasm, she still felt the painfully intense physical pleasure from the memory of the long muscular body and the smell of his sweat. And of course, there had been a double bed and clean sheets and a grown-up's kitchen, bathroom, and living-room in refreshing contrast to student hostel single beds and forced camaraderie in grubby kitchens. She came to herself and looked across at Francesca, prepared to storm out of the room, but the other woman's expression was all right, absorbed and sympathetic.

'He was engaged to someone else. He didn't tell me that then, he just said he was going away for Christmas – it was December when we met, did I say? – to stay with his father and stepmother. They spend a lot of the winter in Spain. And when he came back he told me he'd been engaged and had broken it off because he'd met me.' That had seemed to her the final proof that this wonderful good fortune was indeed hers, that things she had been taught to disbelieve as fairy tales *did* come true. It had struck her then that Cinderella might even *really* have got her Prince.

'Very romantic,' Francesca said, and Annabelle looked at her carefully to see if she was mocking, but she wasn't, she was staring at her empty mug, seeing some vision of her own.

'I sometimes think if we'd got married straightaway it would have been all right. But his father was very angry with him for ditching this other girl, and he didn't – doesn't like me much, and he didn't want to offend him.'

Francesca cleared her throat. 'How old were you both at this point?'

'Antony was twenty-five,' she said, defensively. 'He was only just qualified, but his father was quite old, I mean fifty or so. And he is very well off, and Antony didn't want to get cut out of his will, or well, not *unnecessarily*.' She drew breath. 'So we decided to wait.'

'But you didn't in fact marry.'

'No.' She considered, drearily, the five years between. 'No. I went on wanting to but Antony – well, he changed.'

'And started hitting you.'

'Yes.' She sat, unable to lift her eyes or look away from the small island of spilt tea in the middle of the faded, yellow plastic table top.

'Why did you come here? I mean, rather than to parents or friends?'

'My parents are in – well, they're out of London. My father never liked Antony anyway, and liked him less after he decided to leave the NHS.'

'Your father's a doctor?'

'How did you know?' It was awful to have had to confess to

14

anyone, but far worse to contemplate the prospect of her father knowing.

'One half of all medical students have doctors for one or both parents. I read it somewhere.'

Annabelle was distracted. 'So was *his* father. My grandfather.'

'We are all of us,' Francesca said, portentously, 'more creatures of parental influence than we would be willing to acknowledge. *Aaah.*'

'What?' Annabelle shot alarmed to her feet.

'A face. At the window. A man. I know we don't let any of *them* in under any pretext. Mum told me.'

Annabelle, heart thumping, peered at the man who was now standing at some distance from the windows making gestures to indicate that he would come to the door. Antony could not know she was here, she reminded herself.

'It's all right.' Francesca had got her breath back. 'I can parley with him through the speaker-phone.' She headed up the awkward stairs, Annabelle at her heels. 'Who are you? What do you want?' she said intimidatingly into a box, switching on the outside light as she spoke.

'I'm Matthew Sutherland. Your lawyer. You new here or what?'

Francesca, lips compressed, reminding Annabelle even more forcibly of her headmistress, consulted a list by the box. 'What was your mother's maiden name?'

'Jean Macdonald. You want to let me in?'

'Not enormously,' Francesca muttered crossly, 'but I suppose we have to.' She undid three locks and a chain and opened the door cautiously to reveal a young man standing under the light, head tipped so they could see his face. He was dressed in a baseball cap, and several layers of clothes. Four sets of collars appeared to overlap each other at his neck, the whole shrouded in a long heavy overcoat reaching down almost to the top of his industrial-weight black boots.

'I was out clubbing.'

'I see.' Francesca was sounding more like a headmistress by the minute.

'I saw the light, so I thought I'd stop by, see if anything needs to go to court in the morning.'

'You're an Australian?'

'A New Zealander. None of you Brits know the difference, but you'll learn. You want to let me in, or are we going to hold a discussion on nationality on the step?'

'I suppose so. Not, I think, that we have any new customers.' She visibly recollected Annabelle, standing just behind her.

'Have you had measles?' Annabelle asked, adapting to the confrontational conversational style of the house.

'Yes. And chickenpox and German measles, and mumps. And scarlet fever. And nits. *Now* can I come in?'

They opened the door for him and he shut it behind him, putting on all three locks and the chain. He took his coat and a jacket off and hung them over a chair. He was still wearing a black jacket, a waistcoat, an embroidered vest and two immaculate white shirts, in striking contrast to the brutally cut dark red hair revealed as he pulled off the baseball cap. 'Who are you?'

Francesca, to whom the question was addressed, blinked at him. 'I'm tonight's duty officer.'

'All right, let's try it another way. Where do you come from?'

Annabelle leant against the banisters, meanly pleased to see the infinitely competent Francesca being kicked around.

'I am substituting for my mother, Mary Wilson.'

'Ah *Mary*. She's OK.'

'I'm sure she would be gratified by your opinion.'

'Or rather she's OK now we've stopped her doing that middle-class shit. Why is she not here?'

Annabelle decided to intervene. 'She's ill. Why are *you* here?'

'Ambulance chasing – see if I can pick up any customers. *You* look like a potential to me, lady. Who's been hitting you?' He jerked his square chin towards her bruised right eye, silencing her.

'Mr Sutherland, *is* there a legal service in New Zealand, or did you just come here for fun?' Francesca had recovered herself.

'There is, but I wanted to see the world. So I came here.'

'And you could easily have gone somewhere else,' Annabelle suggested, encouraged by Francesca's return to action.

'Not really. My people came from here, or rather from Edinburgh. My great-grandfather was transported to Australia, before you ask. My grandfather moved to New Zealand. We going to do this bit all night, or you got any real business? Where's the log?'

They stared at him and he sighed and leaned over the hall table for a battered book. 'Let's have a look at this lot. OK. De Souza. She's a client. What's she doing back here? I got her an injunction.' He held the book up to the light. 'Illegible bureaucratic hand-

16

writing. Her old man did what? Oh, rang up her employer. He's in breach, stupid sod. I'll get him. I'll ring her in the morning.' He went swiftly through the rest of the list, offering a running commentary and complaining intermittently about the handwriting.

Francesca, Annabelle was interested to see, did not protest but just watched him. And he was well worth watching, Annabelle conceded; sprawled over two chairs, totally at home. He was quick and authoritative, making notes on the names he knew on the evening's list, and taking details of the ones he didn't, who had expressed a desire to see a lawyer, or had been advised to do so. It was like watching a top consultant at work, one of the good ones. He was so concentrated he might as well have been alone in the room, so she was free to consider him: not good-looking, the eyebrows and eyelashes too pale, but an interesting face, with that dark red hair and pale skin patterned with brown freckles, a good square jaw with a deep cleft.

'Get us a coffee, girl, will you?' he said, returning to the world. 'Long night.'

Annabelle rose to do his bidding, but Francesca waved her down and went off to the kitchen herself.

'So what happened to you, kitty?' Matthew Sutherland said, without lifting his eyes from his notes. 'Who gave you that black eye? The boyfriend?'

'Yes.' It was easy to talk to someone who didn't even have all his attention on you.

'Been doing it for long?'

'No. Yes. About a year. No. Two years.'

'He throw you out?'

'No. I ran.'

'To here. Why not to friends?'

Because I don't have any left to whom I could go, she had realised, bleakly. And if she had managed to stay in touch with Susie or Michaela, or Jennifer, in the teeth of Antony's objection to all of them, how could she have brought herself to explain what seemed to be happening?

'Stupid question. He objected to all your mates, right? Why not a hotel?'

'He . . . I . . . I don't have any money.' *That* had been almost the worst shock, the discovery that Antony had drawn out every penny in the joint account.

Matthew Sutherland closed the log book with a snap and swung round to look at her. 'All you middle-class girls have a bit somewhere. What happened to it?'

It was too much, but she told him between undignified sobs and gulps, and he listened, unmoved, asking the odd question to make sure he had all the details.

'Right.' She gazed at him, sodden with tears, and wiped her nose on the sleeve of her tracksuit. 'You need some sugar. What's Wonderwoman down there called?' She told him, choking back a giggle that threatened to start her eyes running again, and he pulled the door open and enquired where the fuck the coffee was.

'Coming!' The distant voice sounded unoffended, and Francesca, appearing promptly with three cups, sat down in the teeth of Matthew Sutherland's hostile stare.

'You're interrupting a client interview here, lady.'

'Annabelle may have a real lawyer of her own. Have you asked her?'

'He won't be as good as I am. So how about it, lovely, am I your solicitor? Or rather the firm of Graebner and Lewis, since as Wonderwoman here almost pointed out I am not qualified for three months yet. It'll be me doing the work though, whoever's name's on the case.'

'Annabelle, you might want to decide in the morning?'

'No. I mean, yes please, Mr Sutherland, I would like you to be my lawyer.' Antony would *hate* him, she thought, with horrified pleasure.

'Forget the Mr. Everyone calls me Matthew. Now, what do we call you?'

'Annabelle. Annabelle Brewster.'

'Dr Brewster.'

'That's right.'

'Well, I'll go away since you're getting on so spledidly.' Francesca finished her coffee in one gulp.

'Don't be like that,' Matthew advised. 'That's what lawyers are for.'

Francesca considered him, her good jacket dragged on anyhow, white with tiredness. 'How old are you, Matthew?'

'Twenty-six. So what?'

'So I just wondered.'

'You mean why aren't I doing all that deference crap you go in for over here?'

'Something like that.' Francesca, to Annabelle's relief, was smiling, the tired lines lifting. 'I need to go to bed – there's a broom cupboard upstairs next to the emergency room, which is yours, Annabelle. Do you want to come too, or would you rather go on having a client interview with Matthew?'

'I'm done. She can come and do the rest in the morning. What's that noise?'

They all listened to the broken sound of a child with a very sore throat coughing and crying, and Annabelle was on her feet washing her hands at the little basin which seemed to be a feature of every room in the Refuge before the other two had moved.

'I'll stick around,' Matthew said casually. 'Who needs sleep? No, you get to bed, Francesca, can't have you and your ma ill at once. Leave it to me and Dr Brewster here.' He took the cup from Francesca, turned her round and to Annabelle's stunned admiration dispatched her upstairs with a pat on the bottom. Then he rolled up his sleeves and followed her to receive Mrs O'Brien and the four-year-old Francis, brother to Patrick, who had woken panic-stricken, sweaty and covered from head to toe in spots.

2

Monday, 4 April

John McLeish showed his card to the man on the gate at New Scotland Yard and drove his car down the steep slope of the car-park, basking in the first tangible evidence of his new position. Detective Chief Superintendent not only sounded good, it carried the enormous privilege of a car-park space in Central London. That told you that he had the foreman's job at last, he thought, locking the car automatically, though if it was not safe here underneath the detective headquarters of the country there was no security anywhere. He suppressed this wholly improper reaction to the honour that had been done him by this promotion and stopped to straighten his tie and tug at the waistband of his trousers. The suit was five years old but not much worn for the last three and a half while he had been back in uniform as one of two superintendents at Notting Dale. His wife had organised him into buying two new suits on promotion, but some residual superstition had prevented him putting one of them on before he had even seen his office or any of his colleagues. He had also been handicapped that morning; his treasured eighteen-month-old William had wailed and fussed and been feverish until four o'clock in the morning. He had then fallen into an uneasy sleep, waking his mother every hour on the hour. John McLeish had therefore to get himself out of the house to a new job without any assistance.

An hour later nothing much had happened. His designated secretary was held up by a delayed train. His immediate boss was not in, having been called to an emergency conference following the discovery over the weekend of the dismembered pieces of several bodies – the news so far indicated a number anywhere between three and eight – in a terraced house in North London. Two of his staff including his old friend Bruce Davidson, now a detective inspector, were also tied up with the case, so there was a marked shortage of people to talk to. He decided it would be self-indulgent to ring up his wife for a talk, just because he had no one to play with. Coffee and a bun seemed like a sensible option; the first thing any policeman learned was to eat and attend to any other bodily needs when opportunity offered. It was a pity that there was no one to have coffee with, but he was not going to sit in solitary state in the canteen, he would go out and find out if the cash machine he remembered from three years ago was still there, and locate the other necessities of life. He pulled on a raincoat and checked in the mirror to see his tie was straight, bending his knees to get a clear view; at 6′ 4″ mirrors tended to be hung too low for him. He needed, he decided, to get some weight off; his jaw and neck had thickened, and his shirt was tight on the collar. The trouble with a youth spent in hard training was that muscle turned to fat, starting well under forty which he still was. It was difficult to imagine when he was going to find time to fit in any consistent exercise. Unlike most of his colleagues he had a wife with her own career, who would not appreciate his disappearing to play games at weekends, leaving her to the house and their eighteen-month-old son.

He checked at the door; rain was coming down in sheets, and he stood irresolute, undecided as to whether to make a dash to the little Italian café, or wait for a few minutes.

'John?' He turned, assuming it to be one of the uniformed women on reception who had called him, and stopped, frozen in his tracks. 'I didn't realise you were here.'

'I wasn't. I mean I've just arrived. Catherine, how are you?'

She was as beautiful as ever, and looked no older than she had three years ago, the blonde curly hair expensively cut, setting off the pale skin, straight nose and wide blue eyes. Passers-by still checked to look, and no doubt men still sat in meetings with Catherine Crane, resting their eyes on her.

'I'm well, thank you. How are you? How is your wife?'

'Francesca,' he said, just in case she didn't know whom he had married.

'Indeed, Francesca.' She was amused and he felt foolish. 'I heard that you were coming back to C Division, but not when. I'm in the Fraud Squad.'

Well, thank God it's that rather than C, he thought, and realised he was standing gazing at her for the sheer pleasure of her looks. 'Are you a DI now?'

'Oh yes. I have been since ... well, for the last three years. Hoping to make DCI one of these days.'

'Come and have coffee,' he said, resolutely ignoring the memories of the past, determined to treat her as a senior colleague.

'I'd like that.'

'Right. Well, let's see if it's stopped chucking it down.' He looked round and realised that both women behind the reception desk and seemingly all the floating population on the ground floor were watching them with interest, envy or amusement. It had always been like that around Catherine, he remembered, and whisked her out of the door, regardless of the rain.

Seated opposite her, occupying himself with the business of ordering coffee and biscuits, he recovered his poise and managed to look at her properly. They had had a brief but passionate affair, which she had broken off to return to her married lover, leaving him to go to Francesca, whom he had been courting for two years, and to insist that they get married. So in some sense he owed Catherine for the much loved little son he had left behind this morning. He bore her no grudge for the swift slap to his ego she had dealt by leaving him the moment the other man had whistled, but he did observe, with faint smugness, the absence of a wedding ring and the tiny lines around the wide eyes.

'So tell me, where have you been? What have you been doing?'

'Well, I did another couple of years in C after you went to Notting Dale. Then I transferred to the Fraud Squad. The hours are better.'

Then perhaps she was living with the bloke, even if not married, he thought, and tried to decide how to ask.

'It didn't work out with Dave.'

'Oh, I'm sorry.'

'So I decided to change the job a bit, get some more time for myself. To get a life outside the Met.'

There was something missing in this account, he understood, but it would be wrong and counter-productive to probe. 'Is fraud interesting? I've never been offered but it always looks like good work.'

'Oh, it's interesting all right. But dead frustrating a lot of the time.'

'What are you working on now?'

'It's quiet at the moment. Tidying up the Anderson case. I *will* get him one day, so I want everything in good order. And there's

22

one we're watching.' She looked round casually, making sure that she could not be overheard. 'One of these blokes who used to be a bent stockbroker, but the Financial Services Act put him out of business. There was a smell over a couple of things he'd done, and he was told he wouldn't get a licence. So he went into travel and hotels . . . what . . . about three years ago.'

'And people are losing money?'

'We haven't found any yet. But the whole thing looks dicey. You must have seen the ads, John? "Your dream holiday, for ever, one payment secures. Ring Price Fleming." '

'What, you mean timeshare?'

'With a twist. You buy your two weeks, or whatever, and you can go to one of eight places in Majorca. *That's* all right, or has been so far.'

'So what's wrong? The firm not doing well?' He was only mildly interested, but he would cheerfully listen to her recite the London telephone directory for the pleasure of watching that beautiful face and for the envying looks he was getting.

'We've had two or three complaints that people haven't been able to get the places they wanted at the time they wanted. All dealt with . . . you know . . . apologies, offers of compensation, two weeks in the best hotel or your choice of anything a month later. Nothing really for anyone to moan about.'

'But?'

'But my Governor and I both keep thinking Barlow Clowes. And not just because the Price of Price Fleming looks awfully like Mr Clowes – big, burly chap, pleased with himself.'

'Remind me.'

'In the bad old days, before all the legislation, they advertised, offering gilt-edged securities at two or three points better than gilt rates. Everybody wanted to invest with them, particularly retired people.'

'I remember,' McLeish said, interested. 'The whole thing went fine for years, as long as they could sell enough new bonds to pay the interest on the old ones. And lots of people who should have known better invested.'

'That's it. The music only stopped because too many people wanted interest, or their money out to do things with, at the same time. So the proprietors couldn't sell new bonds fast enough to fund them. Nor the yachts, aeroplanes and other goodies they had bought with some of the cash. One of the things that put us on to this particular company – apart from the respectable oldie clientele – was the company yacht.'

Just for a moment you could hear the girl from the Liverpool council estate she had once been, John McLeish thought, as he ordered another cup of coffee each without consulting her. She was well capable of getting through three cups at breakfast.

'You got a couple of complaints, you and your Governor, and started looking. Is that how it works?'

She shovelled sugar into her coffee in exactly the way he remembered, and he felt himself blush as she looked up at him. 'Almost. We thought we'd got something when Teutens – you know, the solicitors – told us on the quiet about a client who has asked for her money back and it was being a bit slow to come. We were just going to do some work when the money came back. Then the headquarters – it's in your old patch, in Kensington Church Street – was done over, safe cracked and a real mess. The head man – one William Price – said that nothing had gone, despite the mess. A loyal secretary had banked all the cash the evening before, and so on. Usually in those cases people claim everything and nobody's been to the bank for weeks. Your old mob at Notting Dale caught it.'

'I've been off in Hull for six months, doing a special,' he said, apologetically. 'So what happened in the end?'

'Since the main victim wasn't complaining Notting Dale stopped trying. Without us pushing them on, they wouldn't have bothered at all. But they did look up their records and found that Mr Price's son, Francis, is a druggie. Conviction for possession of Class A two years ago.'

'So his father maybe thought it was the kid, and decided to protect him.'

'It was his father turned him in the time he was done for possession before.'

'Ah. So the better theory is that Mr Price senior was up to something he didn't want looked at.' He was still not overwhelmingly interested in this history but he was thinking about Catherine. She was thinner than she had been three years ago, which didn't make her any less beautiful, but she had more of an edge, was working closer to her reserves than she had. She looked back at him, and he saw her make a conscious effort to relax, the thin, beautiful, long-fingered hands still clenched round her coffee cup.

'I suppose you wouldn't want a druggie son in the business either,' he speculated helpfully. 'Is anyone else in with him?'

'There are three directors, him, Mr Fleming and Mrs Price. His wife – a second wife – but I don't know how much she does. There's another son, Antony, a doctor, but he doesn't seem to be involved.' She put the cup down and smiled at him. 'You don't really want to know all this, John, and it's time we went back. We could have lunch next week if you like?'

He would indeed, he assured her promptly, and took her back through the chill rain to the Yard, wondering in a corner of his mind when to explain to his wife that Catherine Crane was again working only two floors away from him.

Matthew Sutherland ran up two flights of stairs, and pushed through an open door at the top of the narrow nineteenth-century terraced house. He sank heavily into an ancient, battered chair, whose springs were barely contained by its cover, and tried not to gasp for breath.

'You'll have to give up clubbing, Matt,' the man behind the huge old partner's desk said, through a cloud of cigarette smoke. 'Spoils the wind.' He coughed, rackingly, and hunted amid the piles of papers for a cup half full of cooling coffee. 'How did it go yesterday?'

'We got the order. Took twenty minutes but we waited till three thirty for the judge to get back from his country cottage. I came back but you were gone. I left you a note.' He heaved himself out of the armchair's massive embrace and peered suspiciously at the littered surface of the desk. 'There. Silly me, I only pinned it down under the stapler – couldn't have expected you to see it.'

'Well, I know now.' Peter Graebner, the head of the solicitors Graebner and Lewis, smiled at his only articled clerk, amused as always by the way the red hair prickled and stood up when Matthew was annoyed. 'Any more news?'

'Got another customer. Girl, Annabelle Brewster, beaten up by her bloke. Can we take her on?'

'You got her from the Refuge, I take it. What's the defendant called?'

Matt produced a grubby piece of paper from his coat pocket, stared at it crossly, stuffed it back in and got out of the chair with a sigh, then removed his coat and one jacket and started to search the pockets of the underjacket and waistcoat, unearthing a striking collection of bills and leaflets.

'Do we need to sub you for a briefcase, Matt?'

'Don't be like that, Graebner. This is what I was wearing when I talked to the customer. He we are. Price, Dr Antony. Spelt without the h . . . well it would be, wouldn't it?'

His senior partner stared at him, cigarette in mouth, eyes narrowed against the drifting smoke. 'Mm.' He stubbed the cigarette. 'Got an uneasy feeling there.' He had pulled a keyboard towards him and was gazing doubtfully at a computer screen on the extreme corner of the big desk. 'Price, Beatrice, no, that's a housing case. Price, Wilhelmina, that's a deportation.' He tapped the keyboard. 'Wait a minute, Price, Mrs Sylvia, here it is. A Dr Antony Price, no h, bloke who brought her in after she'd had a beating. From her husband, one William Price. Father of this Antony. Six months ago. The beating, I mean.'

Matthew tried to look stern and unsurprised, but he was as always taken aback by Peter Graebner's grasp of his practice. The man was a physical wreck, greying and stooped, with his chest rattling like the timpani section of an orchestra, but he had all his buttons on, as Matthew had instantly recognised when he had come as a trainee two years ago.

'She got to court?'

'No. Usual thing, we did all the papers, then she withdrew. Paid our bill though.' It was indeed a familiar pattern; about sixty per cent of all cases under the Domestic Violence Act do not get to court. Peter Graebner considered the screen. 'I remember her quite well. Pretty woman.'

'We can act though, can't we? It's this Dr Antony wanker we're suing, not his father, or his stepmother.'

'Better not, Matt. Formally it's just about OK. Bad practice though.'

You didn't argue with Peter Graebner about things like that; it was his firm, built up over twenty-five years and a good one, its partners respected and feared for their efficiency, and Matt desperately wanted to be part of it.

'What can I tell her? Dr Brewster, I mean.'

'Just that we've had dealings with some of the Price family, no need to specify. Give her to Russell Marks, he'll look after her.' He considered his associate. 'Fancy her, do you? Then we're better not acting.'

'That's true.' Matthew cheered up instantly. 'Just hoped I'd made a contribution to the fee income, that's all. And I wanted to do another of those cases. Never mind, I'll give her a call.'

'Matthew.'

'Yes?'

'When you qualify in June, we're going to buy you a suit. We took a vote. Anything you want up to £70.'

Matthew looked across the awful desk, on which Peter Graebner could without fail find any piece of paper, no matter how old or trivial. 'Am I going to stay, then?'

'Yes, Matthew, if you want. Keep off the recreational drugs and you might even be made a partner in due course. Go and dispose of this young woman and come back with the O'Brien papers.'

'Annabelle.'

She turned slowly, understanding that she had been half expecting him to turn up.

'Go away.'

'Annabelle, please.'

'I'm late for surgery.'

'It doesn't start till nine, Annabelle, please. Just come and sit in the car. You're getting wet.'

'You must be joking.'

She had had an interesting three days, living in the Refuge. She had taken two days sick leave from her attachment to the GP practice, claiming a nasty case of flu, and refused the visit offered by one of the partners. She had spent much of the first day in the Refuge reassuring spotty children and their harassed mothers, occasionally retreating to her attic to sleep, waking to the noise of female voices, or children quarrelling, or screaming. There was always someone in the house weeping or shouting, she discovered. The women were not unsympathetic to each others' plight, but they were unwilling to listen to other women deploying the same tactics of denial and rationalisation that they had themselves used. Experienced social workers tried not to interfere, no matter how bruising the dialogue, because a fellow sufferer carried more conviction than anyone else possibly could.

She had also managed to follow Matthew Sutherland's uncompromising instructions to close the joint account she had had with Antony, open a new one somewhere else with £20 issued to her against a receipt from the Refuge funds and arrange for all future salary to be paid into *that*. Which had left her with nothing else to do but cope with sick children and listen to the horrifying histories of the other women in the Refuge. And one of the pieces of hard-won advice she had absorbed was the unwisdom of getting into a confined space with the bloke who had beaten you.

'Sod off, Antony. You'll be hearing from my solicitor if you haven't already.' Another thing she had learned was the pleasure of profanity, and a violent response from a position of safety. She watched him wince, knowing that she should walk through the surgery door and out of this scene but unable to give up the simple joy of being in command. Matthew had told her, somewhere in the course of the long night when they had worked together, that if she really wanted to get out of her situation she would not speak to Antony ever again except through a solicitor. But most women, he had added, couldn't resist, they wanted to go on arguing the toss so they pushed it, usually getting themselves right back in the shit.

'Will you at least let me buy you a coffee? Not that there is anywhere here, but . . .' He looked helpless and miserable and wet, the dark, nearly black hair flattened to his head, and she hesitated, while he looked wildly round. 'There's a café there. I mean, if that's all right. Please, Annabelle.'

He had said 'please' four times in five minutes, or more times than he had used the word in the last two years. Perhaps all it took was for her to stand up for herself.

'Just for ten minutes then.' His eyes went wide with relief and he moved towards her. 'It *would* be better if I didn't have to take you to court to get my money out of the joint account, and all my things.'

'Look, there's no *question* of that. Please, Annabelle, I need to talk to you.'

They hastened to the café, Annabelle keeping a careful distance behind him. He stopped at the door, obviously put off by the tiny crowded room with the strong smell of bacon and none too fresh fat against which a very small fan was labouring ineffectually. She watched in malicious pleasure as he opened his mouth to blast her for thinking of bringing him to such a place and then remembered what his situation was.

'I'm afraid it's a bit crowded.'

'Fine by me.'

He made the best of it, she had to concede, finding a table and placing her at it while he quickly cleared the remains of three people's breakfasts and a clotted ashtray, giving them to the girl at the counter with a quick smile so that her eyes followed him hopefully as he sat down. He looked exotic among the shabby, tired men getting their breakfast down. He was immaculately dressed, pale but shaved, with a clean blue shirt, bringing out the colour in the dark blue eyes. She was still wearing the tracksuit she had found in the clothing cupboard, but she had a clean white cotton polo neck which Francesca had unearthed for her and she had washed her hair that morning. She was comfortable and she did not care if she was not meeting Antony's standards of grooming.

'I cannot tell you how worried I've been.'

Now *that* was typical, she thought, suddenly so angry that she could not speak. His face changed and he seized her hand.

'Annabelle. I meant how worried for *you*. I came here on Friday but you'd called in sick. I rang all the hospitals. I rang the Refuge, but they wouldn't even talk to me.'

'Why do you think that was?'

'Well ... shit ... well, I did think they could have been ...' He stopped, the long mouth tightly compressed, and stared down at his hands.

'Where I have been,' she said to the top of his head, 'men who have beaten women so that they fled for their very lives ring up all the time, wanting to find them so that they can do it again.' She reached, carefully, for her coffee, shaking with anger.

'Annabelle,' he said, hopelessly to the table, and she realised that he was crying. She clenched both hands round her coffee cup and looked over his head. (He always cried, she heard Denise saying wearily, squinting to avoid the smoke from the cigarette stuck to the corner of her mouth, which was never going to look the same since her husband had pushed a broken bottle in her face.) She sat, rigorously ignoring the curious stares, watching Antony find a handkerchief and blow his nose.

'Sorry, Annabelle. I do understand – I've had four days to

understand – that I have behaved like a hopeless shit and you're not going to want to come back to me.'

She was surprised into looking at him properly, and saw that his eyes were red and that he looked suddenly exhausted. He put a hand tentatively on hers. 'I've been under a lot of pressure I couldn't tell you about – no, Annabelle, please, don't look like that, it's not meant as an excuse. It's family things and I should never have got involved, and I've done things I can't imagine how I came to do. Like clean out the joint account.'

'Well, you can't do that again. I closed it on Friday and redirected my salary.'

He winced. 'It's *not* an excuse, but I used it to get Francis out of trouble. No, I didn't buy him drugs, but he was going to get very seriously hurt unless he paid for the ones he'd had. So I paid his debts.'

'You mean I did.'

She watched with interest the pink flush on his cheekbones which had always meant she was pushing him further than was safe. 'I'm afraid that's true, so on Friday I had the conversation with my father I ought to have had years ago and I'll write you a cheque now.' He looked away from her. 'Or get you cash if you don't want me to know where your bank is. I'd understand that.'

'I need all my things – my handbag, my clothes and so on.'

'I'll bring them.' He checked. 'Sorry, I mean, you must come and fetch them any time you like. I'll help you.'

'I'll come when you're not there, with a friend to help.'

The Refuge had taught her that and she watched it go home as he leant his head on his hands. 'I know I deserve all this but it isn't easy after five years.'

'No.' She felt a childish sense of triumph at seeing him so reduced, and was then instantly worried that she was being so unkind that she would lose him for ever. She buried her face in the coffee cup, trying to keep her mind on the hopeless women and the wild children she had tended.

'Can we make a deal? I'll give you the key – I've got your handbag in the car because I knew you'd need it. You let yourself in when you want and move your stuff, but you meet me for dinner on Friday, when you've had a few days to think. We could have dinner every Friday, just so I see you and get a chance to prove I have done some thinking.'

She thought about it, with a delicious sense of triumph competing uneasily with mistrust. After all, it couldn't hurt to have dinner. She picked up the cheque. 'Will this clear?'

'I'm not silly, Annabelle. Behaved appallingly, I agree, but it wouldn't help, would it, if the cheque bounced?'

'I'll come and get my handbag – I'm late for surgery. And I'll ring you about Friday.'

He looked so defeated that she wanted to touch him, but pushed the cheque into a pocket instead and followed him to the car, standing well away from it as her sisters at the Refuge had so urgently advised. He reached and handed her the familiar navy leather bag which he had bought her for her last birthday, and they both looked at it.

'It may seem pretty strange,' he said, painfully, 'but I love you and I need you, and I am truly sorry.' He reached a hand towards her and she stepped back sharply. His face crumpled. 'Annabelle, don't cut me off.'

'I'll ring you,' she said, near to weeping herself, and turned to walk blindly through the surgery door.

3

Monday, 11 April

'The AC wants you, John. At once.'

There went the prospect of coffee, but he was pleased at the prospect of action, after a week of meeting colleagues and sorting out staff.

'Nice to see you, John. Many kind words said round here about your work in Hull.'

This was pleasing; his investigations into the police force of East Yorkshire had produced four resignations and eight disciplinary hearings, and had left that force with not much defence to three civil actions for wrongful arrest. But the stables had been thoroughly cleaned with the minimum fuss, and it was nice to know that his fellow professionals approved.

'Thank you, Commissioner.'

'Right. Got one for you. Brand new.'

'What, already?'

'We don't hang around here, John. One of our lads goes and does one if we're short of work.' There was never any need to manufacture employment for C Division, responsible as it was for the investigation of murders that had features suggesting they might relate to another murder, or were particularly difficult in any unspecified way.

'Bit early in the morning.'

'Not committed today. The preliminary report suggests Friday. Your old manor – Kensington Church Street.'

'Is that why we've got it?' It couldn't be, but Gerry Yates was uncharacteristically tight-lipped and he felt the need to fill the gap.

'No. It's a nasty. The dead man was engaged in auto asphyxia.'

'Sorry?'

'The getting of sexual satisfaction by half strangling yourself, or so they tell me.'

'And he overdid it?'

'Not exactly. He used a heavy table to support himself, but it moved, leaving him dangling. And the house was turned over.'

None of this quite explained why C Division rather than Notting Dale, with its well-staffed detective division, should be involved, and McLeish waited patiently.

'Gentleman who found him is a Member of Parliament.'

'Close friend, was he?'

'Get your mind out of the gutter, John. Deceased was married, it says here, and nothing like that known of the Member. Quite the contrary, indeed, Special Branch tell me.' He passed the single piece of paper across the table. 'You'd better get over there before your old mates trample on the evidence. Or upset the Member even further.'

The last was the point; the AC presumably did not suppose that the well-trained Notting Dale detective force would fail to collect and safeguard everything at the scene of the crime. But a Member of Parliament might easily be treated without the particular deference to which they all felt entitled.

'Francesca well? And the little 'un?'

'William. He's teething, but apart from that he's fine. Francesca sends her regards.'

'Does she now? Doesn't sound like her at all.'

Nor had he reported her accurately, John acknowledged, trying to keep his face straight. What she had actually said, at six thirty that morning in a distracted farewell, was that the blasted Gerry Yates had better not keep him late doing futile chores.

'And the rest of the family?'

The AC had cause to know about his four brothers-in-law; one was a rock star and another had been rescued from the New York police following a drugs charge three years ago.

'All away, thank the Lord. Perry is doing a film in America, Charlie is in Hong Kong, Tristram's touring Eastern Europe with an opera group, and even Jeremy is away – in Japan.'

'Francesca misses them, I expect.'

She did, of course, however pleased he was to have her attention not deflected by four talented, dependent, demanding siblings. He was not however going to discuss this with the AC.

'I'll be off then.'

'Don't let the Member bug you.'

'I won't. Which is it?'

'Ah. London bloke, it's on the paper. Richmond – the constituency, not his name. Miles Arnold. Not a lot known, but not particularly anti-us for once. Said to be on the way up. Your man Davidson is down there already holding the fort, but it needs someone senior quickly.'

'Indeed,' McLeish agreed. 'I'll report later when I've got the strength.'

He slid into the waiting car and looked through the notes. The deceased appeared to be called William Price, and had been found, hanged, in his office which was part of his house. His secretary, who had found Miles Arnold MP on the doorstep, had let them both in to be confronted by a corpse. And a nasty one, McLeish added mentally, if the estimated time of death was three days earlier. There was a phone number on the paper and he rang it to announce his likely arrival within the next quarter of an hour, traffic permitting.

The voice at the other end warmed as he announced himself.

'Bruce. Glad you're on your way, Chief Superintendent.' The pinched Glasgow vowels were peculiarly distinctive on the telephone. 'Would you like to speak to Mr Arnold, who found the body? He's eager to be away to fulfil his parliamentary duties, but mebbe you could have a word over the telephone.'

You would have to know Bruce Davidson well to know that his patience was seriously frayed. It was not an ideal way to make the first steps in a relationship with a touchy MP, whingeing to get away from the scene of a crime, but there appeared to be no choice.

'Miles Arnold here. And you are who?'

'Detective Chief Superintendent John McLeish. I am coming from C Division at Scotland Yard to take charge of the case. I'm sorry you've had a shock.'

'Well. Yes. It was. Look, do I need to stay? I've told your people here everything I know, and I'm late for an appointment at the House – the House of Commons – already.'

'I'm sorry to hold you up but it is important to talk at once to the person who found the body, at the scene of the crime, where I can go through in detail what you saw. I'm not more than five minutes away.'

This was being seriously economical with the truth, but it was effective; you could hear the man weighing his idea of what was due to his consequence against how it would look to have left the scene of a crime five minutes ahead of a senior policeman. He agreed grudgingly to wait. Bruce Davidson came back on the phone.

'Bruce, give the man another coffee and hold his hand. I'm at Marble Arch and the traffic is solid.'

'Ah well, you're not far away,' Bruce said, obviously for the benefit of the audience at his end, and John McLeish grinned in acknowledgement.

'Put the siren on,' he said and the big car pulled out to the right, siren blaring, clearing a path against the oncoming traffic which reluctantly edged over, or stopped, or tucked itself behind the immovable buses.

It took them nearer fifteen minutes, but McLeish still took his time getting himself out of the car and telling the driver where to wait. If you hurried you missed things and the first observations you made were all-important. Bruce Davidson materialised on the pavement to greet him.

'I've sealed the room. It's the kitchen, so we couldna even make a cup of coffee. Doc's just arrived. Be nice to move the body.'

Bruce was not given to hyperbole and McLeish winced. 'Heating on, was it?'

'It's on a clock, so not all the time. But enough, if you take my meaning.'

McLeish did; decomposition would be gathering pace after forty-eight hours in a reasonably warm room. 'I'll go in with the doc. Have we got a scene-of-crime squad?'

'Changing into whites.'

There was always a danger that the scene-of-crime squad – the group charged with collecting every piece of physical evidence from the scene of a crime – might accidentally contaminate the samples. It had taken a surprisingly long time to absorb this fact, but now most forces insisted that the squads wore sterilised white tracksuits, boots, gloves, and Balaclavas to cover their hair.

'Who is in charge?'

'Macdonald. Ye remember him? Older bloke. Inspector now.'

Which would make three Scots in key positions in this investigation, but that was not unusual in the Met; by analogy with the Battle of Waterloo, fought on the pikes of Scottish regiments, crime in London is substantially opposed by the brains and bodies of Scottish-born policemen.

'Get him down. I'll look at the scene and get them started.'

'Could you have a wee word with Mr Arnold first?'

'No, tell him what I'm doing, explain I had to get the body away. I dare say he'll see the sense of that.'

'If he's using his nose he will,' Davidson said, dourly, and went off to do his bidding.

John McLeish stood on the edge of the pavement and looked around him carefully. It was an odd place, this bit of Kensington Church Street, with the typical sizeable Victorian houses now subverted to commercial purposes. This particular house, like the others in the row, was approached by a flight of steps leading to a wide porch. There was a basement, entered from a side entrance, and three floors above. He stood for a moment trying to remember who had been telling him about Kensington Church Street, and saw Catherine's beautiful face in his mind's eye. He made an involuntary startled noise, yes, the chap she was telling him about had been called Price. He walked up the steps to be met by Macdonald, a small man in his thirties with the light step of the runner.

'Sir. Nice to see you back.' He glanced at a closed door just to the right inside the front door.

'Hang on a second before we go down. A bell just rang. You had a burglary here, right, some months ago?'

'Yes. I looked it up before I came. How did you know?'

'A detective inspector in the Fraud Squad was telling me last week. They were involved.'

'That's right.' He watched as Macdonald worked his way through this thought. 'Yes. Well. I just haven't had time to notify them yet.' He looked hopefully at McLeish. 'Thought I ought to get a few facts first.'

'Oh indeed. I only happened to remember this conversation. Leave the call till I've seen what's to do. We'll go down then.'

They had put the impatient MP in the front room, McLeish deduced. He followed Macdonald down the wide stairs, stone, with a good carpet down the centre. Macdonald stopped at the door directly facing them, which had been sealed with paper tape, and as he stopped the door to the left of the stairs opened to reveal Dr Middleton, a forensic pathologist whom he knew. They paused to say hello, and in that moment McLeish caught a familiar smell. It was odd, it was not as if he had had to inspect many decomposing bodies, in most cases the corpse would hardly be cold by the time he got there, but the smell was unmistakable and instantly familiar.

'Right.' He put on the mask handed to him and waited while Macdonald took the tape off and pushed the door open, cautiously standing aside to let him through.

He was ready for it but it was still a grim sight. There was a plastic bag over the head coming down to the shoulders, so there was no neck. From the corner of the bag a rope extended upwards into a hook set into the ceiling, the full weight of the body hanging leadenly, the toes extended, a good thirty inches off the floor. The body was swollen, the belly grotesquely distended as the gases of decomposition pushed it out. He walked closer, trying to breathe shallow, and saw that what he had taken for bruising were transparent black stockings without a suspender belt, the tops cutting deeply into the swollen flesh of the thighs. There was also a pair of black silk French knickers, the elastic waist sunk into the grossly extended belly.

There was a current of air in the room, and he looked for the source. A curtain, narrowly open, hung over a French window which led out into the garden. It was closed, but one of the glass panels had been smashed giving access from the outside to the lock inside. He frowned at the space, not wanting to move the curtain. It was unlikely that in Central London this would be the only method of securing a door with direct access to the garden. Sure enough there were screw-in deadlocks at the top and bottom of each door, two of which must have been undone; the right-hand door was only pushed to. There was no sign the door had been forced, so the man hanging from the rope had not put on all the locks. McLeish considered this small fact. Surely, anyone wanting to engage in an activity in which an interruption would be both embarrassing and disruptive would secure the door first.

He looked, breathing in carefully, at the hands, first the right, then the left. The nails were broken on both hands, and there were what looked like bits of fibre under them. He pointed them out to Macdonald who nodded.

'Poor bugger tried to get the rope off likely,' he observed, voice muffled by his mask.

'Yes.' The three men looked silently at an oblong oak table, lying askew on its side in the middle of the room, beyond the reach of the frenziedly kicking legs of a man trying to save himself from strangulation.

McLeish walked round the body once again, looking for the mechanism that had held the rope so firmly inside the hook and failing at first to find it.

'A ratchet, sir. In the fitting.'

Yes, that was it. And it had held despite the fact that the dead man must have been of the order of fifteen stone, much heavier than the light originally suspended from this fitting.

'Get him down,' he instructed. 'But leave the rope up there so we can get a proper look. Unless you want anything, doc?'

'No. I'll go up and look as you cut him loose, but I need a table.'

He meant, of course, a forensic operating table, but McLeish found himself looking again at the up-ended oak table for which the man's nyloned feet must have scrabbled and kicked in vain.

'How long, roughly, doc?'

Dr Middleton walked round the body and considered it. 'Difficult. More like three days – might be less. Tell you a bit more – perhaps – later.'

'Not Saturday night though?'

'No, no, not possibly, John. Too soon for the gases to get under way as they have. Friday night, perhaps earlier.'

'Right. And we'll need to decide if this could have been an accident.'

Dr Middleton and Inspector Macdonald both stared at him over their masks and looked again at the table on its side. It was too heavy to have been moved by scrabbling feet, but if someone had come through that door, found the householder temporarily off his guard and kicked or pulled the table away, they would inevitably claim that the householder was already dead, having accidentally kicked over the table himself. Dr Middleton indicated that they might as well get the body cut down and removed for analysis. The small breeze from the broken window had made very little impact on the fetid atmosphere; the heavy curtain had kept most of it out and the heating had been on for much of the time.

They closed the door after them and pulled off their masks gratefully. The corridor had filled with Macdonald's scene-of-crime squad, in their whites, individuality stripped away by the white Balaclavas that covered them down to their eyebrows.

'I'm afraid you can't open a window yet, Mac,' John McLeish said, knowing the instruction to be redundant but wanting to give the squad fair warning. Macdonald nodded and gathered the squad around him for instructions, Dr Middleton waiting patiently to supervise the removal of the body.

McLeish ran up the stairs to get out of the way of bearers from the police mortuary clattering downwards past him. He turned off to wash in the little cloakroom he had noticed as he came in. He had touched nothing in the basement kitchen and had in any case been wearing gloves which he stripped off and stuffed into a pocket but his hands felt dirty and the smell of the room was in his nostrils.

'I won't be a minute, Bruce. I need to air off.'

'Not very nice, was it?'

'Well. Probably three days dead. Doesn't do anyone much good. Can you tell Mr Arnold I'm coming?'

He stood on the front steps drawing in air to his lungs, causing a stir among the loiterers who always appeared in London when you put a constable and a couple of police cars outside a house. He had fogotten it was a bus route and was disconcerted to find himself the centre of attention for an entire double-decker. It reminded him that this was a busy street, with people up and down it all the time in substantial numbers, not an anonymous deserted residential area where a house-breaker would be much more conspicuous. He stopped to look at the front door, and indeed it was undamaged, all three of the triple locks properly set in, no signs of any attempt to force them.

He turned to Bruce Davidson who opened the door for him, and announced him. The room was occupied by a tall, blond, rangy man, hunched irritably over a pile of the day's newspapers. He looked up to greet the police party and sprang athletically to his feet. Close up you could see that he was forty, rather than thirty, but it was a credible impression; the blond straight hair was thick and full of colour and the skin hardly lined except round the eyes. He was admirably slim, showing no signs of too much good living, and McLeish furtively sucked in his own stomach muscles.

'I'm sorry we had to keep you waiting, Mr Arnold.'

'No, no, not at all.' The man was burning with suppressed energy, or tension, and McLeish watched him as he got the party sat down at the good mahogany table full of neat piles of magazines which constituted the room's principal piece of furniture.

Coffee appeared with a young constable and McLeish took it

gratefully, heaping in sugar in a way that he recognised would not help his waistline. Miles Arnold accepted but took sweetener.

'Mr Arnold, would you like just to tell us when you arrived and what you did? If I may, I will ask questions as you go along.'

The MP considered him. 'Have you – did you – go into the kitchen?'

'Yes. That is why we kept you waiting.'

'Right. Yes. Well. I arrived about ten o'clock. I was going to meet Bill – William Price – here. It's his office as well as his house. I met Margaret Howard, his secretary, on the doorstep. She's here, of course – have you asked her?'

'Not yet. I wanted to see you first so you could go on to your appointment.'

Miles Arnold took this piece of deference as his due. 'She rang the bell and said to me she always did that just to let Bill know she was here, but when he didn't answer she unlocked the door.' He looked suddenly uncertain as the possible impact of what he was saying struck him. 'So, well ... anyway ... we came in together, I think she called out something like "Good morning" but there was no answer so she turned into her office and said to me she'd find out where Bill was first and then she'd make me a cup of coffee.' He paused, reliving the moment. 'I was starving for a coffee, I'd driven over from Richmond and the traffic was bloody awful, and I'd had a slightly late night, so I decided to go and do it myself. I went down to the kitchen and opened the door.' He stopped to swallow, convulsively. 'It was the smell I noticed first, of course,' he said, shoulders hunched, eyes focused somewhere to McLeish's right. 'I don't know what I thought it was. It was dark, you see, the curtains were still drawn, so I switched on the light. And there was this thing – sorry, but I couldn't even think what it was for a minute – hanging from the ceiling. Then I realised – I mean, not that it was Bill, but that it was a person, but I'll tell you something that really got to me. The legs were different lengths. I mean, one was longer than the other, and it panicked me.' He moistened his lips, the muscles in the long jaw knotting. 'I just made it to the bog before I chucked up my last two meals, or that's what it seemed like. I hope I didn't leave a mess there.'

McLeish glanced sideways at Davidson who got himself quickly out of the door. It would be important that the squad downstairs knew what had happened; the downstairs lavatory could be important.

40

'Where's he gone?' Miles Arnold was tense and alert.

'Just to have a word with the scene-of-crime squad. No need to wait for him.'

'You can take notes, can you?' The man was genuinely if briefly interested, and McLeish understood one of the attractions of a political career was that contact with people of all sorts came with the territory.

'If I need to. We can get it down between us for the record anyway. So when you'd recovered a bit?'

Davidson came round the door silently; he had left it just open and closed it with a click, sliding back into his place without looking at either of them. Miles Arnold looked uncertainly at him.

'Well, I did know I mustn't touch anything.' He looked at McLeish for acknowledgement of his sagacity. 'I mean, it was clear whoever it was was dead. So I just looked enough to be sure whether it – he – was a man or a woman. I thought it must be Bill, who else would it be? And I had some idea of what he'd been doing – I mean, one's read books after all, not to say the News of the Screws. So I just thought, poor sod, thank Christ one's roughly normal.' He gave them a careful look to see that they had registered the point. 'Then I heard Margaret calling me and I rushed upstairs to keep her away – I closed the door again because of the smell. She'd found the office safe had been robbed and couldn't think how anyone had got in and wanted me to come and look round the place with her. So I broke it to her and we rang the police.'

'And you didn't go back downstairs?'

'No, I didn't. I still wanted a coffee – in fact I wanted it even more – so I went up to the corner and brought some back for both of us. I'd hardly got back here before your lot arrived, or rather I suppose the local lads, not your lot. You're Scotland Yard?'

'Yes.'

'Because of me?'

'For a variety of reasons, but certainly your involvement is one of them.'

'When you say my involvement, I'm a parliamentary consultant to Price Fleming. I wouldn't usually be here on Monday mornings. If they want anything Bill rings me or comes and sees me at the House. One gets too busy as the week goes on.' He drank another gulp of coffee and considered McLeish. 'I mean, he must have been dead for days. To smell like that.'

'When did you last see him?'

'Let me think ... sorry, but my life at that place is such a madhouse I sometimes don't know who I *have* seen. No, I didn't see him Friday but I did on Thursday, now I think of it. In my office – my secretary will remember.'

'And you had an appointment with him this morning?'

'No. I came by on the off-chance. There was something I wanted to discuss.' Miles Arnold was fidgeting, shifting in his chair, discharging tension by rubbing the band of his watch; a heavy gold Rolex. 'Look, I wonder if we could possibly do any more you want on another occasion, later today? I will make myself available of course, but I'm running late – I've got a Question down today in the House – and I feel bloody awful, and I think I'd better try and eat a late breakfast, or an early lunch. I've told you all I know about actually finding Bill. Not very useful, I'm afraid, but it's not as if you can't find me when you want me.'

'Of course.' McLeish had been expecting to give ground from the moment parliamentary business had been mentioned, and proceeded to do so with good grace. 'Just two points, if you will. First, when you opened the kitchen door did you see if the French door was open? The one into the garden.'

'No, I didn't. I'm sorry, it was dark, and there was just a chink of light up that end. Was it?'

'It was unlocked and the window broken.'

'Oh, you mean it was a burglar? Who surprised Bill *in medias res*, as it were?'

'We are not yet in a position to draw any conclusions. But could you just, finally, tell us what Price Fleming do, and how long you have been connected with them?'

Miles Arnold stopped fidgeting and looked down at his hands for a minute. 'Well, they started out as financial consultants and brokers in a small way. Then Bill found that all the regulatory stuff that we so carefully put in place to catch the villains was just too difficult to cope with, so he closed that business – much, I might say, to the customers' regret. He did them rather well. My sister was a client, that's how I met Bill. But he'd always been interested in property and he's got a house in Majorca anyway, so he bought another one and a small hotel. Then it just grew, and he's got thirty now, in various bits of Majorca.'

'So he's a hotelier. Or a travel agent?'

'Bit of both. People buy shares in the flats or the hotels for specific times each year.'

'What I call timeshare?'

'Yes. Yes. Essentially. On a large scale.' He hesitated. 'To be honest I'm not closely in touch with all the detail, but it's been very successful. Look, the best person to ask about all this is Luke Fleming, Bill's partner – I imagine Margaret's found him by now.'

McLeish, who knew he was on borrowed time, agreed that this would be a sensible course of action, and saw Arnold to his car, a large Jaguar. Somebody was paying this one more than an MP's salary, and he must as a priority get the Register of Members' Interests looked up. He ran back up the steps to Davidson, who was improving the hour by chatting up a bouncy young WPC. He would be, of course; Bruce was a darkly good-looking Glaswegian with all his Irish mother's charm and had always been spectacularly successful with women. His technique, like all effective methods, was simple; if he fancied a girl he asked her to go to bed with him, achieving about a seventy per cent success-rate which as he said was more than enough for one bloke. Francesca's theory was that as soon as he hit forty – which was five years away – he would marry a dumpy little creature, father eight children and never look at another woman. He caught McLeish's eye and detached himself.

'Dodgy business, you reckon?' McLeish asked.

'Oh aye. *Very* glossy brochures, lots of expensive kit in the office. Bound to be.'

'Lots of perfectly legitimate firms have glossy pictures,' McLeish objected mildly. 'But Mr Arnold was pretty keen to tell us he wasn't involved in the details, wasn't he? What have we got here?'

This turned out to be Margaret Howard, a small, dark woman in her fifties, red-eyed, but with all her buttons on, as McLeish's mother would have said. He invited her to join him after coffee in the waiting-room, and backed out of the room, closing the door hastily behind him, to shut out the sounds associated with four men getting a heavy swollen body up narrow stairs without doing any further damage. He waited in silence as the heavy feet went past the door, glancing up just to see the laden, covered stretcher going down the broad front steps to the mortuary van parked directly outside. There was a delay; someone had misplaced the keys to the back of the van and burdened men were waiting by the stretcher while the driver cursed and hunted for them.

Just then a big BMW, crisply driven, pulled up short of the police tapes. A woman, irritation and tension in every line of her, got out of the driving seat. He watched as she came up the road, expensive black coat tugged by the wind, brown hair in a neat chignon, and realised she was making for the house in which he stood. He stepped back hastily so she would not see him and got a clear view of her as she was stopped by one of the policemen at the edge of the barrier. Older than she had seemed, walking briskly up the pavement; good bones in the face, carefully made up, but the flesh round the jaw was drooping a little and there were lines round the eyes. She looked up suddenly towards the house, and he saw her face on, wide dark eyes, a good high forehead set off by the severe hair-line. A customer perhaps: everything about her spoke of money.

'Mr McLeish.' It was Margaret Howard, panic added to distress. 'That's Mrs Price with the police outside.'

The stretcher was still there, and the driver still seemed not to have found the keys. Galvanised, he got himself out of the door but the young policeman on duty had let Mrs Price through the barrier and was leading her towards the house to find himself face to face with a tableau of grotesquely laden stretcher and four men, frozen in embarrassment. McLeish saw the wide eyes turn up in her head as he ran down the steps and only just managed to catch her before she hit the pavement in a dead faint.

4

Monday, 11 April

Francesca parked on a single yellow line outside the big house with the unmarked door and ran up the steps to ring the bell, watching the car anxiously as if it might escape. When the bell was not immediately answered she rang it again, hard, swearing under her breath.

'I'm coming, fuck it.'

She breathed out, releasing tension, and waited while the person at the other side worked through the triple locks. The door opened to reveal Matthew, dark red hair spiky above a purple velvet jacket of antique cut and a dress shirt.

'Just the man I want.'

'Why? Where's your mum, or is she ill again?'

'She'll be back. I am looking for Annabelle – Dr Brewster, and I hoped you knew where your client was. She moved out of here last week.'

'I know. But she's not my client.'

'What happened?'

'Oh, *that's* not her fault. We had a conflict – minor thing, but we'd acted for one of the prospective defendant's family. Old Peter's very orthodox about that sort of thing. We passed her on.'

'But?'

'But the silly bitch decided not to take the boyfriend to court.'

'Oh dear. Oh, mistake.'

'You can say that again. The boyfriend greased round her by giving back all her things – and the money he'd nicked. *That's* an indiscretion and if you tell her I'll be unfrocked or whatever. So she decided not to do him for assault.'

'She didn't go back to him?' Francesca forgot her own worries in horror.

'No. She's got a room round the corner here. But she'll be working now. She does the nine o'clock surgery on Mondays.'

She looked at him doubtfully. 'I suppose only a tactless old bat would ask you how you know so much.'

'Yes, but I could see you were going to. I quite fancy her but it's one of my little rules, don't mess with them if they're still attached, you waste your time. You're probably spitting in the wind too, trying to tell her what not to do.'

'I am not here to remonstrate with her. I want a medical opinion.'

'Don't you have a doctor of your own?' He peered at her. 'What's the matter, Wonderwoman? You're looking frazzled. Rest the feet, I'll find coffee.'

Francesca sank into one of the Refuge's awful chairs then started out of it as she remembered her illegally parked car.

'Sit down, I'll keep an eye on the car. Now. What?'

She looked into the competent, impatient face and tried to gather herself. 'My secretary – well, I share her – at Gladstone where I work. She's pregnant, about seven weeks, and she told me yesterday. And I can't remember whether I've had German measles. Nor can my useless parent; she says she thought I did but it may have been just the twins. She says some of us did.'

'Francesca. Where is this going?'

'Well, eight weeks is *the* worst time for exposure to German measles, and the kids here who don't have measles have German measles. But I can't have caught it – German measles, I mean – or carry it if I had it once, I think. Only I never knew any biology *and* I can't remember if I ever had the beastly disease and I don't know what to say to Jo. My secretary.' She picked up her coffee clumsily, spilt it and gulped back tears.

'Dear God,' he said, mopping up the mess competently. 'Let's get some facts here. The Refuge does have German measles, one, yes? Take a slug of the coffee and think, don't just witter.'

'Piss off, Matt,' she said, reduced to her teens. 'Yes. Annabelle diagnosed it, and the local practice confirmed it. And Jo *is* pregnant.'

'It's a matter of ordinary general knowledge that you can't transmit the disease unless you've got it. So you don't have it, lady, and you aren't cooking it if either you had it as a kid, or you had the injection.'

She stared at him over her cup. 'The injection?'

'For rubella. You have it, or all the girls in New Zealand do, at about thirteen. Yes? Cast your mind back.'

She put her cup down, slowly turning scarlet, warm all over with a flooding sense of relief. 'Oh Matt, oh thank God. It all comes back to me. Of course I did. Everyone did, it was compulsory, unless you could prove you'd had German measles. And then as now Mum couldn't remember.'

'Will I take you round to your doctor in that posh car just to make quite, quite sure?'

'No, dammit. Nor do I need a sweetie to make me better, although you might be excused for thinking it.' She looked at him, and he was watching her carefully. 'What?'

'How'd you get in such a state, Wonderwoman?'

'I'm tired,' she said, defensively, and closed both hands round her coffee cup. 'William's ill, so he doesn't sleep, and my husband John is very busy.'

'He's the policeman? Well, they are.'

'I do understand that, Matthew, I'm just telling you why I'm tired.'

She was, she could see, cutting no ice with Matthew, who was sitting watching her, large hands quiet in front of him.

'I'll buy you lunch. *I'll* drive and we'll go to a steak place where they owe me.' He had got up from the desk and was shrugging himself into one of his layers of clothing. He took her cup away and led her to the door, leaving her no room to object or demur, and she found herself handing him the car keys and relaxing into the passenger seat with a sigh of relief.

He took her to a tiny restaurant in the back streets of Ealing, leaving the car parked directly outside where he could see it.

'Wouldn't be necessary in Christchurch, but . . .' he said, darkly.

'None of the sheep can drive, of course,' Francesca said, rallying.

'We haven't yet reached the same level of civilisation as the mother country, so we leave our cars out and our simple huts unlocked. Hello. We need two bloody enormous steaks, chips on the side, tomatoes and mushrooms with. And a beer.' He raised an eyebrow at her but she shook her head. 'Water for the lady then.' He introduced her meticulously to the cook, a small middle-aged dark woman who emerged to greet him with joy. He bent to her and said something quietly, intent and concentrated, and the woman shook her head vigorously, beaming at him. 'Good.' He

47

straightened up and steered Francesca to a table, taking her elbow and pulling out her chair for her while chatting with the waiter, six inches taller than the cook but recognisably her son.

'Clients?' Francesca asked quietly when they were left to themselves, with a pile of bread and black olives.

'Mum is. Was. Seems to be OK now. Her old man had been at her for twenty years, so it took a bit of doing.' He considered her across the table. 'As you would not know, women whose men beat them start to think it's their fault.'

'*I* can't imagine putting up with a man who beat me up.'

'No, I'm sure you can't.' He looked suddenly impatient, and she tried to make amends.

'Sorry, Matt, I *do* know that's too easy. My mum is in the business after all.' She found herself very much wanting this man not to think her an arrogant, middle-class matron, but was equally not prepared to compromise. 'And I do see that in the days when the neighbours, the police and everyone else just treated domestic violence as part of Life's Rich Tapestry to be expected in marriage, and something in which outsiders would not get involved, then it was pretty difficult for the women. But then came the Domestic Violence Act. Male violence is, well, officially condemned, and the police do intervene and the courts do exclude battering men from their houses. So why aren't all the women doing something about their men?' She looked at his shuttered face and tried again. 'They've got my mum, and you, after all. And I do know from Mum that quite a lot of these men do stop battering when they are told forcibly they mustn't. And manage to live with their wives.'

Matthew took a long swallow of his beer, and she understood, disconcerted, that he was delaying in order to keep his temper.

'Where to start, that's the problem,' he observed, to the air, and she gritted her teeth.

'No need to patronise, Matthew. You are younger than the most junior of my siblings.'

They glared at each other.

'I'll start with the easy bit,' Matt said, uncompromisingly. 'Some of these men are mad, in the sense that they will not be deterred by anything society can threaten, and the women know that. If they ever have the courage to get to a Refuge, their names have to be changed and they have to live in another town, even when we manage to get the man put away.'

She sat, remembering cases she had read, or heard about from her mother. 'That's a small percentage,' she said, defensively.

'The victims don't quite see it that way. Ah, I see our steaks.' He gave her a look of admonition and warning and she bit her lip in irritation, then exclaimed in genuine admiration of the beautifully laid out plate. She cut into her steak, seeing Matthew wait for her to start.

'Crumbs,' she said, when she could speak again. 'What wonderful meat.'

'Argentinian. Maria was born there and knows what meat should taste like. Like us and lamb.'

'Indeed.' She decided not to risk further comment about New Zealand lamb as experienced by the UK consumer, frozen and shipped 13,000 miles, and worked through her steak, feeling better by the minute.

'Then there's the next group of men.' Matthew's steak had disappeared so fast he might as well have inhaled it and he was spearing chips to dip in the gravy. 'They come from societies where wife-battering is acceptable behaviour. Anywhere in the Mediterranean, much of the Far East, Africa, and Ireland.'

'New Zealand?'

'These get indignant when they're told they mustn't do it, but they do stop. By and large, and if they don't live in closed communities. I have colleagues who aren't having a lot of luck with Punjabis in Bradford, for instance.'

'Are we only changing behaviour rather than hearts and minds?'

He gave her a long, hostile look, a chip arrested in mid-air between his plate and his mouth. 'There speaks the middle-class liberal. Would it be better to let these blokes go on beating up their women – with belts, and hammers, and anything else they can find – until you can persuade them to change their views?'

'I didn't mean that,' she said, furiously, wrong-footed and scarlet. 'What I meant was, didn't they go back to their preferred method of interaction the second the policeman went home?'

'Not if they're in the nick or injuncted from going near the house, no. Works very well mostly.'

'All right,' she said, between her teeth, all too conscious that she had been attempting to defend the utterly indefensible. 'So we are back to my first question. Given that the exercise of society's sanctions works in the majority of cases, why do not all battered women at least try invoking those sanctions?' She considered the sentence, decided the logic was right, and sat back, picking up a chip.

'At last a slightly better question,' he said, balefully, 'if one which shows you don't understand a lot about the upbringing of most women. Even if I didn't know your mother I would only have to look at you to know you had been loved and encouraged and pushed on to achieve from the day you appeared in the world. So if you entangled yourself with a man who beat you, you'd get out again. OK, it might take you a month or so because you'd waste time, thinking that this couldn't be happening to you.' He peered at her and she relaxed her jaw and drew breath.

'What happens to all the others, then?'

'We speak here', he said, stacking her plate and causing them to be removed with a jerk of his head, waiting impatiently while she told the cook how good it had been, 'of women who weren't brought up to think a lot of themselves, who were taught one way or the other that they were on this earth to marry and look after a man.'

'That was held up as an objective even to me,' she objected.

'As a part of your life, if possible, but well second to personal fulfilment.'

'True.'

'Not just little Chinese girls who are of no account at all and made to feel it, but young English women in families where they assume the girls will marry.'

'Oh, Matt. There *aren't* any these days.'

'Don't give me that. Did you know Annabelle has one brother, not nearly as clever as her, but her doctor father dotes on him, and wouldn't even top up her grant to go to university?'

'What you're saying is that women who lack self-esteem get into these battering relationships and can't get out,' she said, determined to evolve a clear hypothesis. 'My mum says that you often find a battering father in these cases.'

'Doesn't do a lot for your opinion of yourself having a father who beats you and calls you stupid or dirty, to justify what he's doing, no. To little boys or little girls. And before you ask, Wonderwoman, I too am the eldest child of devoted parents.'

'That sees itself.'

'But I've got more imagination than you.'

It hit her like a blow and she felt herself turning scarlet. 'When I was your age I'd no time for imagination,' she said furiously. 'I'd been unhappily married for three years and was trying to face the fact I'd have to stop.' She realised her voice had gone up and looked round for an escape. Seeing none that did not involve working her way past three tables of interested faces, she reached for her glass of water.

'He beat you? I got it all wrong?'

She coughed on the water, managed to put it down and calmed herself by blowing her nose, and looked across at the intent, clever face. 'He wasn't supportive or nice to me, he had had a rotten upbringing, but he didn't beat me. I could have left easily if he had.'

'So how did you leave?'

'He left me.'

'Did you mind much?'

'I did, but it was the failure, the loss of the whole idea that made me so unhappy, not the loss of the man. We had been so happy.'

He nodded. 'I've been there. It was so good, why can't we get it back?'

'You must have been about sixteen,' she said, feeling the need to assert seniority.

'Twenty-one. It pushed me into leaving our humble shieling and coming to make my fortune where the streets are paved with gold.'

'To a Refuge in the back of nowhere, excuse me?'

'I got sidetracked. Which reminds me, I have things to do this afternoon, even if I am lunching with the leisured classes.' He shepherded her impatiently from the restaurant, a large hand in the small of her back, and in ten minutes had driven her back home. He saw her to the door, refusing all thanks for lunch, and shook her hand punctiliously. He ran down the steps, several jackets flapping, and stopped to pat the car affectionately before making off down the street.

5

Monday, 11 April

Two miles to the west of Kensington Church Street the sun was illuminating the faded yellow wall and chipped tiling of a tiny kitchen. The place had been advertised as a furnished studio flat, and it met the specification inasmuch as there was a cramped shower and lavatory and a minute kitchen. It was not therefore necessary to cook in the room which held a small double bed, a desk, a wardrobe, one armchair and not much else. The principal point in its favour – and the one that had been of overwhelming importance to Annabelle when she had found it five days ago – was that it was only a two-month let, giving her somewhere to be while she reorganised her life. She stood on her toes to look out of the high, narrow window which lit and ventilated, inadequately, the tiny kitchen.

'Darling, I'll make tea. You get back in and keep warm.'

She smiled to herself as she heard Antony fight his way out of the bedclothes. The heating in the place left much to be desired and they had ended up under her duvet, his car rug and both their overcoats. She felt his arms go round her and leant back against him, resting her cheek on his neck, luxuriating in his smell. It was a miracle, like turning the clock back five years to when they had first been in love. He steered her gently back to bed and crossed the floor again to the kitchen and she sat, the rug round her shoulders where he had put it, duvet up to her chest, and watched as he put tea-bags into the pot and reboiled the kettle. He looked round at her and grinned. He was dressed solely in his own good navy overcoat, black hair flopping over his forehead, his skin looking brown and healthy in the small ray of sunlight.

'I'll tell you what we're going to do,' he announced, handing her her cup, undoing his coat and sliding carefully under the duvet beside her, companionably twining his legs round hers.

'We're going to find you somewhere better to live. I want you back with me, but not just because where you are is too awful. Not that I'm ungrateful to this dreadful bed,' he added hastily. 'Excellent place it seemed at the time.'

She laughed, charmed by him as always. It had been a good night for her too, and she was still moved by the memory.

The process which had ended in the small lumpy bed last night had started two days before on the Friday night when she had agreed to meet Antony for dinner. She had acknowledged to herself before she started that dinner was the top of a slippery slope, but that she was not going to abandon a relationship she had been in since she was twenty-one without at least saying the words that were boiling in her head. She had enjoyed the sense of power; it had been a guilty but delightful pleasure to watch Antony working so hard that he was sweating in his efforts to persuade her that he woude be a changed man.

She had met him on the Friday evening at a restaurant where they had often been before so that initial awkwardness had been dissolved in the professionally welcoming reception. He had wanted to pick her up at her flat, but she had serenely refused to give him the address. She had listened for his reaction, intending to opt out of dinner if he showed any signs of the wicked temper, coming out of nowhere, with which he had terrorised her, but he had accepted her refusal humbly.

They had sat opposite each other and he had tried to take her hand, but she pulled it back on to her lap.

'Sorry. I'm just glad you're here.'

She had been able to think of no response to that but he had gone on, doggedly. 'Look, I want to try and explain. I know I've been awful to live with.'

'You mean you've been beating me up.' She had meant to sit, coldly, in judgement, but rage threatened to choke her.

He opened his mouth to tell her not to speak so loudly but stopped himself just in time. 'Yes.' He stared at the table, and she watched the muscles at the back of his jaw move, a warning sign of trouble. 'I want to explain,' he said, without looking at her, hands clenched on the table.

'Please do try.' She was in a crowded restaurant, she reminded herself; there was nothing he could do.

'It isn't just because I was being hassled by Francis,' he said, finally managing to look at her. She forced herself not to help him in any way. 'Though I've always found him a ... well ... a heavy load. I feel responsible even though I know he's hopeless.'

'He's an addict.' She had not meant to speak but Antony's attitude to his younger brother, combining resentment and absolute refusal to face the key fact, had always infuriated her.

'I do know that. Now at any rate. I understood it finally when I found I was willing to steal from you to pay his debts. I saw that he was an addict and I'd got involved with his habit.'

'Yes.' It was a very fair summary, startlingly so. She tried not to add anything in alleviation, or exculpation, but simple interest overcame her. 'Why do you ... did you ... feel so responsible for him?'

'Ah.' He leant across the table and she understood she had supplied a feed. 'Because of my father – or mother. Both our parents.'

'Bill and your real mother?'

Antony's mother had died fifteen years ago when he was fifteen and Francis twelve. He had never talked much about her.

'He used to beat her up. And us. Francis and me, Francis worse than me. Christ!' He jerked back in his chair, thumping the back legs down so that the people at the tables near them turned to stare. 'Sorry.' He rubbed his face with his hands. 'I can hardly manage to say it even now. I saw a psychiatrist about it when I was younger. Jonty Morris.' He found a handkerchief and blew his nose and she saw that there were tears in his eyes.

Annabelle, fascinated as she was, found herself thinking that of course it wouldn't be any old psychiatrist, like the weary underpaid young man who came in to see the women at the Refuge. It would have been the great Jonty Morris, author and star, now retired.

'What did he say?'

'That I needed help.' He caught her eye. 'Treatment, I should say.' He sniffed and blew his nose again, as she watched, amazed at seeing the confident, dominant Antony so reduced. 'I managed to tell Jonty ... and myself ... that I was ashamed of the whole grubby miserable bloody *thing*. I mean, other people's fathers didn't beat them, make them feel fucking useless. But I was very busy, so was he, and I sort of stopped going.' He was crying openly now and the waiter hesitated with two plates of avocado held above their heads.

Annabelle nodded to him to put them down and reached over

to take Antony's hands, the skin roughened by continual washing in surgical soap.

He looked at her over their clasped hands and sighed so deeply she thought he was going to faint. 'Sorry.'

'Do you want to . . . to go for a walk?'

'Actually, I'm starving. I didn't have lunch, or breakfast. I had a longish list because Peter's a bit off colour and was letting me do most of it.'

They had eaten two courses in virtual silence. He pushed his plate away and reached for the last slice of bread.

'I wanted to find you and persuade you to come back now, tonight.' He was watching her face carefully, but she could not control an alarmed jerk of her shoulders. 'Annabelle, darling, don't worry, please. I know that would be all wrong, I need to give both of us space. So I'm not asking you to do that, I'm just asking you not to cut me off, to go on seeing me.'

She had sat and looked at him, olive skin yellowish, eyes still swollen, and the straight nose reddened. He still looked wonderful, as the covert glances from the two girls at the next table confirmed, and she clenched her hands in her lap. 'I wouldn't dare move back with you at the moment.'

'You're frightened of me?'

'Yes.'

'Oh *Christ*. Like my mother. He killed her, you know. I don't mean literally, but she just faded away. I hate him.' He put his butter knife down, shaking.

'You'll need to get through that,' she said, slowly.

'I don't see how.' They stared at each other. 'Until the bastard dies.'

She fidgeted uncomfortably at the taste of this memory, sitting warmly inside Antony's rug, listening to him struggling with the tiny awkward shower. She had not let him take her home after the scene in the restaurant. But she had agreed to dine with him again two days later, and this time she had brought him back to bed with her. And it had been wonderful; Antony had been gentle, persistent and imaginative, and they had both wept and he had licked the tears from her cheeks.

There was a crash from the bathroom.

'Oh God. We have to get you out of here, darling. I've just wrecked the shower.'

He came out into a patch of sun, laughing and drying his hair,

55

the long, hard-muscled body looking like a sketch for a statue, and she almost opened her mouth to say that she would come back with him to his flat.

'I must go. I've got a two o'clock list. I'll just check my calls.' He reached across the bed to fish in his coat pocket and laid the phone on the bed, pressing buttons and stroking her cheek with his spare hand. 'Three calls.' He raised his eyebrows at her and settled to listen while she wrapped the rug round his shoulders.

'My father's secretary,' he reported, disbelievingly. 'Will I call urgently? No, I bloody will not. Hang on.'

She felt his shoulders stiffen and moved to look at his face. All the lines had suddenly gone straight and he looked alert and wary. 'The Metropolitan Police. Detective Chief Superintendent McLeish or Detective Inspector Davidson. Will I ring in at once?'

They stared at each other.

'I wonder what the bastard's done. Beat up my stepmother perhaps.' He was punching in a number, face tight with concentration.

'Detective Inspector Davidson? Antony Price here. Where am I? Well, in Ealing. Why? My father? Yes, but what has happened? No, I've got a car here. Look, I mean I'm operating at 2 p.m. No. Well ... right.' He put the phone down. He looked simply astonished, eyebrows raised, mouth slightly open. 'Something's happened to my father. They won't say what. That means he's *dead*. I've heard them in Casualty when I was a houseman. They want me now and they want me to cancel my list. So he's dead.'

Annabelle opened her mouth to protest, to dispute, and tried to hug him, but he sat, limp, gazing at the opposite wall.

'You can't find the partner either? Doing well between us. Keep at it. No, Mrs Price is all right. I'm seeing her later.' John McLeish put the phone down and reminded himself that the first day of a murder investigation was often like this; the man in charge kicked his heels while all the procedures were put in place, and the deceased's contacts found. Davidson had located the elder son, the wife was reclining in a bedroom in the house of a woman friend, and he had taken statements from two key players, Margaret Howard and Miles Arnold. Margaret Howard had been of limited usefulness. She had been blamelessly deployed from 4 p.m. on the Friday until 9 a.m. on the Monday – until she had left to meet Miles Arnold on the doorstep – looking after an aged and bedridden aunt, so that the usual minder could have a weekend off. He had considered the slight middle-aged woman in front of him and had decided that while it was theoretically possible that she had left her aunt sleeping in Ealing and crept back to the office to murder her employer, in practice he would not devote much emotional energy to the proposition. In the interests of leaving no stone unturned, however, one of the team he had set up for the case would talk to the aunt sometime later in the day. He would be having the first of the regular daily meetings with the team shortly and he might as well contain his soul in patience and get through the in-tray. Much to his relief the phone rang.

'Davidson.'

'Bruce. Where are you?'

'At Notting Dale. We've got a room here. I have Mr Francis Price with me.'

'Had a chat, have you?'

'Aye.'

'Useful? Where was he Friday?'

'There's a problem about that.' McLeish heard a door bang. 'That's better. He was out of it, he says. He's a druggie, ye remember. Doesna know much after lunch on Friday till about Saturday. He says.'

'He'll have to do better than that.'

'He's given us a couple of places he thinks he was at. I've sent a constable. Trouble is, John, if we let him out on the street we may not find him again that easily.'

McLeish considered the point. 'What state is he in now?'

'Needing a shot.'

'Keep him. I'm coming.'

Bruce Davidson would be right about the man's state; he had put in a couple of years with Narcotics. Both sons were suspects, prima facie, and it would be as well to see this one now on the same day as the discovery of the body.

It took fifteen minutes before the car pulled up at Notting Dale and he plunged up the familiar steps. The young man he would meet was her stepson not her son, he reminded himself, and was not therefore surprised to meet a man much darker than Mrs Price and tall, as she was not. Good-looking bloke, but you could see he was a druggie, the wide hollowed dark eyes in the thin face, the pale skin, the painful, pitted sores round the mouth told you he was an addict. Heroin most likely. He was said to be twenty-seven but looked younger, like a sick seventeen. As Bruce Davidson had said, he was on edge, licking dry lips in between taking impatient pulls at a cigarette which he threw away half smoked as McLeish went through the preliminaries.

'I told your friend here,' he said, moving uneasily in the hard chair. The collar of his shirt was ingrained with dirt, and he smelt, faintly but distinctly. He yawned widely and scratched at his knee, then squirmed again in the chair, rubbing his shoulders against the back. Suppressing the need to have a scratch himself, McLeish explained that his story had hardly been comprehensive or reassuring, to the extent that he might well find himself in custody until he could produce some better answers.

'You can't do that.'

McLeish did not comment and he and Davidson watched as Francis Price pulled the last cigarette from a packet and took three attempts to get it alight.

'I *told* him. I got up about . . . what . . . five in the afternoon. I went round to my brother's flat on Friday about eight o'clock, but he wasn't there.' The wide mouth trembled and he looked suddenly like a little boy whose mother was not at the school gates to meet him.

'Was he expecting you?'

McLeish got a look of instant disconcerting hostility. 'No, he wasn't, but he hadn't said he was going out.'

'When had you last seen him?'

'The day before. Thursday.'

'You're close to him, then?'

'Yes. Yes, he's always helped me.'

'Bought you drugs?'

Francis Price looked at him sharply. 'You can't speak to me like that.'

'You have three convictions for possession of Class A drugs, Mr Price, two of them recent. And you told Detective Inspector Davidson that you could not remember much about Friday evening.'

'I'm off drugs.' He stared at them from the depths of the chair, lips pushed together like a child. 'My brother's a doctor – a surgeon. He doesn't approve of *any* drugs.' He sounded ridiculously proud of his brother's stance. 'I wasn't feeling well on

Friday, I thought I had something really wrong so I went round to Antony.'

'What about your doctor?'

'I haven't got one.'

That was probably true. Hard-pressed London GPs were unwilling to keep an addict on their books. They were difficult to handle, prone to every known illness, and often violent when refused anything. And they were Aids risks, and alarming to other patients. He began to feel some sympathy for Antony Price, surgeon and brother to this human mess.

'So when you couldn't find your brother, what did you do?' He watched the man fidget, reminding himself that he was twenty-seven, although it was difficult to think of him as grown-up. 'You must have been rather upset.'

'I was. Yes, I was.' Francis Price was searching his pockets frenziedly, near to tears. 'You haven't got a cigarette?'

McLeish, a non-smoker, looked round but Davidson had a packet out. He held a match steady while Francis Price managed to co-ordinate sufficiently the cigarette and his shaking hands. He dragged in a lungful and started to cough, the thin chest heaving. Bronchitis at the very least, perhaps nearer pneumonia by the sound of it, McLeish thought, and saw his alarm mirrored on Davidson's face.

'That's a nasty cough.'

'I know. That's why I wanted Antony. I thought he might have let me stay for the weekend. The place I live is cold and there's no one there to bother.'

'So when you couldn't find him what did you do?' He waited while Francis had another fit of coughing. 'You went to see your father?'

'You have to be joking.' Well, that had come out loud and clear, without any scratching, fidgeting or graveyard cough.

'You didn't get on with him?'

'I hate the bastard. Hated him, I mean.'

McLeish caught Davidson's warning look. 'Mr Price, you are aware that we believe your father may have been murdered?'

'I wouldn't be at all surprised.'

'Who do you think would have had cause?'

'Anyone who knew him.' Francis Price was rocking forward, flushed now, arms crossed, hands obsessively rubbing his forearms. 'He was a rotten father and he used to beat our mother till she gave up and died. Even Sylvia – you ask Antony. He tried to make her sue him, but she wouldn't go to court.'

'So you didn't go to your father. Where *did* you go?'

'Back to where I live. I was ill. I took a lot of aspirin – about six, all I had, and I woke up late on Saturday.'

'What then?'

'Well, I tried to phone Antony but he wasn't answering. And he doesn't always ring me back. So I just stayed in bed.'

He was not looking at either of them and both experienced policemen considered the hole in this narrative. This young man was undoubtedly ill, but he was also an addict; had he really managed to get through the whole of Friday night on nothing more than aspirin?

'You didn't go out at all? Did anyone else in the house come and see you?'

Yes, it transpired, rather slowly, somebody had. And he had then felt better and got up for a bit before going back to bed. By Sunday night he had indeed felt well enough to seek out his brother Antony again, but he was out.

McLeish thought about this unpromising recital and decided he was not at all happy with the story. 'Mr Price, we'll get you some tea and something to eat, while your statement is typed.'

'And a cigarette?'

Davidson shook one out of the packet and left it and a couple of matches. 'Not a lot he can set fire to in there,' he observed as they closed the door behind them.

'Just as well. You found the brother?'

'I did. And told him the odds. He's gone over to the mortuary with Dennison. Well, we havenae got formal identification yet, and the bloke's a surgeon. He's not going to pass out.'

'He may not meet many very dead bodies in his line of trade. Where was he, anyway?' McLeish asked, remembering that he had not been at his flat on Sunday night when his brother had called.

'With a girlfriend, seemingly.'

'Lucky man. Get him up here, Bruce. I want someone to take that lad home – the one we've just talked to.'

'If I were him, I wouldn't be keen.'

'I'm not very happy about discharging a sick suspect on to the streets. He could vanish. Or die. I'd like him parked with someone who thinks they're responsible for him.'

'Right. I'll just take a wee look at him.' Davidson turned back down the corridor and peered through the spy-hole. 'I think he's asleep. I'll just check what he did with my cigarette.' He was out again before McLeish could feel it necessary to follow. 'Silly wee man. Asleep but restless. He'll wake up again.'

McLeish found his driver and set off back to the Yard, deciding it was time to talk to Catherine. He had left a careful message that morning with her staff, in the interests of interdepartmental co-operation. But she had talked to *him* about William Price and it was only proper that he should personally repay the compliment. He thought briefly of his wife and decided crossly that he need not. She had been unmoved by the news that Catherine Crane was once more in the same building as him, confining herself to observing that women who only fancied chaps belonging to other people needed to grow up. He had felt this was overly smug, particularly given her own track record, but had decided to keep his head down. He used the car-phone and, finding Catherine at her desk, invited her to join him in his office.

It did feel comfortably like old times, he acknowledged, rising to greet her as she walked in, but now he was senior enough to have three chairs and a low table around which he could invite people to join him. He asked for tea, receiving a quick speculative look from his secretary. The whole building probably knew their joint history, brief though it had been, he understood, resignedly.

'This must be your prospective customer. My corpse, I mean.'

'It is. He is.'

'Are you out of it then, now he's dead? The Fraud Squad, I mean.'

'No, not at all. There's a partner, Luke Fleming. Have you met him yet?'

'He is in Majorca, overseeing some building work, apparently. We haven't talked to him yet.'

Her eyes widened. 'But John, he may have run. I mean, whatever was going on, he must have been in it.'

'It's not as bad as I'm making it. He's touring about six sites, the secretary says. He rang on Sunday and told her where he was, it's

61

just that he's not there now. Not due back until tomorrow, and we've asked the Spanish to find him and break the news. Does he *have* to have been involved?'

He watched with pleasure as she thought how best to present it to him quickly. She was clever as well as beautiful, was Catherine, with a good, clear, hard mind, infinitely better than most of her male colleagues.

'It's a limited company with three directors. The deceased, his wife Sylvia, and Luke Fleming. All directors of a company are responsible for what goes on.'

'What, even if they are non-executive?'

She looked momentarily exasperated. 'There is no difference at all in law between an executive and a non-executive director. The law doesn't recognise the idea of non-executive, to put it another way.'

'So Sylvia Price would be liable too?' He didn't want Catherine finding him slow.

'Yes. But, contrary to what I just said, she might get away with a bit. Juries tend to accept that people put their wives on as directors for tax reasons rather than because they know anything about the business.'

'So where do you go from here? We ... I ... would find it useful to understand exactly what you were looking for. After all, this might be the murder motive.'

'It *is* murder, is it? I mean not an accident?'

Bruce Davidson, he thought resignedly, indefatigable as he was and no doubt still hoping he might be in with a chance. 'It might have been an accident, but it doesn't seem likely. The table was heavy and Forensic report no prints at all on it. Wiped clean. And someone came in through the window. So. *I* think it's murder.'

'That's good enough for me,' she said, with a glancing look under her eyelashes that left him short of breath. 'What we ... I ... thought was that they were at the very least overtrading; that they'd sold more timeshares than there were places for the customers. Now that might have been all right if they could get another couple of developments going quickly, but *that* takes cash and it was beginning to look as if there wasn't enough to go round. That would leave them, assuming we're right, with two choices: go on getting in more cash, or take what they had and run.'

'Which were they doing? Or a bit of both?'

She gave him the measured look of approval which he remembered very well. 'That's right, because whichever way it came out they'd need to get in as much cash as possible. Either to dig themselves out of a hole by getting a new development started, or to give themselves a bigger chunk to vanish with.'

'Where would they go? I felt reasonably happy about Mr Fleming in Majorca *because* Spain's no good to crooks any more, even if they could stand the neighbours.'

'That's right, it would have to be outside the EC. Brazil's still good, so are most places down there. We've never got Ronnie Biggs back.'

'You got any proof at all, Catherine? I mean anything that would hold up to a charge?'

'Not enough,' she admitted. 'But I know it's right.'

'Mm. So why would anyone murder Mr Price? He doesn't *have* dissatisfied customers yet, as far as you know. And anyway, they'd want their money, rather than his body, wouldn't they?'

'That's right, and I wasn't thinking of a customer. The thing about fraud, John, is that it gets everywhere. William Price was the salesman, he took the cheques. He could have been hanging on to some of them for his own personal nest egg somewhere. His fellow directors wouldn't like that, they're all responsible. But if he's dead you can pile all the shit on him.'

'Last thing he did of course. Shit.' He was appalled to hear what he'd said. She looked back at him, momentarily taken completely aback.

'Sorry,' he said, feeling himself go scarlet. 'Forget that. It's been a long day.' He found his cup of tea and drank it down to the bottom. 'Now, you were saying that it could have suited any of his co-conspirators to see him dead, because then they could say he'd been doing it all. Only it would have needed to look like suicide, and it doesn't. Or not enough.'

She had recovered her equanimity, he saw, but she was deciding how to go on. 'Perhaps having him dead was enough, given that I hear there'd been a break-in,' she said, carefully. 'It could have been the burglar after all, none of them need be implicated.'

'When you say "them", you mean Mrs P and the other bloke, Luke Fleming.'

'And just possibly Mr Miles Arnold MP.'

'Now him I met, and I've had him looked up.' He walked over to his desk, glad to get up and move about, and found the piece of paper. 'Seven directorships or consultancies on his sheet.'

She made no movement to take the paper, and he realised that she would have done her homework too. He considered the paper again. 'Hang on. He wasn't a director of Price Fleming. Would that help?'

'In terms of what he could be charged with, yes. In practice, not a lot, do you think?'

No, indeed it wouldn't; in the frenzied atmosphere of current politics, no one would have time or interest in the details if there had been a fraud in the company. A triumphant Opposition would make the most of this, and Mr Arnold's own side would not even go through the motions of defending, not in the present climate of opinion.

'So he's in the frame. Mine, I mean,' he said, reaching the end of his line of thought.

'And in mine. If he was involved. We weren't sure he was. It's possible he was just doing a PR job for them and had no idea of what was happening. He didn't work from that office after all, and might never have seen a customer.'

'If ever I bought a timeshare and found anything dodgy about it I'd go straight for the MP who had his name on it,' McLeish objected.

'Assuming you knew.' She was leaning forward, chasing an idea. 'You might not, he isn't on the notepaper or on the accounts at Companies House, except as "consultancy fees". Doesn't say who they're paid to.'

'But once I *knew*, I'd go for him.'

'Yes.'

They both sat back, pleased with each other.

'Do you want a drink?' he asked, and saw her hesitate so that he became self-conscious again. 'Is that the time?' he asked theatrically, staring at the clock above her head. 'Sorry, I've left it too late, I'm expected.' He sounded like a caricature of a genial uncle, he thought savagely.

'I expect Francesca gets back earlier than you,' Catherine said, pleasantly.

'Sometimes. Tonight anyway.' He managed, just, to avoid giving details of his wife's timetable, and to concentrate on making sure he had got what he, or rather the investigation, needed.

'So, let's see if I've got it. You ... your people think that Mr Price and his associates were running into a siding, too many paid-up customers chasing too few places. And when they hit the buffers, Mrs Price, Mr Fleming and Mr Arnold were all going to be spattered alongside him. So, from my point of view, all three of them might have found it useful if Mr Price was derailed first.'

'That's what we wonder. But if you could let us in to have a look at the books, then we can tell you what's really going on. You'll know then whether you've got three people with a good motive.'

'I'll need to think about that. But don't worry about losing evidence. Everything's locked up, we did that straightaway.' He considered the familiar beauty before him. 'Tomorrow do you?'

She smiled at him. 'Oh heavens yes, John, there are a few other things around on my desk.' She put her cup down and rose, so that he scrambled awkwardly to his feet as well. 'Thank you for tea.'

'Thank you for coming.'

He escorted her to the lift and strode off down the corridor, feeling the need to catch up with the investigation before he went home. He knew he was lucky only to be involved in one; had he been in post for more than a week he would have been dealing with two at least, and indeed another might come in at any moment. It was therefore, he reminded himself, the more important that he did not do all the work himself on this case.

All was however in good order, in fact in excellent shape for this early in an investigation. A control room had been set up and was fully staffed and a reassuring amount of activity seemed to be going on. Detective Chief Inspector Johnson had been posted to the job since lunchtime and he stopped to talk to him; the man would be the key to this job. And he probably was uncomfortable being sandwiched between Davidson and a detective chief superintendent, who had worked together several times before. Johnson was a small, wiry Yorkshireman with stubby blond hair cut apparently with nail scissors, youngish and keen to impress. He and Davidson probably did not get on all that well, but that was tomorrow's problem. He asked cautiously where Davidson was and got shown the board with everyone on the team's current whereabouts marked.

'We can't see Mrs Price till tomorrow, seemingly. Mr Antony

Price is available tomorrow. He identified the deceased for us but he said he had to do his operating list. So Dennison let him, but got his consent to search his flat.' Johnson looked at him for reassurance while McLeish, who had been momentarily transported back to Hull by the familiar flat accent with the consonants spat out, reflected on the contrast with the London accent in which a consonant was a rare occurrence.

'No, quite right,' he said, emerging hastily from this consideration. 'We know where to find him, and he's had since Friday to destroy evidence if he needed to. Tomorrow will do. Anything from Forensics?'

'Report on its way, I understand. Only thing they did say, while it's being typed, is that they looked for footprints where you thought – outside the window. Nothing showing.'

Now that was important, and he was glad to see that Johnson had grasped it. 'Whoever it was could have been in there, or come through the front door then,' he suggested, just to make sure.

'Mebbe.'

Now that was Yorkshire for you, he thought, amused. Just like the men of Hull. 'Where are you from, Johnson?'

'Goole. Hear you were in Hull.'

'I was.'

Both men observed a respectful silence for Hull, where John McLeish's report had resulted in a wholesale clearance in which no one had been allowed to retire early on grounds of ill health.

'Who are we going to send to Majorca to find Mr Fleming?'

'Oh me, of course. Needs a senior man. The bugger is we've found him. He's getting on a plane now.' Johnson was grinning.

'I might as well go home since you've got it all in hand. You know where to find me.'

Johnson confirmed that he did and McLeish got out the car and drove home. He would be on time for supper, and early enough to see William. On the days she worked Francesca had instituted a system of a long rest in the afternoon, which suited their young nanny, so that William could stay up to see her from five thirty when she got home and with luck have some time between seven and eight with his father. McLeish felt guiltily that he might have preferred a stiff drink and a comfortable chair in front of the TV to reading with actions and gestures to a demanding small son, particularly when he had already entertained said son for much of the night. But that was family life, and he was lucky to have it.

'William's asleep, sorry,' she said, meeting him on the doorstep, and he felt a guilty lift of the heart. 'And Susannah is just off.'

He greeted their young nanny punctiliously and wished her a good evening, then padded into the kitchen following the smell of cooking. 'Dover sole?' he said, enquiringly, knowing what they cost.

'Mm.'

'*And* wine?'

'Yes.'

He considered his wife, who had poured wine for them both. Even with two professional salaries coming in they were not in a position to buy Dover sole and wine every day, not after paying a nanny, a cleaner and a mortgage on a house big enough to hold a flatlet for living-in help. Francesca was looking preoccupied and tired.

'The lads all right, I hope?' He decided to head into the likely area of trouble.

'Yes, I think so.' She sounded surprised.

So it wasn't the brotherhood. He cast his mind back and slowly remembered. 'Oh, I'm sorry, I forgot to ask. German measles. Did you have it?'

'Ah. That. No, or rather I don't know, but it doesn't blessedly matter. I had the injection for rubella, and it would be really unlikely apparently that I'd get the disease. So that's OK.'

'When did you find all this out? Why didn't you tell me? You were upset this morning.'

'Oh darling. I only worried for three hours, until that kind boy who works as the Refuge lawyer – Matthew – sorted me out.'

'That fierce arrogant New Zealand lad you told me about?' McLeish asked, struggling to get his facts straight.

'All of that, but a kind boy too. Fed me lunch. Now, do sit down and eat your lovely supper.'

He sat, gratefully, just as the telephone rang. He listened, watching the table and his wife's set expression, put the phone down and started to eat, rapidly.

'You have to go back.'

'I'm sorry. Yes, I do.' He reached a hand over to take hers, but she was not mollified. 'It's always like this the first day of a case. You remember.'

'Can't it wait?'

She knew the answer to that, he thought, angrily, she'd known it when they married. He ate doggedly, the beautiful food tasteless in his mouth.

6

Tuesday, 12 April

As the plane taxied slowly to the stand, the tall man sitting in the front for the leg room reached for his jacket. He stood up to put it on, defying the painstaking instructions not to move from his seat, or undo his seat belt.

The speaker system rustled into life. 'We have a message for Mr Luke Fleming. Could Mr Fleming please identify himself to one of the cabin staff?'

The man tensed, all his anxieties crystallising, and looked over to where two members of the crew, wearing fixed expressions of bright helpfulness, were standing in the corridor between him and the door, which was now being manoeuvred into place at the air jetty with a set of metallic bumps and crashes.

'It's me,' he said, hauling his jacket on.

'Mr *Luke* Fleming?' one of the helpful young men asked, as if there might be several of him. 'You're being met on the air side, I understand. Would you come with us? Excuse me, sir.' He held back, civilly but firmly, a hopeful Majorcan who wanted to find himself on English soil as soon as possible. 'Do you have baggage in the hold?'

'No. Just hand luggage. This.'

The young man took his case and Luke Fleming followed. He was expecting to find a policeman at the other end of this process and was mildly surprised to find himself and his luggage handed over to a man in the uniform of the British Airport Authority, who opened an unmarked door by the edge of the air jetty and took him down a ramp to a waiting Airport Authority car.

'Luke.'

'Miles. What are you doing here?'

'In a minute. They want your passport.'

Luke handed it over, and the man who had met him examined it carefully before handing it back. 'Thank you, sir.'

'I wanted to have a talk before you got to the office,' Miles said, levering himself into the back of the car and jabbing a warning finger at the driver's impassive back. 'We're going to the VIP lounge – it's quiet there.'

It was, Luke conceded. The place was enormous, and comfortable with chairs and sofas grouped so that you could talk, and enough space between each grouping to give privacy for any conversation conducted below megaphone level. And it was empty but for a small group of men in long robes and *keffiyeh*, who sat, contained and silent, in one corner. Coffee arrived instantly; Miles Arnold drank his thirstily while Luke sipped his and considered the room.

'Easiest way out of an aeroplane I've ever found at Heathrow,' he observed. 'Can MPs always do that?'

'No. I asked a favour. It's done for ministers of course all the time.'

Luke noted the change of tone; long years of working in contracting in countries all over the world had made him acutely sensitive to the sound rather than the words. He had always assumed Miles Arnold to be ambitious, and now he knew how much and for what.

'Who found him? Bill, I mean.'

'I did. It was awful. What did they tell you?'

'The Garda? Not a lot other than that he had been found dead yesterday. I tried to speak to Sylvia but she was laid up, poor girl, and I couldn't find you.'

'They reckon he'd been dead since Friday. Margaret Howard said goodbye to him at four o'clock on Friday, so he was OK then.'

Luke Fleming waited, but Miles Arnold seemed to have said all he was going to. 'So how did he die exactly?'

'I found him hanging from the ceiling with a bag over his head, wearing stockings and a pair of silk knickers. And smelling not very nice.'

'Poor bugger.'

'I've never asked you, Luke, but did you *like* him? Or was he just someone you worked with?'

'I didn't think about it that way. He was a bloody good salesman, no doubt about that. He messed you around if you let him, but everyone does that in the building trade. And he was a good laugh, you know, went to the clubs, people liked him. Drank a bit too much, but we all do down there.'

'How did you meet him?'

Luke needed urgently to get to the office and talk to the bank, but he had been around long enough to know you could only do business when everyone involved was comfortable. 'It was about eight years ago. Bill came to look at a flat in a development I'd just finished for Wimpey. He didn't like the one we had so I took him off to another one. He didn't like that either. He travelled around a bit – Syliva was with him by then – looking, and after, what, about a couple of weeks he came back and bought me lunch.'

'And?'

'And said he had sold his business and was looking for another. He had looked everywhere for a flat down there and kept thinking that it really wasn't quite what he wanted. He loved the place but he didn't want the bother. He'd looked at conventional timeshares and he thought that was OK but a bit limited. So he came up with this idea. Said what he wanted was to be able to get into somewhere nice, in a place he knew, whenever he wanted to. So why wasn't there a company that owned enough places to offer that?'

'And that's what we sell?'

'That's right. You pay a premium sometimes, but most of the time we can give you a flat in one of the thirty we've got down there when you want it, and at the worst we can get you into one of the hotel flats. It's worked pretty well so far. But you know all this, surely?'

'Not the details.'

Luke, who had not thought his description of the business detailed, found a previous conviction confirmed. Miles Arnold was paid a salary that would have enabled the business to afford a second site agent in Spain, and had done very little for it other than advance Bill Price's social ambitions. And Sylvia's, he conceded, reluctantly.

'I mean, the customers have all been pretty satisfied, haven't they? No one's found themselves in a building site, or anything?'

'We've had times when we got the plumbers out about an hour before the punters arrived, but that's not unusual down there.'

'Yes, of course.' Miles Arnold MP was struggling. 'Look, I'm trying to ask if everything is all right – financially,' he added.

'What do you mean?'

'Well ...' Miles Arnold poured himself coffee, mouth tight in concentration. 'I suppose I'm asking, are the assets for which the customers have paid actually *there* on the ground? I've seen most of them, but ...'

Indeed he had, Luke Fleming thought drily, on several free holidays, some with his wife, some with other women. 'Most of them.'

'What?' Miles Arnold's hand jerked as he poured milk into his coffee.

'A business like this has debts, as you know.'

It was gratifyingly clear that Miles Arnold MP wished he had not embarked on this line of enquiry, and Luke watched him wriggle. Well, it was no time for weak brethren.

'All right, Luke. Tell me the full strength.'

'Why?'

'Because I'm in a certain amount of shit already and I'd better know where the next lot is coming from. And because it turns out some of my money is in this business.'

'Now *that* I did not know.'

'Nor did I. I thought my cash had gone into buying shares, in companies quoted on the Stock Exchange. I'm not an entrepreneur, what I understand is how to earn money from putting people in touch with each other. And I wanted it safely invested so I'd have an income behind me if I got into the government. You know what they pay a junior minister? About the same as a junior bag carrier in a merchant bank, and you have to give up all your other jobs. I've seen too many of our lot come to grief if they don't have a bit behind them.'

Luke thought his way through the information and went back to the key point. 'So how much of your cash is in the business?'

'About £80,000. Yes, well, I'm not actually that careless.' Luke supposed he must have been looking as incredulous as he felt. 'The thing *is*, about a year ago I had £20,000 from a fee, and for once in my life I didn't immediately need it, so I invested it through Bill. He turned it into £50,000. No, he did, I saw the certificates. *That* was all right.'

'Then you gave him some more?'

'I left that with him and gave him £30,000 more. Another fee.'

'Nice money.'

'Legitimate, therefore taxable – I mean, I owe the tax on both of

72

them now. Twenty-four bloody thousand. When we say we're the party of low taxes it's only relative to the other lot, you know.'

Luke ignored this expedition into fiscal policy. 'What did Bill do with it?'

'He *told* me he'd put the lot into shares in three of the water companies, and sold at a £50k profit. The certs were with the brokers and £20,000 in cash was in the safe. He said – but the brokers don't have certificates. Indeed, they'd never taken an order for any shares, all the money from the sale of the last lot went to Bill. As I'd instructed, more fool me.'

Luke, in silent agreement with this judgement, thought for a minute. 'Why the cash? I mean, why didn't he send you a cheque if you wanted some of it out?'

'Ah, well.' Miles Arnold leant forward, the fair hair flopping over his forehead. 'I wanted cash to pass on.'

'Where to?'

'A friend of mine.' Luke stared at him and he flushed. 'A lady friend.'

'A pay-off?'

'No, no. So she could get her own flat.' Miles Arnold was staring at the coffee table, jaw set, back teeth clenched.

Luke remembered sharply a much-needed subvention of £80,000 arriving, five months before. He had been worried sick, but Bill had seemingly worked his usual magic, and this £80,000 had enabled him to blag enough cash out of the local bank to get the place finished and trigger the next lot of payments from the punters.

'I take it there was no cash in the safe yesterday,' he asked unhopefully.

'There was nothing in the safe at all. But it could be that the chap, or chaps, who broke in cleaned it out.'

'Then you can claim on our insurance. I mean, it wasn't funny money, it was yours, you can explain.'

'I suppose so. But I'd have to prove it was there. It'll take time and I need the cash *now*, and I need it without having to explain the whole thing to Caroline.' Miles Arnold threw himself back in his chair and semaphored to one of the distant British Airport Authority employees.

Luke, who did not want his fifth cup of coffee that day, let Miles Arnold get out of his chair the better to communicate his needs; the man needed to discharge energy, and he needed to think. It was becoming more and more important to get to the office and find out where, if anywhere, there was any cash outside of the rainy-day money sitting in a bank in Geneva. He watched Miles Arnold come back, jacket flapping, with the politician's fulsome smile for a BAA employee doing no more than his job in clearing away the coffee cups.

'Who is Bill's executor?' Miles asked, as he sat down and reached for coffee.

'Sylvia is one, I'm the other.'

'Really?' Miles Arnold stopped, arrested in mid-movement. 'Is that usual? I thought there'd be a lawyer.'

'If you want to ensure a small business fails when the main proprietor dies that's a good way to do it. Bill knew that. He didn't think he was going to die, well, none of us do, but he agreed Sylvia and I, who are the only other directors, had better be executors. The business was all he had to leave, after all.'

'What about that great house?'

'It belongs to Sylvia. The business is there on a yearly licence.'

'Is *that* usual?'

'Not unusual. If you're a businessman you try and keep some assets outside the company. So when you go belly up because the government's decided to hook us on to the Deutschmark, or some other insanity, then you can start again.'

Miles Arnold opened his mouth, presumably to produce a defence of recent government actions, but thought better of it.

'So unless you can hide the asset you put it in the wife's name, where the company's creditors can't get at it. You have to get your timing right; they can get the deal cancelled if you go down within two years of making the transfer.'

'And how long ago was the house put in Sylvia's name?' Miles asked.

'Well, it's at least three years since they bought it. And she put up some of the money herself – she was a widow when Bill met her. Of course it left a problem for the company.'

'What?' Miles Arnold was very jumpy; well, anyone would be rattled by finding himself £80,000 lighter.

'Banks won't lend a small company much money unless they can find a solid asset as security. Bill always had a problem there; the bank kept him on a very tight rope. They've lent all they're going to on the overseas stuff.' He waited patiently to see if Miles Arnold was going to get to the point by himself.

'Oh Christ. So all my money, including the cash in the safe, may have been used somewhere, and Sylvia – who has the house – might not be prepared to do anything about repaying it.' The man had turned white, and Luke Fleming took pity on him.

'When you're in business, Miles, you don't necessarily think you'll live for ever.'

'Of course, he was insured.'

'As am I. Key Man insurance, £2m for him, £1m for me, it being thought you could get someone else to do what I do, easier than you can get someone to do what Bill does – did. Used to be only £1m and £500,000, but we upped it, thank God, sometime last year.'

'But where does that money go?'

'Into the company. The insurance is in their name. *And* the premiums were paid. I checked, first thing I did.'

Miles Arnold was watching his face like a lover. 'And will it be enough?'

'It'll help.'

'You mean the company could still go down?'

'Depends on the bank. They'll want to hang on to all the money but they have to give the other creditors a chance. I can suck my teeth and sound dead gloomy about the properties in Spain, and persuade the bank they'd be better letting me finish up the ones we've got, get the punters' money in and trade our way out.'

He saw that Miles Arnold had understood exactly what he was being told and decided he could afford a pee. He rose heavily from the low chair, hitching his trousers and thinking he badly needed to play a bit more tennis and drink a bit less, but none of that was going to happen until he had this lot under control.

He did his teeth and washed his face as well, and put his glasses back on and contemplated himself in the mirror. Looked less than forty-seven, he thought, all his own dark hair, brown eyes and the sallow skin that was much improved by his permanent suntan.

He paused outside the door and looked through glass and tall, green plants over the expanse of silver-grey carpet to where Miles Arnold sat, very still, leaning forward, hands clenched, and decided he would have to get this one off his back.

'More coffe?' Miles Arnold looked up, hopefully.

'No. I have to get on. I'm expected. Look, your spot of bother. You've got a timing problem. I'll have to talk to Sylvia of course, but yes, unless the situation's much worse than I think, I'll get you the £20k you need now.'

'Oh yes. Thank you. That *would* help.' He looked momentarily like a man reprieved from the electric chair.

Luke said his farewells and strode off through the maze of Terminal 1, hoping that Sylvia would see the advantage of keeping Miles Arnold sweet while they grappled jointly with whatever mess Bill had left this time.

John McLeish had agreed that he would interview Sylvia Price in her own living-room, rather than at Scotland Yard, or Notting Dale. It had been a choice between that and waiting until the next day, or the day after. Her solicitor, Peter Graebner, whom he knew of old, had made it civilly clear that medical certificates would block any attempt to get his client off her own base. The deceased's wife was going to be able to tell them about the business and, assuming Catherine and her colleagues were anywhere near right, *that* might shed more light on the murder than anything else. He had read the pathologist's report in the car, and it contained not a lot he did not already know. Bill Price had had a slightly enlarged heart – indicative of possible heart disease and indeed the narrowed arteries that went with it. But that had not been what killed him. He had died from strangulation; the neck had not been broken, which indicated that he had not dropped suddenly and sharply as hanged murderers once had, with their hands bound behind their backs so that they could not claw vainly against the rope as Bill Price had done. McLeish, imagining the stifling darkness inside the inverted plastic bag, the sickening terror as the table went from beneath his knees and the rope tightening against the jugular, hoped that it had not gone on long.

He thought about his notes as he went up the stone steps; he needed to know who had known of Bill Price's sexual habits, and could have planned to take advantage of them. If his wife had been ignorant of them she was no longer; plenty of people including her own solicitor would have enlightened her. And if she had known, what had she felt about it? And had the dead man related sexually to her at all, or was the activity in the basement his sole outlet? The police psychiatrist, consulted in haste, had told him that the Prices might well have had at least the semblance of an ordinary sexual relationship. 'Whatever *that* means, John, but lots of chaps have things they do to amuse themselves and still fuck the wife in a pretty straightforward way. Or they might have had a version of that game – deprivation of oxygen – that they played together and he just did the do-it-yourself variation when she wasn't there. Or they might not be doing anything at all together and he got all his entertainment this way. No, it's not a silly question, John, I just don't know the answer.'

Bruce Davidson was waiting for him inside, passing the time by chatting to Margaret Howard.

'That was Mr Fleming,' she said, with unmistakable relief. 'He's at the airport. He'll be here in about an hour.'

'We'll let him get his breath then,' McLeish said, pleasantly. Whatever messages Luke Fleming had wanted to convey to the company's secretary he had already passed. And a couple of his squad were on the spot, in the office, sorting through papers and answering the telephone under Bruce Davidson's eye. Luke Fleming would not be able to move anything around unseen, assuming that he wanted or needed to.

'Mrs Price is upstairs, sir,' Bruce Davidson said formally, for the benefit of the youngsters in the office.

'Let's get to it.' He nodded to the lads to sit down again, and realised wryly as he went upstairs that he now expected men only ten years his junior to stand when he arrived in a room.

There were three people waiting for him, two standing already and one who did not get up to greet him.

'I thought I would not faint in your arms again today, Detective Chief Superintendent.' Sylvia Price was arranged gracefully on a sofa so that he had to avoid a low coffee table to take her outstretched hand. She was indeed a pretty woman, he thought, his first impressions confirmed, a little on the plump side perhaps, but that was a matter of taste, and she had the confidence of a woman who had always been to someone's taste. She did dye her hair, blonde streaks on dark brown, but it was done with style and suited the slightly sallow skin and blunt features. If the late Mr Price had not been engaging in sexual activity with this one, then someone else had, McLeish thought and saw much the same conviction in Bruce Davidson's face as he, too, took her hand.

The other two people were male, one being Peter Graebner, looking as always tired, grey, stooped, and dressed by Oxfam, in a suit a size too large for him which sagged in folds. This derelict

77

appearance concealed one of the most careful as well as one of the sharpest legal minds in London, and John McLeish considered him warily.

'This is my articled clerk, Matthew Sutherland.'

You didn't see that particular dark red hair much outside the North, McLeish thought, interested, shaking the offered hand. The lad appeared to be wearing fancy dress and several layers of it, but Graebner's firm had always been a law unto itself. A New Zealander from the accent. Now, where had he heard *that* recently?

'I've met your wife, Detective Chief Superintendent, and your mother-in-law. At the Refuge.'

'Mrs Price is aware that Matthew has some acquaintance with your family, Mr McLeish.' Peter Graebner was sounding more exhausted than ever. 'He is, however, the only articled clerk we have just now. Since we do not have the honour of acting for any of your family I could see no conflict.'

'If it's all right with Mrs Price, it's OK with me,' McLeish said, stolidly. The lad had obviously behaved with kindness and efficiency and Francesca would be amused to know that they had met. Just so long as this wasn't a substitute for her absent brothers, he thought severely, as he looked for somewhere to sit.

It was difficult to achieve an appropriate arrangement; three sofas, plump, pale gold and yielding, were arranged round the three sides of a vast square glass coffee table. A large marble fireplace in which flickered electric logs ornately set in an iron grate, bedecked with legs and curlicues, sat opposite the fourth side. This arrangment took care of much of the floor space, but the walls were lined with side tables and chairs. And every surface including the low glass table was thickly populated with objects: little china boxes, larger wooden boxes, china figurines, ivory statuettes, and photographs – an eclectic mixture. Some of it, he recognised, was good, or at least valuable, like the Dresden piece in the middle of the mantelpiece and a pretty Japanese ivory figure, but the rest looked as if it had been bought in an up-market tourist shop.

He and Bruce Davidson sat on the sofa to Sylvia Price's right while her legal advisers placed themselves to her left. Davidson found space for the police tape recorder by pushing gently at a raft of objects; a china box threatened to fall off the other side, but Matthew Sutherland saved it, reaching awkwardly round his knees to do so. He was having the same trouble as McLeish, fitting his knees between the squashy sofa and the coffee table and, like McLeish, he had tried sitting back, realised that would not work and was now perched, back strained and knees placed sideways, at the front edge of his sofa. Peter Graebner, with six inches less in the leg than either of them, was sitting in apparent comfort, watching his client.

'First, let me say how very sorry I am about your husband.' McLeish knew that the words were important whoever you were talking to, and Sylvia Price responded with a nod of acknowledgement and a tear, mopped up with a clean white handkerchief. 'I'd like to ask some general background questions before I ask about your movements, if I may. Quite ordinary things, like how long had you been married.'

She was very tense, and it was not helpful to be interrupted by Margaret Howard bringing coffee, but at least it gave him and young Sutherland a chance to rearrange their knees.

'Sorry, what did you ask? Ah yes. I was married eight years ago. I was a widow.'

'Were you born in this country?'

'No, in Austria. My first husband – before Bill – was also English so I have lived here since I was twenty-six.'

'And you are how old now?'

'Forty-five.'

Ten years younger than the dead man, whom she had married when she was thirty-seven, having presumably plenty of experience of men and their sexual behaviour. McLeish reminded himself that her own arrangements might be pretty strange; there was nowt so queer as folks' sexual preferences. 'Did you have children by your first marriage?'

No, it appeared. They had hoped but nothing had happened.

'And Mr Price's children? Do you see much of them?'

'Francis we see only sometimes. He is an addict, and hopeless. I am sorry for him but there's nothing to be done.' The tone was absolutely dismissive; Matthew Sutherland twitched uncomfortably and McLeish remembered that he must be much the same age as Francis Price. 'Antony yes. Not at first but more lately.' She looked under her eyelashes at Peter Graebner who made a barely perceptible sign of prohibition, and she shrugged and fell silent.

'So you and your husband lived here and the ground floor is the office and waiting-room?'

'That's right.' She leaned forward to get her coffee; her grass-green woollen jacket was dotted with yellow and white flowers. It ought to have looked overdone but on her it seemed properly decorative. 'We have two bedrooms and two bathrooms on the next floor, and this room and a little kitchen here just for coffee and breakfast. To eat properly we go all the way downstairs, to the basement.'

And not just to eat, McLeish thought, irresistibly, and found himself wondering how she was managing for meals at the moment.

'I shall sell this house when it becomes possible. When all is over.'

McLeish, unable to think of an adequate response, made none, but let a pause elapse before he asked her about her movements on Friday.

She looked at him warily. 'I leave here at about four o'clock in the afternoon. I go to a little cottage – no, it is not ours, it is rented, near Bosham. I wanted . . . we wanted to find out if we liked the . . . the pattern . . . the going away at weekends.'

'So Mr Price was not going with you?'

'No. He did not want to this weekend. He had a meeting with two people – Mr and Mrs Rayner – who wanted to buy into our places in Soller on Saturday morning and he wanted to play golf here on Sunday. He belongs in Mill Hill as well as in Bosham.'

There had been a message on the office answering machine from a Mr Rayner cancelling the Saturday meeting. He had been interviewed and his and his wife's presence at a lunch party eighty miles away to the east in Norfolk confirmed.

'When did he . . . did he die?' She extracted the handkerchief from a concealed pocket and held it to her nose.

'Probably in the twelve hours after Miss Howard said goodnight to him at four fifteen on Friday. But this is only an estimate.' McLeish believed that the deceased's spouse was entitled to his best idea of the truth.

'I reached the cottage about seven. I had hoped to be earlier but the traffic was terrible.'

'Did you see anyone? Your cleaner, or a housekeeper?'

'The man in the garage. I know him. I must have been there perhaps fifteen minutes before seven. Then after that, nobody.'

'You saw nobody after seven in the evening?'

'I was there by myself, I watch the television. I have supper – this I have in the car with me – I go to bed. Then next day I get up and go shopping. I was in the butcher's, and he will remember. But Bill is by then dead, no?'

'Almost certainly.'

There was a silence which McLeish finally broke to ask if anyone had telephoned her at the cottage. No? Would the car have been visible, or lights showing?

'You mean, to prove I am there?'

'Yes,' McLeish said baldly, and felt rather than saw Matthew Sutherland shift in his seat.

'The car was outside the front door. And of course I have lights on, but I draw all the curtains – it was cold. But I was there, where else would I be? I would not drive about in the middle of the night.'

'We will need the address of the cottage, and the names of your garage and your butcher. You can give them to Inspector Davidson afterwards,' McLeish said, calmly. 'Tell me, did you and your husband get on well?'

'What do you mean? Why do you ask this?' Peter Graebner stirred minutely at her side.

'As I am sure Mr Graebner will have told you, your husband was discovered hanging from the ceiling with the table that should have supported him out of his reach. Did your husband ever try anything like this before?'

There really was no good way of phrasing that sort of question, he and Bruce Davidson had agreed. 'She'll have known about it, though. The wives always do,' Bruce had said, with the blunt assurance born of his legendary sexual experience. And Bruce had been right as usual, he saw, suddenly alert – the woman had known it, or some of it, and was not going to deny it totally.

'He was interested in . . . he liked . . . to do things which meant he could not properly breathe.'

'Did he do any of them with you? Or ask you to help?'

'When we were first married, then yes. Sometimes. But I did not like it. I was frightened by it, so I say no. But never like *that*, never hanging himself in that way – in the way you say he died. Or now I think perhaps he may have done when I was not there, but I never knew.' She was weeping, dabbing at her eyes, and the four men in the room gazed at the table, waiting for her to recover herself.

'You had a full sexual relationship with him still, is that what you are saying?' McLeish asked, gently.

'We did the things ordinary people do, yes. He ... he seemed to like them too. As well, I mean as ... as the other things.' She stared miserably at the crowded table top and blew her nose again. 'I did not know,' she said, sniffing inelegantly. 'I did not know.'

It was, of course, a key point, but he did not think he would get any further with it at this interview.

'So you got on with your husband reasonably well?'

'Oh yes. We have had our difficulties. Mr Graebner says I need not speak of them but I wish to. I came to him six months ago because Bill had sometimes hit me when ... when he was drunk. And one night he hit me very much. I was most frightened, so I went to Mr Graebner who tells me I could bring action against him. But it was not necessary. Once I knew that, you understand, I said to Bill that if ever he would do such a thing again I would take the action, and he was very, very sad and he promised never to do such a thing again.'

McLeish looked enquiringly at Peter Graebner, who confirmed without any emphasis at all that he had indeed advised Mrs Price that action lay against her husband under the Domestic Violence Act, quite apart from the general law, and that she could seek an injunction banning him from the matrimonial home.

'So you see,' Sylvia Price said, 'I tell Bill this and he apologise very much and buy me some ear-rings. And it never happen again. You may be thinking that I have a reason to kill Bill. But he never did again.'

Now I wonder, McLeish thought, I wonder if I believe that. She owned the house from which the business operated and her husband could not afford to lose her, but he was in the habit of hitting her – on her own admission. He looked over at Graebner who confirmed, in the same emotionless way, that Mrs Price had not consulted him again from that day until yesterday when she had sought guidance and advice in her current situation. And that spoke for her too; there were plenty of lawyers in London and she need not have gone back to the one who knew that her husband had in the past given her cause to wish him dead.

'Thank you for telling us all this,' McLeish said, deploying one of the generally useful soothing statements he had learned as a young detective. 'Now can you tell us anything about your husband's relationship with his sons?'

'You should ask them.'

'That will be done of course, but I am interested in your view.'

'You think one of them could have ... could have caused this thing?'

'At this stage, Mrs Price, we don't have any firm views. We are just covering the ground.' He waited, but she was not embarrassed or uneasy, just considering her answer.

'He have very little of a relationship with Francis. I told you, he is a hopeless person. He also stole money from his father – from us, from the business. But Bill did not persecute.'

'Prosecute.'

'So. Yes. He decide just to change the number of the safe and not to let Francis come to the house. Antony is closer – he is a doctor, you know, and beginning now to be well known. I believe there were difficulties when they were young boys and the mother was ill. You should ask Antony, it was he who tell me. He came with me to see Mr Graebner and he said then that Bill had been hitting Francis and him when they were children.'

'Did Antony come to the house often?'

'Not very. He come, I know, the week before last to talk with Bill, but I was out. I hear it was that he has quarrelled with his girlfriend Annabelle. But you must ask Antony. I am talking only of things heard.'

'Hearsay,' McLeish said, irresistibly, and apologised, noting that Matthew Sutherland was evidently trying a new position to get comfortable.

'Just one more set of questions if I may. You are a director of Price Fleming as was your husband. Is that right?'

'This is correct but I am director because there is some of my money in it and I have a salary and it is easier for tax. Bill's partner Luke Fleming, who is usually abroad finding and making new the properties for the business, is also a director. But I am William's executor, with Luke Fleming.'

'So you would have known the combination of the safe?' McLeish asked blandly.

'Yes, because my jewellery was kept in there. There is a list with the insurance company.'

'Who else did, do you know?'

'Margaret Howard, Luke, Bill.'

'You know that the safe was found open?'

'I hear. Bill perhaps had not yet closed it, when ... when ...' She reached for the handkerchief.

'Indeed,' McLeish agreed hastily.

'Or perhaps the breakers in knew how to open?'

'That too is not impossible. You've been very patient, Mrs Price, and we will now get a statement typed for you to sign. When you have consulted Mr Graebner of course. And I am sure we will need to talk to you again at a later stage, when we have more idea of what may have happened.'

They said their farewells, and McLeish and Davidson left, followed down the stairs on to the steps by Matthew Sutherland.

'Got to get to West London Magistrates,' he said, to their enquiring look. 'Peter will tidy up.'

'I hope so indeed,' McLeish said, amused. 'I see you had trouble with the legs as well.'

'Couldn't have borne another five minutes. And you've got a couple of inches on me, it must have been worse for you.'

I have perhaps been a senior policeman too long, McLeish thought, finding himself just slightly affronted by being addressed as an equal by this lad.

'Give Francesca my regards, will you? It's good to have her mum back, but she wasn't a bad substitute.'

'I'm sure she'll be glad to hear that.' McLeish decided he *was* being stuffy. 'And thank you for helping to reassure her about German measles.'

'Pleasure,' Matthew said, grinning, the personality springing to life. 'Here, taxi!' He was gone, in a clatter, down the stone steps, long coat flying, briefcase clasped under one arm, and was in the back of the taxi issuing instructions before they could say goodbye.

7

Wednesday, 13 April

Francesca, picking at a slice of toast, butter and jam, shifted her chair irritably away from the high-chair containing her son. He was waving a strip of toast, getting some of it into his mouth, but a good deal more down his front and on the floor. He was having a nice day and it would be even better if he could escape from his chair. He beamed as he saw a way out and stretched out his arms in greeting to his father who was edging cautiously round the kitchen door.

'Do I unharness him?'

'Please. See if he'll go away and play.'

Her son gave her a look of sheer amazement and plastered himself to his father's chest, distributing toast crumbs and butter down his towelling dressing-gown.

'I'm sorry,' McLeish said over his head. 'Has he been up long?'

'Since five o'clock. I've had four lots of breakfast just to keep going. Tomorrow it's your turn.'

'You should have woken me today. I never heard a thing. I got in just after you'd gone to sleep. I'm sorry, I just needed to pull the bits together on this Price case. You lose things otherwise.'

His wife looked at him dully, and he sighed.

'You don't *look* very good.'

'I'm not. I'm operating at crawling pace and eating everything I can see just to keep going. How *are* we going to manage with you working this hard?'

'Perhaps William will get better at staying in bed in the mornings.'

They looked unhopefully at their son who beamed back at them and made a grab for his father's tea.

'In about half an hour,' Francesca said, bitterly, 'just when Susannah gets here, he will decide a bit of a sleep would be nice and will go out like a light having been entertained and fed for the last three hours. I feel like a sleep too, but what's left of me has to totter out to Gladstone to tell the auditors which way up to hold the accounts.'

McLeish reached to hold her hand and she moved her chair towards him so that she could rest her head on his shoulder and get a buttery kiss from William, who then decided to go and unpack the saucepan cupboard.

'How *is* the Price case? I ask only because I hope it will be over soon and you can get back for supper.'

'Coming on. I met your Matthew Sutherland yesterday. His firm acts for Mrs Price. Cheeky bugger.'

'Matthew? Well, I told you. He's just the same with everyone, absolutely direct, no use for conventional manners. All crusaders are like that.'

'Is that what he is? A crusader?'

'Oh yes, bless him. Prop and mainstay of the Refuge for all he's so young. Never loses a case. I imagine you have to keep him away from all employees of Social Services, or anybody who might give money to the Refuge.'

'Does he find that taking the blokes to court – or threatening it – does any *good*? Are there some cases where the bloke stops beating the wife or girlfriend after he's been taken to court, and they settle down together like ordinary people?'

'You mean, does law change behaviour?' She poured him tea, reflecting on her lunch with Matt.

'Yes, I suppose I do.'

'Well, as Matt says, it's very useful to change that behaviour. And if you do change behaviour, in the end, you change hearts and minds. He says. What an odd conversation to be having with a policeman.'

He cuddled her to him and their son looked up from his task of extracting the last saucepan from the recesses of the cupboard and decided to join in, so McLeish hauled him on to his knee and redistributed his forces. 'I should have put the question direct,' he said, meekly. 'If someone told you that their man had beaten them but on being threatened with court action had desisted and had never done it again, would you believe them?'

'Yes. Particularly if it was the first time he'd really hurt her. Bit like potty-training – speaking of which, William, come along darling, think how pleased Susannah will be. Then we can get dressed.'

McLeish, left in the kitchen, guiltily reached for the paper and his cup of tea and sat, savouring the warmth of the spring sun and the domesticity surrounding him. He decided there could be no point in replacing the pans and lids that littered the kitchen floor since William would get them out again immediately, so he read the sports pages to the accompaniment of his wife's congratulatory cries from the hall cloakroom. He looked up to applaud as she came back, carrying William, but she was looking worried.

'Not all right?'

'Oh *that* yes, what a clever boy. Such a help.' She considered the littered floor, replaced William in the middle of it and handed him a bowl full of dried beans and a spoon so that he could distribute them between containers. 'What I need to tell you is that there is an Awkward Connection. You remember I told you about Annabelle, the young doctor who was so good about the measles. *Her* doctor boyfriend, the one who was beating her up, is called Antony. Blow me, when I read the *Mail* this morning – in a blessed pause, you understand, while Will watched *Breakfast News* – I see a picture of Annabelle holding the hand of someone called Antony Price, said to be the son of your murdered William Price.'

'Have you seen her except at the Refuge?'

'No, but Matthew Sutherland has, because he told me that she wouldn't press charges against this Antony. Matt isn't acting for her – I mean, it isn't too awful, is it?'

'No,' he said slowly, thinking it through. 'So the son beats his women as well.'

'Ah.' She was on to the point with very creditable speed, given how early her day had started. 'So your Mr Price – the deceased – was a wife-beater?'

'Yes, but only once seriously, apparently. Then she went to a lawyer. Now, Fran, this is absolutely confidential.'

'You need not remind me.' Nor he need, he thought gratefully; there was a lot to be said for a wife who had always had her own professional confidences to guard. 'The only other thing we know about domestic violence is that men mostly learn how to do it from their fathers,' she said, carefully.

'The wife in question is a second wife.'

'He maybe beat the *first* wife badly and gave it a go with the

87

second one, who wouldn't have it. So in order to get his kicks he took to hanging himself from the ceiling.'

'And someone kicked the table from under him, or that's how it looks.'

'Mm.' A particularly loud crash drew their attention to their infant son and they looked at each other guiltily.

'He can't possibly understand,' McLeish objected.

'I suppose not. So this Antony is the son of the *first* wife. Whom presumably Mr Price deceased did beat seriously. Where is she?'

'In a graveyard in Ross-on-Wye, these fifteen years past. Died of cancer.'

'Not a credible suspect then. But this Antony might have waited until he grew to man's estate to avenge her.'

'Indeed. As might his brother Francis.'

'Oh *dear*. That silly Annabelle must have gone back to the son just like Matthew thought she had, and now she'll have difficulty in walking out again if he's a suspect. Is that the time? If I do not get out of here, the A-level rejects who constitute the junior staff of our auditors will start without me. And we'll never find anything again. There's Susannah, look, Will.'

'Dr Brewster.'

Annabelle looked doubtfully at the man who approached her, smiling. His hair was as dark as Antony's but curly, and he was comfortably built, bursting out of a light grey suit, tie flapping as he came towards her.

'Detective Inspector Davidson.' He beamed at her, confident of his welcome, and she found herself relaxing just a little under the pressure of his interest. 'You're young to be a doctor.'

A Scot, probably Glasgow, she thought, feeling an access of confidence. 'I'm not that young. You wanted to see me.'

'I did. We did, and it's very good of you to come up here to the station, it saves us time and means we can be private. Now, this young man here is Detective Constable Richey.'

The young man appeared to be about seventeen, and Annabelle nodded to him kindly. They were assembled by the staff sergeant's desk at Notting Dale police station, and at Davidson's nod the man swung open a section of the counter to let them through, without diverting his attention from the two sullen, black adolescents facing him.

'See about some coffee, would you, Richey?' Davidson said, comfortably, settling her in a chair on one side of the plain table in the small room. 'Now, what we do here is we record all interviews, so if there's any disagreement at all about what was said, there's a tape.' He smiled at her kindly, the tape recorder held in his square hands, and she nodded. 'The lad'll take a wee note as well, to keep him in practice. Ah, thank you, Richey.'

Davidson helped her to sugar, chatting gently, appearing not to notice that she was too tense to answer.

'So then, Dr Brewster.' He went through the formalities, noting her full name and address. 'You'll know that Dr William Price died probably sometime between Friday evening and the Saturday forenoon. We are asking everyone close to the deceased, either family or in his business, where they were at that time. And Mr Antony Price told us that he was with you, from about seven thirty in the evening. Can you confirm that, please?'

'Yes indeed. He collected me to go out to dinner at just after seven thirty.'

'You'd mebbe looked at your watch?'

'Yes. I'd got out of evening surgery at six forty-five and I'd had to hurry.'

'Fair enough. And you were at dinner at the Crabtree Restaurant?'

'That's right. Then we went for a little walk and he dropped me back at my flat at ten thirty.'

'He didn't come up for coffee?'

Her heart thumped. 'No.'

'And you're sure about ten thirty?'

'Yes. I was very tired and needed an early night, so I'm sure that was the time.'

'That's very helpful, thank you.' His expression of bright interest had not varied at all, and she did not seem to be able to say anything or ask if he had all he wanted.

'Dr Brewster, how long have you known Dr Antony Price?'

'Oh. Five years. About.'

'And ye knew his father?'

'Not well at all. They didn't see very much of each other.' She looked into the bright brown eyes. 'Antony must have told you all this.'

'Have you lived long at your present address?'

'Uh . . . oh, not long at all. I am getting a proper flat . . . this is just temporary.'

'And you were living where before?'

She hesitated, hopelessly, and looked away but he waited so that finally she had to speak. 'I was living for some of the time in Antony's flat. But we'd always envisaged . . . I always meant . . . to get my own place.'

The dark peaked eyebrows went up. 'Did you have an argument?'

'I don't see that it's any of your business. He was with me, at the times I said, last Friday.'

'But not later than ten thirty.'

'No, I'm sure,' she said, defiantly, on safe ground at last.

'Mr Price told us it was a little later than that.' She looked at him, horrified, opened her mouth to suggest that it might have been and closed it again as the exact nature of the pit dug for her became clear. 'And did you see him on the Saturday?' Davidson had waited courteously.

'No, no. Not till the Sunday.'

'What time would that have been?'

'I thought you said Antony's father would have been dead by the early hours of Saturday,' she said, near to tears.

'We're interested in knowing where people were at any time from Friday through till Monday morning when the body was found.' He let the pause stretch. 'What time on Sunday would you have met Dr Antony Price?'

'About 7 p.m. I'm fairly sure that's right. We had dinner and we came back to my flat and Antony was with me until he left about eleven o'clock on Monday morning.' She felt under the bright gaze as if she had been found committing some small but squalid crime.

'Thank you, Dr Brewster.' Surprisingly, he was not sounding unsympathetic and as she managed to look at him he smiled at her. 'Now, DC Richey will write all that down for you to sign, if you'll be kind enough to wait a few minutes. We may want to talk to you again, so please let us know if you change your address again.'

She looked at him sharply. Long eyelashes for a man, she thought, irrelevantly.

'Specifically the officer in charge of this case, Detective Superintendent McLeish, may want to see you.'

'McLeish?'

'Aye. A Scot like myself.' He waited to see if she had anything else to say, then handed over to the desk sergeant and vanished, followed by his acolyte.

Twenty minutes later, her statement signed, she found a phone box. She made one call to the Refuge then rang St George's. Antony mercifully was not operating that afternoon and she found him in his office.

'How did it go?' he asked, sounding anxious.

'Not well. I told them you left at ten thirty on Friday.'

'Did you? I thought it was a bit later than that.' He had a tight hold on himself.

She went on doggedly, 'I'm afraid I knew it was ten thirty so I told them so. But look, Antony, it's worse than that. The man in charge is called McLeish. He's married to Francesca. The woman I told you about. At the Refuge.'

'Oh *Christ*.' The silence hung between them. 'I thought you said she was an academic.' He sounded furiously accusing and she had to remind herself of the reasons why she had met Francesca at all.

'She's actually a civil servant in the DTI, on loan to a college. But in any case she *is* married to this man.'

'Well, it's bloody well against the rules for them to talk to each other.'

'The thing is, Antony, I don't think we can keep everything secret. I mean the man I talked to, called Davidson, got out of me that I'd lived with you until recently and *he* asked if we'd had an argument.'

'You didn't *tell* him about . . . about . . . ?'

'No, but I'm not sure I was very convincing.' It was just like Antony, she thought, suddenly enraged, to try and force her to lie to protect him, because *he* had beaten her up. She remembered suddenly Ellen from the Refuge, married to a barrister, describing with incredulous anger how she had to put on make-up and long-sleeved dresses while the husband who had blacked her eye and left savage bruises on her upper arms criticised her incompetence, because the marks still showed.

'Annabelle, sorry. I'm sorry you had a difficult time. I'm just worried stupid, have been ever since yesterday, and it's all got on top of me.' He was sounding desperate. 'And I really don't want all . . . well, all of that to come out. It would be bad for me – for us, I hope – professionally.'

Silence was a new weapon for Annabelle, but it had proved effective every time so far.

'And the trouble is, I had a bloody good reason to kill my father, quite apart from what he did to Mum and us. Mum left her money to him for life, then to Francis and me. My father was a trustee. And he's got at it, I knew he would, that's why I had to take yours when Francis was in trouble. The old bastard had spent it, I could see he was lying when I went to see him. I've just talked to the clown who is the other trustee – it's all gone, he can't find it. A clean £100,000.' It was a wail of anguish and disappointment, and Annabelle felt sick.

'Do they suspect you?'

'Well, of course they bloody do. I could have left you and gone to the house, found him there and kicked the table away sometime in the night, couldn't I? And I can't prove otherwise.' Because you had driven me out, Annabelle supplied, painfully.

'My card's running out, Antony. I'll see you tonight.'

'Detective Inspector Crane would like to see you, sir.'

John McLeish nodded. Catherine had rung him yesterday, asking hopefully if she or one of her team could join his squad at the house in Kensington Church Street, in case the wherewithal for a fraud prosecution was lying around for the taking as it were. McLeish had refused; he had a reason for being there, the Fraud Squad would have been on a fishing expedition. And he had been quite clear as he put the phone down that Catherine had been asked to put this irregular request to him because something – enough – was known of their past relationship. He told his secretary to go home; there was nothing else for her to do tonight and it was only sensible to let her go early to get a credit against the days when he would have to ask her to stay half the night. He decided he, too, would try to get home; it had been a long day. He needed to – wanted to – go over the various bits of information that had come in, but he could do that at home, so his wife could at least have the pleasure of his physical presence and he could relax and have a drink. He looked up at a noise from his outer office, and Catherine appeared in the doorway. She was wearing a pale green suit that he recognised from three years ago and she looked fresh and untouchably beautiful.

'John. I came to plead with you to let my Guv'nor talk to you.

We have – or we had – in our hands an actual person complaining of being defrauded by Mr Price.'

McLeish considered her. 'Your man hired him from Equity,' he suggested.

'No. He's real. Please, John. Peter – Detective Chief Superintendent Clark – is waiting, biting his fingernails at the other end of the telephone.' She was very pretty and very pleased with herself, and if they did have a real customer it was absolutely his duty to talk.

'I've just the one call I must make then I'll come down and see him. Third floor, isn't it? Will you tell him ten minutes?' He watched her elegant rear view out of the office, thinking that it was impossible not to feel proprietary about a girl you'd been to bed with, even three years ago. It was true what they said about sex, it was like a chemical reaction, it changed things, people, relationships for ever, even if it hadn't gone on for very long, or seemed to cut very deep. He rang Francesca, who was not prepared to be mollified and told him his supper would keep very badly.

A review of the available evidence at lunchtime had led him and the team to the conclusion that the field was uncomfortably wide open. Neither of the Price sons had anything that looked like an alibi for late on Friday; Sylvia Price had, in theory, been sixty miles away at Bosham but could only be placed there at six forty-five on Friday evening and ten thirty on Saturday, leaving more than twelve hours unaccounted for. The remaining business partner, Luke Fleming, had been in Majorca, but it was emerging that he, too, had been out of touch with anyone who could give him an alibi. One of McLeish's squad was sweating over airline schedules to see whether Mr Fleming could have got back to murder his partner without anyone realising he was in England and back to meet contractors on Sunday evening in Puerto Soller. And Miles Arnold had come sharply into the frame with the discovery that his wife had been away with the children on Friday and Saturday night and Mr Arnold had stated that he had watched the television alone at home both nights. 'He was lying all right,' Bruce Davidson had reported, cheerfully. 'Holed up with a lassie somewhere, is my guess.'

The trouble, or one of the troubles, was that this looked like an opportunistic crime. The victim had arranged himself in a position where all it took was someone combining motivation with being on the spot to pull the support from under him. Both sons met those criteria, and indeed they were right at the top of his mental list; their father had been a brute, the two Price boys were close and Francis was an addict and Antony a doctor, a good combination if you wanted to commit a murder. He considered a note on his crowded desk; Francis had been released that afternoon, there being no reason to keep him in a prison cell. Antony appeared to be carrying on his duties as usual, and the patients on his operating list to be recovering as expected. Sylvia Price and Luke Fleming had no firm alibis, and he didn't know enough about their motivation. Any assistance that the Fraud Squad could legitimately give ought to be welcomed with both hands.

He walked down two flights of stairs to do just that, regretting his lost supper with his wife. He found Peter Clark with Catherine seated demurely at his right and an older man, tight-mouthed, at his left. Peter Clark did not stand but nodded in grudging welcome; pissed off, McLeish judged, by not being allowed to crawl all over *his* investigation just for the asking.

'We have a promising lead here,' Peter Clark said, and McLeish inclined his head in indication of willingness to hear more. 'A customer of Price Fleming; a chap who bought a unit on the basis of a set of pictures. Here.'

McLeish considered the three pictures; all looked exactly like each other, five-storey, pleasant blocks with the sea in the background and groups of trees.

'As I understand it you don't exactly buy a unit. You buy the right to a week or two weeks in the company's Majorcan properties,' he said cautiously.

'That's correct. But our man – a Mr Fabian Mastry – was interested particularly in these three blocks because they are in a part of the coast where he'll meet lots of other chaps like him. So he paid his money for two weeks in June and, on impulse, flew down at the weekend just to have a look.'

'And?'

'And there is a site on which stand the outlines, as it were, of those three buildings. Walls about three feet high, no one on site, no one's been on site for six weeks. He has enough Spanish to have asked. So he rings up the office on Monday afternoon and gets a secretary who tells him that Mr Price is indisposed and Mr Fleming is in Spain. He sits and worries until he sees the papers this morning and it took him the rest of the day to find his way to us. Our feeling is he may be one of several.'

They were looking very pleased with themselves, McLeish thought, except Catherine who had her head down in contemplation of a pad of paper. This was not a new complaint, he understood suddenly, they'd had this Fabian worrying them before and they'd told him to go and see what was on the ground. And finally he had, and after that the story ran more or less as he had been told. And they'd just been lucky – better not to suppose they might have orchestrated it – that their man rang when the office was in total disarray in the aftermath of William Price's death, and there was no one to reassure him.

'Well, I assume all that has given you cause to interview the directors of the company,' he said, briskly.

'When you've finished with them of course. I don't know how far you've got.' Clark looked hopeful.

'I've interviewed Mrs Price, but we didn't talk about the company because she was still under medical supervision and I just wanted to know where she was when her husband died. I'm due to see her again tomorrow. One of my lads interviewed Luke Fleming who got back yesterday; I read his statement and I'm to see him tomorrow as well. If you want to hold a different conversation, I wouldn't want to stand in your way, but I think we – the Yard – have to be a bit careful. I don't want to be accused of harassment.'

'Nor do we.' Peter Clark was into the breach at once. 'That's why we hoped we could just have a look at whatever papers and records you got out of the office, or put one of our people in there.'

McLeish sat and thought; a thing he never minded doing publicly, although it caused his excitable, over-reactive in-laws great difficulty. 'I'll take a view on that after you've interviewed the directors,' he said, and saw their faces fall. 'Sorry, but we need to find a murderer more than we need to sort out a fraud. You can see all the statements you want, of course. And if I were you I'd interview Luke Fleming first. Mrs Price has Peter Graebner as her brief.'

'Thank you for that.' Peter Clark was prepared to settle for the inch he'd got and try and take the ell tomorrow. 'I'll send Catherine up with you now to get them if that's all right.' He looked speculatively from her to McLeish.

'Of course, Detective Inspector Davidson will get them out for her – he's still here. I'm late for supper,' he added, and wished he hadn't; it came out very defensive.

He handed Catherine over to Bruce Davidson and retired to his office to collect his bits and pieces together. Francesca was exasperated because he always carried a briefcase full of papers whether he could see a time when he might read them or not. The point was that a policeman's life left you odd lumps of time, unexpectedly, in funny places, and it was in *those* patches that he could catch up and often would suddenly see a pattern. None of this cut any ice with his wife, who led a regular life, went to her office every day and was moreover – he had to concede – ferociously disciplined in her work habits.

He looked up to find Bruce Davidson had joined him, and was silently watching him pack.

'I thought I'd have a wee word. I saw Dr Brewster – Dr Antony Price's girl. Something odd there; she'd moved out just before all this happened.'

'I forgot you were seeing her. You're quite right, there's a lot wrong there.' He relayed what his wife had told him.

'Francesca gets around, doesn't she?' Davidson said, shaking his head. 'What about my godson?'

'She's not doing the Refuge any more. Her mum is back on duty.' He was aware he was sounding edgy.

Davidson let a pause elapse. 'I've just given Catherine all the statements and the freedom of the photocopier.'

'Good. That's what I agreed. And we may have to do more but not yet.'

'She's looking tired.'

'Catherine? Is she?'

'The clack is that her bloke – the one she lived with, what's his name . . . Davies . . . used to beat her.'

McLeish straightened and banged his shoulder on the edge of the desk.

'I don't believe it. She'd not have put up with it.'

'Well, as to that . . . Well, in the end, she didn't. Got an injunction under the Act and got rid of him. But she'd had a bit by then.'

'How do you know?'

'WPC in the unit at Haringay.' Davidson was gazing at the huge pin board on the wall with apparent interest.

'But she went *back* to him after . . . after the Morgan case,' McLeish said, stunned.

'Where you met her. Yes. He promised to stop, seemingly, and she gave it another go.'

He found he felt slightly sick and extremely angry. Poor Catherine. Beautiful Catherine, who could have had anyone she wanted, including him.

'I didn't want you to hear it in the canteen,' Davidson said, still engaged in a minute inspection of the board.

'No. Thanks, Bruce.' He collected his two briefcases and banged his way into the lift down to the car-park. But he had to sit in the car for a full five minutes before he could collect himself.

Matthew Sutherland turned into the pub; he hadn't used it before but it looked cheerful and well kept. He had spent three hours with Peter Graebner, sorting out a witness statement in an assault case, and needed something to take away the taste of the stewed tea, served by the prospective witness's mother. And he needed a pee and had not felt able to ask for the bathroom in the dirty flat, overflowing with children.

His immediate needs attended to, he sat in a corner with a second pint and looked round him. It was a nice room with a decent gas-powered log fire, whose artificial flames looked pleasantly real, and polished glasses on the bar. It was busy, as pubs were in that part of London at nine in the evening, but not noisy, people who had come out for a quiet drink after supper, rather than people who had come out to get drunk. It was a peaceful, middle-aged, slightly eccentric place, and Matthew sat enjoying the quiet.

The door opened and a man of about his own age came in, turning clumsily to close it after him. He made for the bar jerkily and sat heavily in the manner of a swimmer just succeeding in reaching the shore. Had a few, Matt thought, and watched as the lady of the house alerted her husband with a jerk of her head, and the man carefully put down the glass he was polishing so his hands were free before approaching the prospective customer. He had to bend forward and ask the man to repeat himself, Matthew saw, and even then he wasn't sure what had been said. He straightened up, looked to his wife for guidance and at that moment the man fell off the bar stool, straight over sideways, not moving a hand to save himself, just flat down on the floor, with a

97

thud, so he lay sprawled, unmoving and limp. The rest of the customers sat and stared while the barman peered disbelievingly over the counter. His wife banged up the flap on the counter; she was obviously furious. 'John, Fred, give me a hand will you? We'll just put this one out in the street where he came from.' Mine host, recovering from his astonishment, came round to help and he and the bulky man, who had been sitting nearest, bent to help, tugging at the fallen man.

'Hang on.' He had not meant to have anything to do with this scene, but he had seen the man's head go back and his eyes roll as they tried to move him. 'Excuse me, sorry.' He was out of his seat and squatting by the man, turning his head gently, the stertorous breathing very loud.

'Are you a doctor?'

He ignored the question, delivered as it was in tones of utter disbelief, and forced a dirty shirt and sweater up above the elbow on the man's right arm, so that they could all see the pitted injection sites inside the elbow. He looked up into their horrified faces. 'No, I'm a lawyer. But you need an ambulance. It's an overdose, tell them. Heroin probably.'

'Is he a friend of yours?' the landlord asked between hope and distaste.

'Never seen him before. Has someone called that ambulance?'

'Wouldn't he be better in the air outside?'

'He'd be better not moved too much.' He saw open rebellion on the landlord's face. 'You don't want to find yourself being sued.'

'By you, for instance.' The man had gone suddenly scarlet, his hands clenching, and Matthew gaped at him.

'Nothing to do with me, mate. That's free advice you're getting.'

'John.' The man's head jerked round at his wife's sharp, alarmed summons, and he went reluctantly over to the bar, with one backward look full of venom at Matthew. No wonder there was no one under fifty in the place, he thought, taken aback as always by middle-aged male aggression. The man on the floor was breathing at least, so he made sure the airway was unobstructed and that he didn't seem to have broken anything. He looked up but the landlord and his wife were huddled behind the bar, muttering, and several of the customers leaving. So he went over and got his drink and sat stolidly on the floor beside the limp body.

The ambulance arrived before he had got more than half his

beer down; he explained succinctly to the crew and declined their invitation to join them in the ambulance. He stood back to watch them loading the casualty on to a stretcher and found himself hemmed in by two men in suits and short haircuts, both youngish.

'Friend of yours, sir?'

'Never seen him before.'

'But you called the ambulance.'

'No, no. Landlord here did that.' He nodded to the man behind the bar and got a look of hatred in response.

'We'd like to take a statement about the incident, if we may, sir?' They both showed him warrant cards which he had been expecting since he saw them on either side of him.

'Nothing to make a statement about. He fell off the chair flat, as you saw. I said an ambulance would be needed. It came. I'm not sure why *you* did, nobody was exactly wrecking the place.'

The two did not so much as look at each other. 'So you are unwilling to come to the station with us?'

'Damn right I am. I was just a spectator and I want to get home. Ask anyone.' He waved an arm round the pub and realised he was in enemy territory. The half-dozen remaining patrons looked away, or buried their faces in their drinks, while the landlord and his wife busied themselves over glasses, their backs to him. He looked at the policeman incredulously. 'You're not serious. Why don't we sit down here and I'll tell you what happened? It'll take about a minute and a half.'

'It would be better for you if you accompanied us, sir.'

'*Crap.*' It was, he knew, not wise, but he was outraged, and saw too late the gleam in the senior man's eye. He heard through an incredulous haze himself being arrested on suspicion of trafficking in drugs and cautioned. 'Bugger that,' he said, recovering his voice, 'what do you stupid shits think you're doing?'

He never saw the blow that caught him in the stomach and doubled him up, but he was in the waiting police car, sicking up his beer, before he could register any further objection. He was whisked through the streets and bustled into a police station he recognised; it was Notting Dale and the sergeant on the desk knew him at once.

'If it isn't Mr Sutherland! What's he done? Drugs, is it? Well, well, well.'

Matthew had himself in hand despite the sickness and the pain in his stomach. He knew he was not among friends here, as a lawyer in the firm that represented much of the local criminal fraternity. 'No, it isn't. I just stopped one of your local citizenry dumping a sick man in the street.'

'He's been charged, Bill. Obstruction.'

The sergeant, lips compressed, assembled a pencil and paper and Matthew, objecting loudly, turned out both pockets and spread the contents on the desk. The four of them, and several members of the general public, contemplated a heap of handkerchief, keys, change, four pens, a notepad, and finally a small plastic bag full of a dark lumpy powder.

'Is there anyone you would like to telephone, Mr Sutherland?' the sergeant broke the silence to ask.

An hour later, he was sitting in a cell, hunched over, feeling deathly cold. He heard the clear commanding voice from the passage and sat up, disbelieving.

'And how are you, Bill?' she was asking as cheerfully as if she had dropped in for tea. 'I'm sure John would have sent his regards if he'd known I was going to be here. How nice of you. What were the chaps called again who made the arrest? Killigan and O'Brien – I'm sure John will remember them.'

He managed to stop shivering and get his head up as the door opened.

'Ah, Matthew. Come along, you must be hungry. I understand you have to appear tomorrow somewhere. West London, Bill? Thank you so much.'

The Seventh Cavalry was wearing the same yellow jacket as she had the night he had first seen her. She'd had her hair done since Monday and was wearing expensive executive-type jewellery and carrying an aggressively shiny black leather briefcase. The desk sergeant, who seemed to have shrunk, avoided his eye and the two detectives were nowhere to be seen. He followed her through the waiting area, getting a fleeting impression of people falling back before them. They were in the big McLeish Volvo before he felt able to speak and then he swore for two minutes consecutively.

'Dearest Matthew, quite yourself again, I hear.' He blew his nose, noisily, hoping he wasn't going to cry, or be sick, eyeing his driver's strong profile and spiky dark hair. 'Silly me,' she said, swinging the big car past a bus, 'I'd expected, oh I dunno, some cries of how clever of you to get here, how lucky you happened to be around.'

'Aha,' he said, gratefully realising he wasn't after all going to fall apart. 'But then I recognised you as Wonderwoman the very first time I saw you. Your cunning disguise as an ordinary person never fooled *me*.'

She grinned in acknowledgement. 'You gave my poor mum a hell of a shock. She couldn't think what to do when you rang, struggling as she was with three new battered women.'

'But she remembered that if she rubbed a lantern you'd pop up?'

'That's right. And by great good luck Susannah was in and is listening for William.'

'And your husband? The copper?'

'Don't say it like that, we traded heavily on his name to get you out. Why didn't you call Peter Graebner or someone from your shop? Matthew, have you died on me?'

'Because they were going to keep me when I qualify. Partnership prospects. Only I'm not qualified, not yet, and with a conviction for drugs I never will.'

'Get off. There's lots of criminal solicitors.'

'You're thinking of admitted solicitors who abstract all the clients' monies, or who give crappy advice which just enmeshes them in further shit. Not solicitors who do drugs. Your Law Society won't even let me get to the starting post with a conviction.'

'Ah.' He did not, she noticed, protest his innocence. 'It was cannabis they found on you?' she asked carefully. 'That's not a Class A, I do know that.'

'Doesn't matter for this purpose. It's still a conviction for drugs.'

A harder mind than her siblings, she thought, respectfully, for all he was younger even than the twins. He had faced his situation instantly and without evasion.

'So you need not to be prosecuted, or if prosecuted to be found not guilty?' she asked, determined to match his standards.

'That's about it.' He was huddled against the window of the big car, hugging himself, and she speeded up, flying down the familiar streets to her house.

'Come in, Matt.' She took his hand as he hesitated, disconcerted, on the steps and led him downstairs to the kitchen, and heated up soup for him and occupied herself with tidying the kitchen while he ate the soup and the remains of a chicken and half a cake.

'I can't immediately work out what to do,' she said, finally, when he had finished and was drinking coffee, 'but I'll think of something.'

'Not your problem.' The response was swift and decisive. 'You're a good girl to come and get me, and hang on to me, so I didn't go and spill it all over Graebner. But you forget about it, I'm not one of your siblings.'

'No, indeed. Though now you mention it, it was just like old times. Only with Tristram it was heroin, and in America, which made the whole thing that much more difficult.'

'You mean you had to get into your tights, Wonderwoman, and fly across the Atlantic? What did your husband, the policeman, say?'

'We weren't married then.'

'He was totally pissed off, in short. Don't you worry about it, Frannie.' He was sitting at the end of her table, elbows planted, the red hair looking flat and dejected, and as she watched him he fished out a handkerchief and blew his nose, lengthily.

'Matt,' she said, her heart wrung, and sat down beside him, and managed awkwardly to put an arm around his shoulders. He sat, stiff and tight, then turned his head to look at her. I need to move, she thought, frantically, and leant over to kiss him briskly and in a sisterly manner on the cheek, then disengaged herself and got to her feet. 'Get some sleep,' she said, idiotically, and pulled her voice back to the normal register. 'I'll drive you home, I know it's near the Refuge.'

'I agree, I can't afford any more trouble tonight.'

She peeped at him anxiously, but he was shrugging himself into his layers of jacket, so she was able to hunt for the car key and call to Susannah that she would be back again very soon.

8

Thursday, 14 April

Luke Fleming arrived early, but Margaret Howard was there before him and made him coffee. He stopped to enquire about the welfare of her aunt. The business needed to keep Margaret in place, not too much agitated by the policemen who seemed to infest the office. He decided that they had nothing to worry about in this quarter; the murder had acted on her like oxygen and she was looking younger and fitter by the minute, bright-eyed and cheerful as she described the three days non-stop of phone calls, and the armies of nice young policemen, customers and neighbours that she had entertained.

'And it's good to have *you* in charge now, Mr Fleming. Poor Mrs Price is of course not able to deal with all these things.' She gave him a flirtatious look and he remembered she was only five years his senior.

'Mrs Price and I need to spend a couple of hours together, then I'll need you to help me ... us ... with letters and so on ... You know the people this end better than I do. Can you organise your lunch hour accordingly?'

Nothing, it turned out, could be easier. Miss Howard had felt it her duty, from the day the death had been discovered, to defend her desk against all comers. To which end she no longer left the building for lunch and brought in sandwiches from home, in which Luke would be most welcome to participate.

He thanked her and pushed through the interconnecting door which separated the office from the staircase to the first floor, and went up the thickly carpeted stairs. He was expected; Sylvia was not much of a one for surprises, and she opened the door to him, carefully dressed and made up and smelling deliciously of a flowery perfume.

'Did you lock the door downstairs?'

'Of course I did.' He closed the living-room door behind him and took her in his arms. 'You're looking better,' he said into her hair. 'Did you sleep?'

'Yes, I sleep. And you?'

'Not well. I wanted to be here with you.'

'This would not be proper.' She detached herself from him in order to pour him coffee. He took the cup and put it down on the mantelpiece. It was important to discuss the business but he had one need more urgent than any of that. He took her cup away as well and held her, hands moving over her body.

'Luke. We have not time.'

'Oh yes, we have. We'll work much better after.' He felt for the nipple under the silk blouse as he kissed her mouth, and felt her lean on him.

'Well . . .'

'Upstairs quick then, unless you want it here on the floor.'

She didn't, as he knew, preferring a decent bed. Well, he had no complaints, he was happy to do anything she wanted in return for her compliance in anything he'd ever asked for, and a couple of things he hadn't thought of before.

He lay back in bed afterwards, listening to the noises in the bathroom, grinning to himself. It had been very good. And it would be even better to be able to do it when he wanted to, in a decent climate, as an acknowledged couple.

'Luke, you must get up now.' She appeared in the doorway wrapped in a travelling dressing-gown, looking soft and elegant. He made an effort and swung his legs out of bed to intercept her as she went past him to her dressing-table, and cuddled her to him.

'You should have waited. I wanted to have a shower with you.'

'Another day, Luke, yes, I too will want. But I am not easy here today. I know we will have many visitors. The police again, I am sure.' She had removed herself firmly from his arms and was putting on foundation in careful small circles, concentrating on the task. He sighed, recognising that she could be right, and padded into the bathroom, finding a huge white towel, just the sort he liked, laid out for him. Sylvia knew – had always known – how to make a man feel comfortable, though he could have done without the small bits of china and little brightly coloured bottles of bath oil, skin cream, and shampoo, arranged decoratively on every surface. He thought without regret of his ex-wife, and their permanently untidy farmhouse on the cold side of a Yorkshire hill. Not at all what he had wanted, and he was paying out a lot of money to keep the place in being. He gritted his teeth against an old bitterness, but there was nothing to be done, or not yet.

'Luke? I will be in the living-room. I hear the phone.'

It took him not more than fifteen minutes to shower and dress again. He was glad to see a slice of cake waiting with fresh coffee; it was like Sylvia to acknowledge that a man might need a little sustenance afterwards, rather than a plaintive request to fix whatever had last fallen off the house. He hauled a solid pile of paper out of his briefcase, in earnest of his good intentions, and ate the cake, cleaning his fingers on the immaculate lace-edged napkin provided, watching Sylvia as she made little adjustments to the various objects on the sidetables.

'Sylvia? Look, I went to see the Nat West yesterday.'

'That man Mr Rawling?'

'Rawlings, yes. I brought him up to speed with where the police were, i.e. not very far but inclined to think that . . . that it was an intruder – someone breaking in – who killed Bill.'

'I, too, think this.'

'Yes.' He looked at her under his eyelashes. They had been lovers for a year; it had been clear to him that she hadn't been getting what she needed sexually from Bill, but she had seemed to get on well enough with him from day to day. And while the situation had not exactly been what he wanted, it hadn't *not* suited him either. It left him free to live as he wanted in Majorca, having another girl every now and then. He had been coasting along in this relationship, he recognised, but the business out there had needed all his attention. 'Anyway, he'd reread the insurance policy – he'd got it in the bank's safe – and he was quite pleased. It had a suicide clause, but even if there had been any question of that with Bill it would have been OK. From their point of view, I mean. It only applied for a year after the policy was taken out, or increased.'

'And it is more than a year since we raised the amounts. This I looked at. So we have £2m.'

He had never known how much Sylvia was involved in the business, but he suspected she had always had a sound under-standing of the essentials. 'Well, not necessarily. We have an overdraft of nearly £1.5m and we owe £15m in loans. Nat West are the lead bank, but there are others. If he wanted all his overdraft back that would leave us only £500,000 to play with.'

'Can you get twenty new units for this summer?'

'With just that?' He fished out three pieces of paper stapled together, and made some rapid calculations. 'We got out of the ground, just, on all of the Soller blocks.' He looked at his figures again. 'But I couldn't do all three, not at once. If I did two, it'd be end of June before they were finished and fitted out. I've lost the contractor, you see. Couldn't pay him, so he went on somewhere else. But if I could write a cheque for £500,000 on condition he started back on site now, he'd come back.' He looked up at her to find her gazing at him with the trusting-little-woman look he liked so much.

'I think Bill has said that it is twenty units at least that we need. Otherwise we will have too much problems here, at this end.'

'He'd oversold?'

'I believe, yes.'

He sat back, thinking how much easier it was to deal with her than with Bill, who would have gone off on a long speech, full of metaphor, refusing to acknowledge that he had taken money for a product he was not going to be able to deliver when it was wanted.

'If there were more cash would the work be able to go faster?' she asked, frowning, and he put an arm round her.

'You mean is there a way I could be sure of twenty units in . . . what . . . three months?' He looked down to think and when he raised his head saw that she was watching him expectantly. 'I wasn't expecting the question – that's why I'm slow,' he said bluntly. 'I didn't know how much Bill had sold, nor how much cash I might get, so I haven't worked this out.'

'What was originally planned?'

'Ah. To have these three blocks – that's thirty-three units – at Soller ready for the end of May. I'd have done it too with a start last September, only *that* got delayed. I'd still have been there for the end of June, but we had to stop again, in January.'

'But you have surely had some money from Bill since then?'

'Oh, I did. About £200,000, but £100,000 went to the contractor for Soller, and I had to use £80,000 to finish at Cartina – we had bookings for that in April, and Bill and I agreed that that had to be done.'

'What cash do you have out there?'

'£17,000 odd,' he said, suppressing the £20,000 in Geneva. Not even to Sylvia was he going to disclose that. 'But we need it for the office wages.'

'I will need to come to Majorca, yes?'

'Good idea, when we're organised here. Something I haven't told you, though. I know where Bill got £80,000 of the cash I had, and *that*'ll have to go back. It's Miles Arnold's money.'

'Miles?' she said, incredulously.

He relayed the story as told to him by Miles, following her into the tiny kitchenette where she went abruptly to make more coffee.

'He thought some of his money was in cash in the safe,' he said, in conclusion.

'Because Bill had told him so,' she observed, and they looked at each other. 'I wonder how the insurance company will behave? Miss Howard, she did not know? No. Why did he now want cash? Miles, I am talking about.'

'Well, to put the deposit on a flat for a lady friend, apparently. And cash, so it wasn't traceable, by the wife, apart from anyone else. It seems it's all true what you read about MPs, they're all at it.'

'For a woman he wanted this cash?'

'Seemingly. Anyway, Syl, the point is that if he's telling the truth – and I bet he is – he has papers and he can sue us. So I said to him that we'd try and cash flow him out of the present embarrassment and give him £20,000 in cash so he could do the necessary. There's no point overlooking someone who can actually sue us. Not if we want to keep the business going.'

She was fidgeting with the cups, her back to him. 'Perhaps we should not go on with the business if all is so difficult?'

'You need an income, don't you?' he objected.

'This house is mine. And it is worth at least £1m. And I do not yet know that we can meet these bookings, and if we cannot then I will not go on. Peter Graebner says that I can say it was the business of my husband and I knew nothing.'

'Sylvia, it is my business too.'

'You will be able to say you knew also not much because you were not here. Perhaps you will be in a little trouble, but not so much.'

'Well . . .' He was disconcerted. 'It's a good business, it's just that Bill lived off it and took too much cash out. I joined him because I could see it working and making very decent money. Look, Syl, if you and I work it together and get over this hump we could be making serious money in three years.'

She sat elegantly on the end of the big sofa and put her coffee cup down on the mantelpiece. 'Peter Graebner says I should not be in a hurry, Luke. Already today Margaret says there is another police person wanting to see you. Or me. Not about murder but about the business. A woman, an Inspector Crane. We put her off but tomorrow you must see her. We need to do a cash flow, he says, so I can see how it will be and whether we can do this. You shall have the bookings and the letters file – they are waiting for you with Miss Howard. I will deal with Miles if he makes problems.'

He put his hand on her knee, below the tight skirt, but she was cross and unresponsive, and after a moment he removed the hand and pretended to look for his coffee.

'I'd done a cash flow of course, but not quite on that basis. After lunch do you?' He tried and failed to make it sound humorous.

'No, no, dear Luke, I am sorry to be cross but it is all so difficult and I am not yet knowing what to do for the best.'

'We'll work it out,' he said, reassuringly. 'Better tomorrow.'

Francesca McLeish turned the key in her own front door, furtive as a burglar. She had been seeing officials at the Department for Education and had realised as she left them that papers she needed for a meeting at Gladstone were still at home. But if her William realised she had come back she could hardly get in and out in ten minutes. The house was silent as she stepped carefully on to the door mat and she remembered that it was Thursday, the day of Susannah's regular get-together with another young nanny and her little charges. She let out her breath and dropped her coat on the floor.

'Francesca?'

She gasped in shock and turned to see Matthew Sutherland, standing on the step behind her looking tired and bedraggled, long coat scraping the top of black Doc Martens.

'Sorry, didn't mean to frighten you. Can we talk?'

'I'm not really here.' She looked at his face, dejected under the dark red hair. 'But come in. Tell me all. Did you appear this morning? Have you seen Peter Graebner?'

'Yes and yes.' He had followed her downstairs, sat himself at her kitchen table and started to pick at a bit of dried food off the high-chair with obsessive concentration.

'And?'

'I pleaded Not Guilty. Trial date set three weeks away. Graebner sent me home; says he can't have me on drug cases which is mostly what I've got, and that he must consult his partners about what to do.'

She considered his profile as he dug at the chair with a blunt knife he had found on the table, and decided soup rather than coffee would help the situation. 'He can't really do otherwise, Matt, just at the moment.'

'Yeah. So then I went to St Mary's to see if I could find the lad I got the ambulance for.'

'Why?'

'To see if I'd been wasting my time.' He put the knife down, to her relief, and accepted the soup, unseeingly. He still wasn't looking at her but he was eating hungrily.

'Did you find him?'

'Yes. And that's why I'm here. Among other reasons.'

She brought a bowl for herself and sat beside him in a patch of sunlight.

'I went to the hospital, see. Typical. Couldn't find anyone who knew a bloody thing, but then I got talking to a casualty nurse. She remembered him coming in and she had his name. Francis Price.' He looked at her meaningfully, but she shook her head. 'Francesca. What happened to Wonderwoman? Your husband, the policeman, is dealing with the murder of someone called William Price. This is one of the sons.'

She gaped at him. 'What? How do you know? Is he all right?'

'*I* knew because I'd talked to Annabelle this morning. I found her outside the Refuge. She's looking rough. So we had a coffee and I told her my troubles since she didn't want to tell me hers. She says it's likely to be Antony Price's brother – he's a druggie, and the age is about right. And no, he's not all right.'

'Not dead?'

'Unconscious still, not in good shape, my little girl at the hospital said. She rang a friend on the ward.'

'I hope you bought her a coffee.'

'I am seeing her again, yes, since you ask. But the Man'll want to know. Your husband.'

'Yes, he will. Did you tell them at the hospital? Didn't the Met have someone there?'

'They did and you must be joking. I'm a *criminal*, they're not going to listen to me.' He winced. 'Jesus Christ, what a bastard thing to happen.'

She opened her mouth to say something consoling and drew his bleakest look. 'Ignore that,' he instructed her. 'Lack of sleep.'

'Of course,' she said. 'Shall I ring John?'

'You told him the rest?'

'No. He came in too late and left before I was quite with it. I could not get out of bed in the morning.' She looked at him.

'Ring and tell him. And get him to ask Francis Price – if the poor sod ever comes out of it – where he got the drug. That much of it, I mean; my new friends at the hospital said it was a stonking great dose.'

'That'll be a technical term, I expect. Where do *you* think he got it?'

'His brother.'

She looked at him carefully. 'Do you *know*? I mean, did you get that from Annabelle?'

'No.'

'Is this pure prejudice?'

'Pure I don't say. I *am* prejudiced against him with good reason. These wankers who beat up women do it because they want to control, and there's nothing much less controllable than a druggie, particularly if he's your brother. It would be convenient all round, that much I can gather from Annabelle, if Francis could be postulated to have wandered in, stoned, and kicked the table from under his brutal father.'

She eyed him warily, and he scowled at her. 'No need to look at me like a social worker. Just ring your old man and tell him where one of his suspects is.'

She picked up the phone but did not dial. 'We've got a bathroom,' she said, pointedly. 'Two in fact. And a cloakroom. First door you come to in the hall.'

'I'll find it. Do you want me to get out while you ring him, is that it?'

'Yes.'

'You could give it to me straight next time.'

He went off, dropping his coat on the chair behind him, and she rang the Yard and explained the situation to Bruce Davidson.

'. . . And tell John I'm sorry,' she finished, obscurely. 'I'm sure there's someone at the hospital from Notting Dale, but they may not make the connection.' She put the phone down and looked, agonised, at her watch.

'Can I come back?' It was Matthew from the hall.

She sat, uneasily, listening to his footsteps coming down. He stopped in the doorway; much slighter than John, she saw, but nearly as tall; square, strong shoulders and the athlete's poise, weight distributed properly. She rushed to assert herself. 'Matthew, are you saying that Antony Price murdered his father? And has now tried to kill his brother? You don't think you're a bit OTT?'

'Antony's a better candidate than his brother. And Annabelle wants keeping an eye on. And I haven't any work to do.'

'So you're going to meddle.'

'If I hadn't fucking meddled, your husband would be a suspect short.'

'Anyway, I've told them.' She considered Matthew anxiously. 'So you're not working? Well, you need something else to do as well as assist the police to find a murderer. I mean, my husband has a team of about thirty on this case, all falling over each other, all needing his guidance late into the night, they can't need you full-time as well.'

'Bit pissed off, are you, Wonderwoman?'

'Will you *stop* calling me that!' He looked at her, startled, and she felt herself go slowly scarlet. 'It is you who needs employment, not me,' she said, trying to get back the ascendancy. 'Couldn't you do something useful for the Refuge? I mean, more than what you already do.'

'Thought of that.' He shrugged off a layer of clothes and reached a large hand for the sugar. 'No one has put together the stats for years. They're all so busy they just write things down and lose them. When they want to do an appeal they pick whichever tear-jerker they've got in hand.'

'You mean instead of a sober set of facts, such as might convince people with real money, like Government?'

'That's it. So I could get our statistics into order and on to a proper data base. You'd never know the computer had been invented if you look round the office. They did get the data on about three years ago, but no one uses it.'

'Mm,' Francesca said, shiftily. 'I'm afraid that's people like my mum.'

'I'll teach your mother. Capable lady, for all she over-indulges her children.'

'You're looking better.'

His head jerked up, and he looked at her, unsmiling. 'You know what? You need to distinguish me from your delinquent siblings.'

'How?' she asked, coldly, and watched as he went slowly scarlet in his turn.

'Right,' he said, tight-lipped, and swallowed his coffee as he got up. 'I'm going to the Refuge. Now.'

'Matt. Sorry, but *no one* attacks my brothers in my presence. Childhood habit. In practice I have to say you are being much more, well, clear-headed and active than they have often managed to be when in trouble.' She considered his unyielding face and got up to see him off, sadly.

'I'm not in any position to take offence, fuck it,' he said, the scarlet fading patchily, 'but I'm hurt in my feelings.' He stopped and looked down at her. 'I'm not coming back till I feel better, either,' he warned, 'or not till I've got somewhere with the Refuge stuff and done something.'

She looked into the light blue eyes and put a hand on the back of her chair. 'Will it take very long?' she asked, trying for a light touch. He didn't answer, just went on looking at her and she caught her breath. 'I must go, Matt, the office needs me.' She let go of the chair and looked round her.

'Francesca, you're off on Mondays.'

'Yes?'

'It's Thursday today, yes? I'll ring you Monday.'

'Yes. That'll be fine. I'll be here.' She managed to look up at him again and for a moment they both stood there, then he shrugged himself back into his coat, bent to kiss her, on the lips, and was gone.

John McLeish could still taste the canteen lunch; he had eaten chips, beans, sausages, bacon and two eggs, piled high and eased down with tomato ketchup. Francesca had reacted as if he had asked her to cook something nice with cyanide in it when he asked for this combination at home and it turned out she was dispiritingly right; the days when he could get that lot down without a cross word from his digestive system had gone. It was, however, the news embodied in a note left on his chair with 'urgent' stickers all over it that was causing maximum gastric unease. A man he slightly knew, a political journalist, had rung with urgent information about Miles Arnold MP, but had refused to talk to anyone else. McLeish had, when superintendent at Notting Dale, intervened to prevent an over-zealous detective sergeant from pursuing a case against four men – of whom this had been one – who were engaged in behaviour which could have been held to threaten public order only if you were very insecure about your own sexuality. McLeish had stopped the whole business dead in the tracks, ostensibly to protect the Met from being ridiculed in court, but in practice because his sense of justice was offended. The man, who had been the oldest and best known of the group, had been grateful and had tried to pay him back with information. He would have to ring him back; Miles Arnold was a suspect in a murder case without an alibi, but if Arnold was also homosexual everything he thought he knew about human sexuality was way off. Well, *that* had happened before and no doubt would again, so he reached for the telephone.

He was hailed with éclat, and his full title, no doubt for the benefit of the newsroom, but his informant asked him to wait two minutes until he found a private phone.

'Thank you for ringing back.' The deep voice was devoid of any camp mannerisms, and reassuring. 'I hear that Miles Arnold is in a spot of bother with your lot about that murder in Kensington. He was a consultant to the travel firm, yes?'

'That's right.'

'Don't know anything about *that*, but one thing you need to know about Miles is that his life's a bit complicated just now. There's a woman, runs her own image consultancy. Susie James. Word is that Mrs A doesn't have any idea, poor girl.'

'The wife? The poor girl, I mean.'

'Oh yes. Ms James is a tough little piece, whereas poor Mrs A is rather sweet – you know, local girl married him on the way up.'

McLeish sat silent, trying to work out where this left him and what else he might usefully ask; he didn't want to have to ring back later.

'Don't know if this is useful.' The man was sounding mildly miffed, and McLeish bestirred himself.

'I'm sure it is somewhere.' He considered and decided to risk going on. 'People in that sort of situation need money, of course.'

'He should have enough. He's got about ten consultancies, so-called. But yes, they always seem to need more, don't they? Sorry, as we speak, it doesn't sound much, but I wasn't sure that this sort of information came to you in the ordinary way, as it were.'

'Not easily,' McLeish acknowledged. 'Thank you.'

'You're always welcome.'

Which left him, McLeish thought wearily, with the clear duty of seeing Miles Arnold again and putting pressure on him to come up with a better story about where he was on Friday and Saturday nights. The vision of that lively, restless, driving personality sitting at home with the television for two consecutive nights had never been convincing, and now a possible explanation had appeared which could eliminate one suspect, and stop his team wasting a lot of time. To tell Miles Arnold MP that the police were unconvinced by his story was a task for the detective chief superintendent in charge of the investigation, but he was not going to advance directly. He picked up the phone.

'Chief Whip's Office.'

'May I speak to Jim Waters?' This was a civil servant not a politician he was after, an infinitely experienced and careful professional, younger than himself and a fellow Scot, with a long career as Private Secretary to Chief Whips of both political colours. He arranged to have a drink with the man later that day. He looked round for his team; Davidson had gone off to a hospital for some reason, but he would catch up with him later.

He was standing, fidgeting, in the damp hall by the receptionist's desk, surrounded by filing cabinets, looking much younger than thirty.

'Annabelle, sorry to drag you out. It was him. *Is* him. He's in a coma.' He was sounding desperate, right at the edge as he did so often these days, and she wondered how she could ever have thought him such a monolithic tower of strength. Like so many husbands and lovers of the abused women at the Refuge, he was a desperately dependent child when things were not going his way.

'Antony, come in for a minute. I'm sorry, Jenny, five minutes.' She pulled him into a decent-sized office, with the inevitable furnishings of weighing machine, blood-pressure machine and battered desk.

'Very decent office,' he said, surprised. He looked dazed and pale, and smaller than usual.

'My senior partner's. I don't have an office. Was Francis hurt when he fell?'

'No, it's entirely the drugs. Rubbish from a crooked dealer, I expect.'

'Where did he get the cash?'

'I have no idea. I never give him any. Well ... it would go on drugs. I pay anything I have to for him direct.'

She knew this to be true and realised that she was only stalling while she thought. 'It's a good hospital, Mary's,' she said.

'Yes.' He sat heavily on the edge of the desk. 'I can't cope with all this, Annabelle. I just want to be a doctor and look after patients.'

Who are properly grateful, not related to you and not on drugs, she supplied, silently. 'Well, you can't do anything for Francis until he comes out of a coma,' she pointed out patiently.

'And the police are probing me about Friday night.' He looked at her sideways, lips compressed, a quick testing glance.

She decided she did not quite dare to remind him that it was hardly her fault that he was without an alibi. 'Great Ormond Street have offered to interview me,' she said, instead.

'Why? What for?'

'I did tell you that I had decided to try and get back into paediatrics. This being a GP – isn't what I wanted to do.'

'Oh Christ. Can't you think of anyone but yourself?'

It was a cry of pure rage and she gaped at him, utterly taken aback. He had turned scarlet and was trembling, and she was the other side of the desk before she had consciously thought, so sure was she that he was going to hit her. His mouth squared like a child starting to cry and he banged the desk with the edge of his hand. It was a frightening study in frustrated rage, and she edged another step away and put her hand on the comforting weight of a silver ink-well, gift of a grateful patient.

'You'd better go,' she said, trying to steady her voice.

'No, wait.' He was struggling with himself and she watched, horrified. 'I cannot believe that you're not doing it deliberately. Winding me up.' His voice broke, and she could feel the power of his wanting to hit her, or break something. She understood in one liberating flash that all this had not very much to do with her, she was just there, a necessary focus for this uncontrollable anger. She waited, quietly, the heavy ink-well in her hand, because she understood that if he came after her she would have to knock him out or deflect him long enough to get out of the door, because he had no control. She watched him fighting with himself, fighting against the spurts of pure uncontrollable rage and misery. It was like watching a two-year-old coming out of a tantrum only this was a grown man with the strength to batter those around him as a toddler could not.

'This must be how you felt about your father,' she said, when she was sure he had himself in hand.

'Yes. I wanted to kill him and I couldn't, I couldn't. When I saw him hanging there I wanted to pick up the chair and batter him.'

She must have made a noise or moved, because suddenly he was staring at her across the desk with dark blue eyes. 'He was *dead*, anyone could see that. So there wasn't anything I could do.'

'Why were you there?' She was almost too frightened to speak, but instinct told her to keep a conversation going.

'To look for the file on the trust. My mother's trust. And see what I could find. I knew he'd stolen the money and we needed it – Francis and me. I couldn't find anything, so I went away.'

'Why didn't you call the police?'

'I didn't want to. I wanted to leave him hanging there. I knew he was dead, but I didn't want him cut down. And I thought they'd think I'd done it.' He looked at her, limp suddenly. 'They *will* think I did it.'

She walked round the desk, her legs still shaking but in control, and put her arms round him and he clutched at her convulsively. 'I didn't. He was *dead*. It was Saturday morning. I thought he was away with Sylvia, you see, so I went round. I got a key cut.' He sounded six years old and scared, and she held him stiffly, wanting to comfort but passionately not wanting the terrified little boy.

'We'd better go to the police. The one you've already talked to – Francesca's husband.'

'Will you come with me?'

'Of course,' she said, regretting helplessly the new life she was beginning to find for herself. 'Of course, darling. We'll go first thing tomorrow morning.'

9

Friday, 15 April

'No, I haven't done much about Francis Price. He was still unconscious yesterday, but I did make sure Notting Dale knew I had an interest. And the hospital.'

John McLeish had just come out of the morning meeting of the team on the Price case, and was aware he was sounding cross. He had seen his wife very little for the past week, and it was hardly Francesca's fault that the Price case was not following the usual pattern in most murder cases, in which the likely murderer emerged quickly from the surroundings. 'I'm due to see his brother again,' he offered, in partial explanation.

'I didn't mean to nag,' Francesca said, coldly. She was at her desk in Gladstone College; he could hear the clock-tower strike in the background. 'I just wanted to be quite sure Bruce had passed on the message. I forgot last night, due to your getting back so late.'

There must, he reflected, be some wives who would let their policeman husbands work the hours a difficult case needed without a continual barrage of objection.

'Notting Dale aren't going to charge him. Well, they can't, for a start nothing on him and nothing at the place he lives. And it's not him they're after anyway, it's the supplier.'

'And he was still unconscious. That must have made it a bit more difficult.'

'It did. And I haven't got very far with your Mr Sutherland either. I'll have a word with the DS there later. See you tonight.'

'That would make a nice change.'

Matthew Sutherland strode confidently up to the nurses' room in the Minto ward of St Mary's and greeted the uniformed rear view of a young woman, scrabbling through papers.

'Excuse me. My cousin Francis Price is here somewhere and my aunt, who is abroad, has asked me to come and see him.'

'You can't.'

'He's still unconscious? Could I possibly just look at him so I can tell my aunt?'

The nurse turned round, revealing herself as very young and very cross, and he gave her his most winning smile.

'You can't see him. He's too weak for visitors.'

'You mean he's come round?'

She took him in this time, slowly recognising a personable young man not much older than herself. 'Yes, he has actually. Not long ago, but he's very weak. He's on the ward because they needed the bed in Intensive Care. You're his cousin, you said?' She looked doubtfully at the dark red hair, and bent to look at a schedule.

'It was me called the ambulance when he collapsed. Please. I won't fuss him. And my aunt would be so relieved.' He cast a mental apology in the direction of his father's only sister in faraway Rarituka, New Zealand.

The girl was still hesitant, but he smiled at her patiently, so she came round the counter and led him down the corridor, her heavy black shoes thumping on the hard floor. She threw open the door. Francis Price was lying on the bed, his head slightly raised and a drip running into his outstretched left arm. He was deathly pale and still, but back in the world, his eyes opening momentarily at their arrival. The nurse checked the drip and looked carefully at her patient and reflectively at Matthew.

'It's all right,' he said quietly. 'I'll just stay five minutes, if I may.'

She nodded and left, and he hitched his chair close up to the bed.

'Francis,' he said, 'you don't know me, but when you fell over unconscious in the pub night before last I called the ambulance.'

The eyes stayed closed but there was something in the face to show the man was listening.

'I realised you'd overdosed. Smack, was it?'

The eyes flickered open and closed again, firmly.

'I'm not a policeman. I'm a lawyer. And you're in dead shtuck, mate. Who gave it to you?'

A faint twist of the mouth and Matthew strained to hear.

'M'man.'

'Wrong question. Who gave you the cash?'

'Fuck off.'

Matthew sat back, acknowledging a reasonable rebuke and decided to start again. 'I'm not sure how much you're hearing, Francis, but I know you're one of the people suspected of killing your father, and I know that because we – my firm – represent your stepmother.'

'Sylvia?'

'Yes.' Matthew considered the pale eyelids. 'So you don't want to open your eyes. Fair enough, I only need you to hear. You had a load the day before yesterday when I saw you take a dive off a bar stool. I know what smack costs. What I've been wondering was whether someone among the group found it convenient to have you overdose. That way it could be *you* who killed your father.'

The man on the bed remained silent, but the rhythm of his breathing had changed, and Matthew knew he was hearing the words. 'So I asked myself who gave you the cash? Was it your brother?'

Francis Price started to cough, painfully and Matthew reached to prop him up in bed, cautiously working round the drip.

'Who, Francis?' He watched, frustrated, as the man performed the difficult trick of coughing up his lungs with his eyes closed. He heard footsteps in the corridor. 'Listen, mate, I'm on your side. I've done smack in my time. Think about it. If you didn't kill your father someone else did. And it's a bit easy to pin it on a naughty druggie like you.'

Francis had managed to stop coughing but he wasn't going to speak.

'I'll have to go, but I'll be back. I've told them I'm your cousin, OK? I've left my card in the drawer here. Call me and I'll come running. And don't take any presents from anyone.' He straightened up as the door opened and greeted the entering ward sister with an anxious complaint about Francis's cough, so that she went straight to her patient and let him get out of the door without her registering anything more about him.

John McLeish wasted no time in getting to the interview room in which Dr Antony Price was waiting. This was the break he had been waiting for, when the pressure applied by the sheer weight of an investigation started to cause cracks in the original accounts to appear. And this was a structural fault that was being revealed; what Antony Price had already told Davidson placed him by his father's suspended body on Saturday morning. He stopped only to make sure he had everything Davidson knew.

'The wee girl's here,' Davidson added, at the end of his account. 'In a waiting-room.'

'Not with Price?'

'No. I thought he'd better be on his own. Face up to where he is.'

'How long's he been there? Twenty minutes? Give him another coffee, I'll just have a word here.'

A few minutes with a suspect's girlfriend would give him useful background against which to view the man. And besides, he was curious about any young woman who had managed to impress his wife.

'I'm John McLeish, Francesca's husband,' he said, extending a hand to the exhausted young woman who looked up at him, eyes wide and wary. 'Are you reasonably comfortable? Can we get you anything else?'

'No. No, thank you. Will it ... will you ... be very long?' He considered her, trying for a sensible answer, and she flushed. 'You don't know, of course.'

'I'm sorry, I don't. I would be grateful if I could talk to you after I've talked to Dr Price, but do go back to ... well, wherever ... if you'd prefer that, just tell us where we can find you.'

'I'd rather stay. I've got ... I had an interview but I've rung up and cancelled.' She looked at him. 'I couldn't do it anyway.'

'What was it for?'

'It was at Great Ormond Street. To see if I could get on to the research staff there.'

'You're training as a GP, Francesca tells me.'

The girl considered him and he saw that she had a good strong jaw. 'Tell her ... tell Francesca that I *am* going back to paediatrics, I am going to try to be a consultant. Just as soon as I can.'

'I will. Now, I must go and talk to Dr Price.'

She nodded, her face pinched with anxiety, and he left her sitting tense on the edge of her chair. He collected Davidson and went into the interview room.

Antony Price looked quite different today from when they had interviewed him four days before. His face was thinner, the good bones showing so that he looked older and less charming. And there was something unfocused about the wide dark blue eyes, so that instead of looking confident and easy he looked driven, tense and braced for a struggle. If he were a dog, McLeish thought, one would go a long way round him. But this was a suspect in a murder case and the strategy that usually worked was to go in hard. He glanced at Davidson to make sure the tape was running.

'Dr Price, I understand you want to change the statement you made to me on Monday,' he said, formally, and was interested and mildly surprised to find that Antony Price had nerved himself to this task and, without apology, described his arrival at his father's house on Saturday and discovery of the body hanging from the ceiling hook.

'Did you have a key?'

'Yes. Bill didn't know I had, before you ask, but Sylvia had given me one after the incident when he beat her up. She thought it was a useful precaution, so she could ring me up if it happened again.'

'Rather than ringing the police?'

'Sylvia doesn't have much confidence in the police. She's Austrian and I understand the police there might not be very receptive to a complaint of that nature.'

He was looking past them both, jaw tight. The knowledge that he, too, had beaten up his woman, presumably in the faith that the police had no role in the matter, hung in the room, leaving McLeish a tempting side path down which he decided not to go. It was this man's father, not his girlfriend, who had been murdered.

'So you came through the front door?'

'Yes. I didn't expect to find anyone there. I thought Bill and Sylvia were both away, and Margaret Howard doesn't work weekends.'

'Even though it is a travel business?' The point had worried McLeish and the team and he thought it was worth a minor diversion.

'I don't think Bill wanted to be accessible to anyone just at the moment. As I'm sure you know by now, he'd oversold places abroad and owed a lot of money here.'

'I understand that neither you nor your brother were involved in the business.'

Antony Price considered him, mouth tight. 'That's right, and of

121

course I only knew what Bill chose to tell me. I'd been to see him a week before to find out what had happened to the trust funds held for me and my brother. When I tackled him both about the trust and some cash for Francis, to pay off the rest of his debts, all I got was a long whinge about how tight cash was, and how every penny was needed in the business. So, as I was about to say, I decided to come back and have a look round myself.'

'So you let yourself in with the key given you by Mrs Price.' McLeish wanted this story in detail and in order, and this witness who had lied flatly once already could damn well answer questions this time. 'Then what?'

'Well, I thought I'd better check no one was around, so I called out something like "Anyone at home?" and got no answer. So I went upstairs to the flat and knocked there. Again no answer, so I used the other key and just checked there. Then I went back to the office.'

'And did what?' McLeish asked, after a pause.

'Well, actually I just stood. The safe was open, you see. First thing I noticed, so I thought that somebody *must* be in the house and I'd better check the kitchen downstairs, in case they hadn't heard me. I mean Sylvia, or Bill, might have been out in the garden.' He stopped again, and McLeish waited, listening for the hesitations or the change of tone that would tell him when the man was lying again. Antony Price was sweating round the hair-line and while he had his hands out of sight under the table the hunch of his shoulders told both experienced observers that all of him was clenched in resistance. 'So I decided to go downstairs.'

'Did you look in the safe?'

Antony hesitated and flicked a look at McLeish's unmoving face. 'Yes, I did. Of course I did. It was empty.'

'Completely?'

'Yes. Nothing in it at all.'

'What would you have expected to see in there?'

'Oh. The petty cash box. Margaret Howard was very keen on putting *that* away, though petty cash wasn't what my father – Bill – was interested in. Grand larceny was more his form. And the Books. I've no idea what was in them, but it was some sort of accounts.'

Davidson shifted position, to signal that he thought his senior officer was missing something.

'But what exactly had you come to look for, Dr Price? And why did you expect it to be in the safe?'

'I wanted the trust accounts, or any correspondence about my mother's trust. I thought he might have put the file in the safe, because I'd been asking about it. I didn't know what the file looked like, but ... well ... I thought it would look like a *file*, I suppose. It doesn't matter what I thought, it wasn't there, nothing was, and so I went down to the kitchen. I didn't dare poke around in the office and have a good look, because I thought someone *must* be in the house.' He looked at them, then looked away at the walls.

'You went downstairs,' McLeish prompted.

'Yes.' He looked down at the table, then up again at their professionally expressionless faces. 'Yes. Downstairs.' He stopped again and they waited, listening to the tiny whirr of the tape. 'When I opened the door I could see it straightaway.'

'It was light then?'

'It *was* nine thirty in the morning. Oh, no, sorry, I see what you mean. The curtains were drawn, but the lights were on.'

Two days later, on the Monday morning, Miles Arnold had come down those same stairs to total darkness, with the thick curtains drawn across the French windows.

'Go on.'

'It was just hanging there, I just saw the feet, and then you could tell straightaway what it was, I mean, it became a body.'

'What did you do then?'

'I went over. I knew it must be Bill, it was built like him, great fat stomach, and he was dead.'

'You were certain of that?'

'I'm a *surgeon*, for Christ's sake. He was dead. And stiff and cold. I felt the legs.'

'Stiff as well as cold?'

'As a board. Rigor mortis – you know, it sets in about eight hours after death.'

'We are familiar with the phenomenon,' McLeish said, suddenly furious with a man who could have established the time of death very much more closely and with less trouble than the police pathologist. Assuming, that was, that he was telling the truth. 'Did you form a view about how long he had been dead?'

'I didn't really. He was dead, so there was nothing I was obliged to do. But I've thought about it since – of course I have, all the bloody time – and he must have been twelve hours dead at least. Rigor was still well established.' He flicked a glance at them.

Twelve hours took them back to nine thirty on the Friday evening when Antony Price had a solid alibi, vouched for not only by the young woman in the waiting-room but by half the staff of a London restaurant. McLeish looked into the wide dark blue eyes thoughtfully.

'So why didn't you ring the police?'

'I was honestly just about to.' The eyes widened even further, but McLeish had ceased to expect the truth even without this signal; the use of 'honestly' or 'frankly' by a witness invariably signalled exactly the opposite intent. 'Then I got scared.' His faint inclination of the head acknowledged the small-boy frankness. 'And I thought, my God, no one's going to believe this. The other trustee of my mother's trust knows I had a blistering row with Bill last week because I went and saw him too. And even without *that* there's enough people know that Bill and I hated each other. And I'd just had – Annabelle had – we'd split up.' He looked at them under his eyelashes to see how much they knew about that, but neither man moved a muscle. 'So I didn't dare. I thought I'd better just get out as quickly as possible.'

And out of this interview too, everything in the body language shrieked, and McLeish decided the moment had come to push. 'So what did you think when you saw your father hanging there?'

'What do you mean, what did I think?' Antony Price had gone suddenly scarlet, and was leaning forward.

Both policemen waited, stolidly. 'Well, did you think he'd committed suicide?'

'Oh no. No, that's the point, that's why I was terrified. It was quite clear what he'd been doing. I mean, he had a bag over his head and he was wearing women's underwear.'

'You thought it was an accident?' McLeish suggested.

'I did, you know, for a minute or so. But then I realised that it wasn't that. Something else had happened. The table was turned over and the door was open.'

'The door was open?'

'Yes. And there was some broken glass.'

McLeish leant over and spoke into the recorder. 'Sorry, I want to stop. I want you to look at some pictures taken on Monday in the kitchen.'

They waited, McLeish looking at his notes and Antony Price fidgeting while Davidson came back with a set of envelopes.

'Did you move anything?' McLeish, asked, when the tape was running again.

'No. Sorry. Yes, I pushed the door shut and drew the curtains across the gap.'

'Why did you do that?' No fingerprints belonging to Antony Price had been found on the door, or indeed anywhere in the room.

'I wanted to look through the office.' His hands were on the table now, clenched to each other. 'And I thought anyone could see that the basement door was open. There's another house backs on to the garden, it's not very big. So I pushed the door – I really didn't disturb anything, you know, I just pushed it with a handkerchief and drew the curtains over.'

'You didn't touch the table?'

'No. Or the body except that once, on the leg.'

McLeish spread the photographs, taken by flashlight on Monday, and watched Price as he leant forward to look.

'Take your time. Was the table in that position?'

'Yes. Yes, I think so. I'm sorry, it looks a bit different when it's dark.'

'I'm sure that's true.'

Antony Price's head came up. 'I wasn't trying to make your job more difficult. I'm sorry, I was, frankly, shit-scared.'

No, you weren't, McLeish thought. If you are telling the truth, and genuinely walked in on the aftermath, you did not give one blind damn about anything except finding what you'd come for. You don't think the rules about obstructing the police have anything to do with you.

'So you went back to the office?'

'Yes. I turned the lights out at the door of the kitchen and then I had a look in the office. It's got Venetian blinds, you can't see in from the street. I couldn't find the file – I didn't know where to look but I tried the obvious places, and I even had a look in the flat.' He looked at the table. 'I wore rubber gloves.'

'Did you bring the gloves with you?'

'Yes, I did.'

'Although you couldn't know the place had been burgled before you started.' He watched the sweat shine just above Price's eyebrows.

'I suppose I've just been reading too may detective stories. I just thought I'd better not leave any traces.'

'Were you going to take the file?'

The relief on the man's face could have served as a commercial for indigestion pills. 'Yes, yes, I was. *That's* why I needed not to leave fingerprints, so if Bill had called the police they wouldn't have found my fingerprints.'

It was not convincing and all three people in the room knew it, but he couldn't be shaken. No, he had not found the file and he did not know where it could be, except possibly in Bosham at the rented cottage. And he hadn't dared go there and look because he thought Bill and Sylvia were there. And no, no, and no, he had not killed his father, nor seen his body before about nine thirty on the Saturday, when he had been at least twelve hours dead. They couldn't move him, though he was sweating and wild-eyed, and losing his temper by the end.

McLeish was just about to call a halt when he checked his notes and recalled that there was a key question not yet asked.

'Right,' he said into an exhausted silence. 'Thank you, Dr Price. Now I need to ask you about your brother.'

'Francis? I'm going to see him after ... after this. He's out of Intensive Care, you know.'

'Yes. And doing all right, but St Mary's say he was lucky. Where did he get the drug, Dr Price, do you know?'

'Not from me.' It was said wearily without stress, and McLeish believed him. 'Getting drugs for a habitual user is just a question of cash.'

'So I understand. You give him money sometimes, I understand.'

'Only in very small, meal-buying quantities. I normally pay his rent by cheque – he never would when he's on drugs – and I gave him £50 this time because what with everything I hadn't sent a cheque. And I've paid off people who threaten him. Twice. But I don't give him much cash because I don't want him killing himself.' He stopped to examine this statement. 'Or not with cash *I've* given him.'

They ended the interview formally and left him sitting there while they repaired to another room and gave the tape to a police typist.

'Charge him,' Bruce Davidson said, definitively, in answer to McLeish's questioning look.

'What exactly do you think he did, Bruce? Knocked his father off on Friday, late, or early Saturday after dinner with his girl, and then came back in the morning to tidy up?'

'I'm not sure he was there on Saturday at all. Killed his father on Friday after he'd said goodnight to his girl, cleaned out the safe, smashed a bit of glass and sauntered off, and waited till Monday. Only *now* he thinks mebbe he left a wee trace somewhere, so he'd better find a story about how he was there after all. *And* it means he can suggest that his father had been killed at a time when he was still eating with the girlfriend. He's a surgeon, and he could be convincing in the box. No?'

'It's a very good insurance policy against us finding any traces of him,' McLeish conceded. 'But I don't think we can make a case stick yet and I'd rather give him some more rope. After all, he's moved on some since Monday and he's windy. If we charge him he'll clam up.' He sat, thinking, unhindered by Bruce Davidson who knew when not to speak. 'He's not going to run, is he? Nowhere to go.'

'You're not convinced?' Bruce was not fooled by all this.

'No, I'm not, but I'm buggered if I could tell you why. Let him go, Bruce, but tell him not to go far. Keep the pressure on.'

Bruce Davidson sat still, looking miserable.

'What?'

'You believe him about the lad – his brother? You don't reckon he gave him the cash to overdose with?'

'No, I don't.'

'Mm. And the wee girl? Out there. You reckon she's safe with him?'

'If he killed his father – and I say *if* – it was opportunistic. He found his dad playing a game which satisfactorily incapacitated and blinded him, he saw his chance and shifted the table. He didn't plan it ahead. And he knows we're watching him now. The girl isn't living with him. He's the type to crack if he did do it, and we may be saved a lot of work.'

'So you're not one of Chief Superintendent McLeish's mob then?'

Luke Fleming was sitting opposite Catherine Crane in the room looking on to the street, which served as a waiting-room for visitors to Price Fleming Associates. He was leaning forward slightly, with an expression she knew very well, somewhere between lust, incredulity and hope, as he took in her neat suit with the smart blouse and the carefully manicured hands.

'No. I am a detective inspector with the Fraud Squad, and I am here today to follow up a complaint made to us about the conduct of Price Fleming.'

'People can do that, can they? Come to you if they're not a happy camper?'

'No.' She gave him a carefully rationed smile. 'We can only move if there is some prima facie evidence that a fraud has been committed.'

'And you think there is here. What's the complaint? Or rather who is the complaint?'

'What is being alleged is that you have sold a holiday that you can't deliver. Or won't deliver.'

'We're not going to get anywhere unless I know who it is who reckons he hasn't got what he paid for. And why hasn't he – or she – complained to us, so that we could put it right?'

'They have. We have copies of the correspondence. Or rather copies of the letters he wrote. He didn't get many answers. He last rang earlier this week.'

'Wouldn't have got much of an answer earlier this week with Bill dead and me on the way home.'

He had a point of course, which was why she had come by herself, not mob-handed. She considered him: a big chap, thick hair going grey round the ears, only just not leering at her.

'He tried to reassure himself by more conventional means, Mr Fleming. But found that the last set of accounts at Companies House are three years old.'

'Ah, well, I'm not in London much, I am afraid I depended on Bill for all that. I'll get the accountants on to it straightaway.'

'Late filing of accounts is of course an offence.'

'I don't doubt it. I expect there's a few of us in the same boat.'

There were, of course – several hundreds of them – and, as he rightly supposed, there was not official time enough to do other than write increasingly rude letters. She was, however, paradoxically heartened by his straight-bat response; it was characteristic of the truly fraudulent. Those who had got into a more or less innocent muddle tended to collapse in tears and confusion.

'Your customer was sold a two-week holiday in Soller in June, in one of the new blocks you advertised you were building.'

'We are building at Soller.'

'Not very fast, I understand. The informant went down last week and could find only a site with no buildings on it at all. He didn't fancy his chances of having a holiday there in June.'

The big man smiled at her, kindly. 'He hasn't read his contract, has he? I've been working in Spain a very long time, and what with the unions and the local bad lads you can't guarantee finishing a building when you hoped you would. So we always put a clause in which says if we haven't finished a particular building you get something else. Something better as often as not.'

'If the company can afford it.'

'I don't think anybody is suggesting seriously that we are going to let this customer down, are they? Not aloud, where anyone else can hear them, like our solicitor.'

Another salient characteristic of the fraudulent, all the Squad agreed, was the threat of libel action in response to any questions, and Catherine was further encouraged.

'*I'm* suggesting it, Mr Fleming, here to you. Your accounts are adrift, your auditors resigned six months ago, and I don't believe you've replaced them, and you've got three actions for unpaid bills pending in Majorca. Oh, and you're a year behind with your rates here, and there are two County Court actions pending against the company by trade creditors.'

Luke Fleming did not move but the smile faded, and she had a strong impression of a system going into overdrive.

'I'd have to say that cash has been tight, but I was not aware how tight.'

'You must, however, have been aware of your liability as a director under the Companies Acts.'

'Oh yes. And my duty to customers, and our suppliers.' He was watching her intently, looking for an opening, and she presented him with her best, unsmiling, mask. 'Bill was always an optimist,' he said at last. 'I'm afraid he may well have been too hopeful about me getting the Soller apartments finished, but we won't let the customers down, Detective Inspector. We expect to have some cash shortly for a rather sad reason, but I'm sure you know that in any small business the principals are heavily insured.'

'For £2m in Mr Price's case, increased to that last year.'

'You've been busy.'

'Your fellow director was murdered.'

'So they say, although I don't know if that's right. But the Key Man insurance pays out to the company whatever happened to him, and it'll pay all the bills I know about. And see any disappointed customers into the best hotel in Soller.' He shifted position, without taking his eyes off her. 'That's what I told Miles – that's Miles Arnold MP, I expect you know of him. He was sure everyone would be supportive, provided we could pay our way.'

Catherine had been waiting for the political card to emerge and wondered again at the propensity of backbench MPs to take paid jobs with companies run on less than the soundest commercial principles. She considered Luke Fleming. Where the simplest course of action was the businesslike one he would take it, she decided. In a year in the Fraud Squad she had met many men and women who lied for the sake of it, and who walked an incompetent and crooked line, even when a perfectly straightforward route offered itself. Something of this must have got through her professional mask, because Luke Fleming had relaxed, fractionally.

'Come back in a couple of weeks, Miss Crane – not Mrs, is it? – when the insurance money is in the bank, and I've written a few cheques, and got the accountants up to speed and found some auditors. You won't have anything to worry about and nor will the customers.'

'What about the sites in Spain?'

'They'll be moving, I can tell you that. You ever been there? No? I've worked all over the world – well, that's what happens with civil engineers, and there's only one rule. Pay your debts or you'll never work *there* again. I've got a house there, and they're not very interested in legalities. If the company I work for doesn't pay its debts, they'll go after the house. Or burn it down. Happened to a friend of mine. So you can rely on me there.'

'How are you going to get them to build the apartments on time?' This was unwise; she was involving herself with a possible fraud, just as you were all warned not to in the squad, but she was confident in her own abilities and interested.

'They're short of work. They'll build out for me, on spec, if I can keep them going with a bit of cash.' He grinned at her, and she saw that his teeth had been expensively capped. 'So. Why don't you send the chap who has been worrying you to me, and we'll put his mind at rest. Or give him back his money if he'd rather. We don't have to but I will, just send him in. And come back yourself if you'd like, to see fair play.'

'We have the power under the Acts to make an investigation to determine if you are overtrading. We can put accountants in.'

He was not smiling now, but he was not rattled either. 'Entirely up to you. I've called accountants in and they are producing a report right now, and you can have that. Save a bit of taxpayers' money, wouldn't it? Mr Arnold will get a copy of course.'

Catherine Crane sat still and thought her way through. It would indeed be difficult to move in on Fleming Price in circumstances where a sum of £2m, enough to settle any short-term debts of which there was a public record, was about to come into their accounts. And if they could satisfy this complainant – and any others who might appear, alarmed by Bill Price's death – then the Fraud Squad was on weaker ground than they liked. Not hopelessly weak; the Squad had moved on less obvious cases than this one, but it was not a large company, it wasn't obviously another Barlow Clowes, and it had an MP working for it who would presumably put up a fearsome squawk if he found himself in public trouble as a result of over-enthusiastic action by the Squad. The rational course might well be to wait a couple of weeks, as Fleming was suggesting, and see what happened. It wasn't her decision to make alone, she needed to report and seek guidance. Time was always useful in a difficult situation; give it a few days and things could be very different. And it could be argued that no creditors of the company would be disadvantaged by waiting for an insurance payment.

'Sleep on it?' Luke Fleming had been watching her.

'I'd like to talk to your accountants,' she said, stiffly.

'Fine.' He named a good small firm. 'They're only just started on the books. I'd want to talk to them first – I mean before you did. I don't want them resigning before they've started.'

'I know them. I'll wait until they've had their heads down a bit longer.'

'Up to you.' He waited to see if she had finished with him, and held the door for her when she indicated she had. 'Can I get you a taxi?'

'I have a driver.' This was only partially true; it was the chief superintendent's driver, but he was there, having a quick sleep, which was how they all managed to work long into the evening. Luke Fleming shook her hand, holding it too long, as they all did, and she walked slowly down the steps, starting to compose her report.

He watched her into the car then went back to the office and checked Margaret Howard's methodically set out log of callers for the week. It was long and repetitive, as different grades of policemen had checked in and out and rung each other up. He finally found what he was looking for on Monday's log and went through the pass door to the flat. Sylvia was seated at a small square table, considering the spread-sheet he had organised for her earlier that day.

'I've got one we may have to add,' he reported. 'Mr Mastry. Went to the Fraud Squad. I told the policewoman they sent that we'd give him his money back if he wanted.'

'Can we afford that? What was she like, this woman?'

'A dazzler.' He sat down beside her and kissed her ear. 'Ask anyone. A very, very beautiful blonde.' He felt her stiffen; she was not one for having other women praised to her face.

'Natural?'

'Well, I didn't investigate that far. But yes, I'd think so. Or mostly natural, she may have helped it a bit.' He nuzzled her neck.

'She is how old?'

'Young. Early thirties, if that.' He could feel her tense and angry, and decided to stop teasing. 'If she comes back you'd better see her. But *if* we can get Mr Mastry off our backs and settle the worst of the claims against us then I don't think she will be back. We're small beer for them.'

They both considered the sheet.

'I'll put Mr Mastry in on the computer,' he said, frowning. 'But I'd guess that if we give him his £30k back, Mr Arnold'll have to wait.'.

'Or your builder in Spain?'

'Can't do that, darling, if we want those apartments. And we do; there's going to be a few more besides Mastry when they wake up and read the Sundays, and wonder if their holiday's going to be all right. In fact, I'm surprised more of them haven't, with what's in the papers.'

'They have. I took three calls myself this morning.'

'Shit.'

'No, it is all right. They were all embarrassed that I who am widow am talking to them, so they did not ask very much.'

'They wouldn't, would they? We'd better have you in the office full-time.'

'This I think too. For the moment. And Mr Arnold will most definitely have to wait. Our problems are more serious.'

'He could sue.'

'And tell his wife where there is money and why he wants it?'

'No, no. Poor bugger, though – the girlfriend won't be pleased.'

'It is foolish of her to be with a married man.'

He blinked, but the absence of emphasis with which she spoke made it clear that she recognised nothing odd in the statement. Women who took up with married men were fools. *Married* women could do as they pleased, but where did it leave the men who took up with them?

'I'll have to tell him. He's phoned twice. And I must talk to the insurers. They have all that they need and they are raising the cheque. They have tried to tell me that they are waiting because of the murder, but your solicitor gave *that* one short shrift. He reminded them that it is the company who insure and a company cannot murder people. They had to concede they knew this, it is only a delay.'

'So the company will have this £2m.'

'No, not all of it. The bank wanted £1.5m to pay off the whole overdraft, but I think I've negotiated them down to £1m. Margaret has written a letter in confirmation for me to sign. I must go down. I'll need to ring Miles.' He paused.

Sylvia was looking mulish. 'Please, Luke, do not yet talk to Miles; I need – we need – to discuss all these things before we pay anything. It is right, is it not, that both of us must sign any cheque?'

It was indeed right, he realised; she was joint executor with him. He opened his mouth to argue that this particular debt was overdue and difficult to stall but decided not to bother today, time enough to get Sylvia facing forward tomorrow when she had got used to having him around again.

10

Monday, 18 April

'John? Guess what we've found?'

'Another body? Make my day.'

'The trust file.'

John McLeish gazed unseeingly at the telephone then remembered. 'Ah. The late Mrs Price's trust. The one for the lads. For Antony and Francis. Well done, Bruce.'

'Not me. That wee Jenny. She decided the best place to hide a file was in a filing system, in the wrong place.'

'How right she is,' McLeish said, interested. 'So she found it?'

'Aye. Took her a day or so. We talked about it and decided the file might be labelled something else, so she'd to look in every one. But we have it; I'm on my way with Jenny as soon as it's been printed and photographed.'

They appeared in his office an hour later, both looking very pleased with themselves and very conscious of each other. Davidson was looking sleek, and the girl, a young DC from the Potteries, was trying a little too hard for a businesslike approach. Useless to feel reproachful, this one would just run its course, ending in tears in about three months' time like all the others in which Bruce Davidson was involved.

'Any prints?'

'Mr Price, Mrs Price, Miss Howard, no one else but a few smudges. As if someone wore gloves.'

'Mm. Why Mrs Price? She isn't a trustee.'

'I asked her, once we'd found it. She said of course she had seen the file before. Antony had asked her about it and, indeed, she had started to look at it but Mr Price – her late husband – had taken it away from her and she'd not seen it again. She thinks it must have been him who hid it, because Miss Howard would not do such a thing. Convinced me.'

'How did you feel, Jenny?' McLeish, always mindful of junior staff, asked, and the girl blushed.

'I don't particularly like her, sir, but why would she have hidden it?'

A good question, McLeish thought and raised an eyebrow at Bruce.

'Because it shows that trust assets went into the company.'

'You've read it?'

'DI Crane has. Well, John, it would be fraud, and that's their angle.'

'Yes. Yes, that's all right. Catherine is sure, is she?'

'You could ask her,' Davidson suggested.

'I'll get her to write something so we all know,' McLeish said, repressively. 'So Antony Price was right; his father *was* taking trust assets. And he did need to find that file. I mean, it makes a bit more sense of his visit last Saturday.'

Davidson nodded. 'Now, I've had a bittie time, while Jenny here went through the files, and I'm wondering about the other lad, Francis. It's a bit easy to forget he's a druggie. He'd no cash on him when they picked him up, but he could have spent what was in the safe, couldn't he?'

'Twenty thousand quid in less than a week?' McLeish objected.

'Could have owed a lot of that.'

'All right, Bruce, but why would *he* hide the file?'

Davidson gazed at him. 'No, no, John. Might he have been looking for it too? We've not asked him whether he knew about it.'

'Is he still in hospital?'

'Yes. They've got a problem about discharging him. They're trying to kick him out but he says he wants to get off drugs, and they're trying to find a place in a drugs unit.'

'That's interesting. Why?'

'Why does he want to get off drugs? Well, he's had a fright, hasn't he? Could easily have died.'

'I wonder if that was it? Or whether he had a fright of another sort.'

'Walked in on Dad's dead body, you mean? Possible. Anyway, Notting Dale aren't going to charge him on the drugs unless you insist – there's a bit of a problem with the drugs lads on the CID, I understand – but if he gets into a unit we'll know where to find him.'

'Until he walks out,' McLeish, said, from long and difficult experience. 'Sorry, say it again, Bruce. Something up at Notting Dale CID? Jenny, you didn't hear this, mind. Who is it? Oh, *those* two. I thought they'd been very successful.'

'They had. There's mebbe a problem about how they'd done it.'

McLeish nodded; members of the CID concerned with drugs ran more risk of joining the criminals than most. The difficulty of getting a conviction combined with the sheer amount of money involved could result in the steadiest policeman straying over the line. He made a note to check what was happening about Matt Sutherland's case.

'We might go and see Francis Price again, Bruce, if he's able.'

'He's doped up – no, painkillers and the like – but coherent.'

'In better shape than last time?'

'Oh yes.'

And so it proved. They left Jenny to tidy up the records and to go back and check through the rest of the filing system to see if they could find anything else that shouldn't be there, and visited Francis Price who was sitting in a chair on a balcony looking pale and hostile, and in no shape to be out of bed.

'I gather they're trying to find you a unit,' McLeish said, having reintroduced themselves.

'Yes, but I hate those places. I hope I can go tomorrow to ... well, to a friend's place. He'll look after me, he says.'

'You might be better in a unit.'

'It's never worked before.'

McLeish considered him; he looked terrible, but more solid than when they had last seen him, and as he watched the young man reached for a banana, peeled it and ate it hungrily.

'I seem to eat all the time,' he said, catching McLeish's eye, 'but it's better than stomach cramps.'

'We've come', McLeish said, deciding to get to grips with the subject, 'to ask about the trust your mother set up for you and your brother.'

'Antony said the file was missing. He was here last night.'

And Francis was a great deal more gathered than when they had last seen him, McLeish observed. 'He'd been looking for it, had he?'

'Yes, because he said that there would be *something* in it, some letter to someone that told us what had happened.'

'You weren't looking for it?'

'I told you. My father and Sylvia wouldn't let me near the house. So Antony was the only one who could hunt for the file.' He looked momentarily puzzled, then shook his head.

'The file has been found. Just.'

'Where?'

'At the house.'

'And does it help? Us, I mean?'

'I understand it makes it clear that funds or assets of the trust had been shifted into either your father's company or his own account. Either as loans or for purchase of shares in the company.'

'And Cousin Bruce agreed, I expect. Our so-called trustee.'

'That's not quite so clear, I understand.'

'But we could probably sue my father's company,' Francis Price said, wincing. 'Excuse me. I'll try another banana.' He peeled it and missed the wastepaper basket with the skin. 'Or would that not do any good? My father wasn't safe with money.'

A just verdict, even coming from a drug addict, McLeish thought, and considered Francis Price. He was showing no signs of unease, apart from physical discomfort, and he seemed to set no particular store by the missing trust monies. But ten days ago, desperate for another fix and organised by a stronger personality, he might have done anything. There was no more to be gained today; just possibly if this lad stayed off drugs he might remember something useful about the events of the last week, but they were no nearer a solution.

Francesca was sitting, half asleep, with her son heavy on her knee, watching Susannah clear up the kitchen, whisking round with the undiminished energy of a nineteen-year-old who got seven hours' sleep every night.

'Will is asleep, Francesca. Shall I take him?'

'Please. I have to go out. That is, I may have to, I'm waiting for a phone call.'

I wouldn't care, she told herself earnestly, if Matt were somehow prevented from ringing me today. I could go back to bed for a couple of hours and not feel so terrible. Will was teething, interminably, seeming to have as many as a crocodile, except she could not believe that any baby crocodile had this much difficulty. She needed to see Matthew Sutherland. She had not managed to stick to his timetable, but had taken William round to the Refuge the day before, ostensibly to see his grandmother who was taking the unpopular Sunday day-shift. (Unpopular with the staff, that was; the customers flooded in, victims of a long Sunday with their men setting about them as a result of a liquid lunch, or a Saturday night hangover.) She had found Matt, as she knew she would, patiently entering data on the computer, pale and cross, but with a smile of pure pleasure when he looked up and saw her and William. She had felt the whole of her face lift in response and they had managed a few minutes together, earnestly discussing the problems of data entry before a desperate Asian mother with three weeping children had needed everyone's attention.

The phone rang as she was handing William over, gingerly, praying he would not wake, and she watched Susannah out of the room, the child burrowing into her small nineteen-year-old bosom.

'It's me, Matt. I've finished. The whole thing is on a hard disc, and I'm taking a copy home, so I can run it on the lap-top. You can't think in that place.'

'Was it a busy night?'

'Yes. Your mum stayed till nine, bless her, but I made her go home then. Do you want to see the preliminary runs? I could bring them round, or you could come here, since you've got the car.'

'I'll come round. I need to get out of the house for a bit.'

She rushed into the shower, then cleaned her teeth again, telling herself that anyone who had been on the go since 4 a.m. needed to make a bit of an effort before rejoining the grown-ups. Her nicest jeans and shirt were ready and ironed, and apart from feeling sick, she was in good shape. She drove the twenty-minute journey, rang the bell and listened to the sound of footsteps coming down the stairs. Matt opened the door to her, and they looked at each other, silently.

'Come in, Fran. It's not quite as tidy as I would wish up there. I'm going to have a house guest tomorrow for a few days.'

'Who?'

'Francis Price. The druggie I got to hospital. He wants to stay off and he doesn't want to go to a unit. Been there, done that, didn't work at all.'

'But Matt – how will you manage?'

'It's only for a couple of weeks. He's going to live with me and do some work for a mate of mine at the poly, sorry, university.

138

Keep him occupied, which he needs. So I'm having a bit of a sort-out up there, and I'm not quite done.'

She followed him up three flights of stairs and into a huge high-ceilinged room, with a bed at one end, the walls lined with books and elaborate sound machinery. A young man's room, she thought, trying for some distance, just like any of her brothers. The pictures however were in a different class, violent red and purple landscapes, desolate but beautiful. 'Australian.'

'Yeh. There isn't any New Zealand art worth having. Or not yet. You want coffee?' He was nervous too, she saw, watching his hands as he came close to dropping the jug of water. 'I'm putting Francis in the bedroom on a Z-bed, and I'm moving my bed into the living-room. He'd need to sleep more than I do.'

'Are you going to switch that percolator on?' she asked, and he stared at it.

'I've got some wine. Would you like that instead?' He was carefully not looking at her but rummaging in the fridge, and she took a deep breath and uncurled her fingers from the kitchen counter.

'Matt.'

'What?' He straightened up from the fridge, smudges of colour on the high cheekbones, and looked down at her.

'A drink would be a very good idea. I'm nervous too.'

He looked at her carefully, put the bottle he was holding down on the counter and wrapped his arms round her. 'Fran, I suddenly thought I'd got it all wrong.'

'No, you didn't. You were putting on clean sheets when I arrived.'

'Just stay here, and don't go away while I open the bottle.'

They both fell asleep afterwards, having confessed to each other that they had both had sleepless nights and neither of them had any tolerance for wine at eleven o'clock in the morning. Francesca woke first, with a headache, and found some orange juice which she took back to bed with two glasses. Matt was sitting up, watching her.

'You OK?'

'You know I was.'

'I meant now. You're looking sad.'

'I don't feel it,' she said, climbing back beside him. 'I wanted you very much.'

He wrapped himself round her. 'Now me, I wanted you from the first time I saw you, all gussied up in your executive suit.'

'And I thought you fancied Annabelle.'

'Oh I did, but I fancied you more.' He swallowed his orange juice. 'Better. How long have we got?'

'Mr Sutherland. Art not satisfied? I have to go at five.'

'I were satisfied, lass, I were, but I could manage again. Besides, I've got a house guest from tomorrow, and I . . . I don't know how you're placed.'

She leant against his shoulder, comfortably. 'Oh, nor do I, Matt. I did not think this through.'

'Me neither.' He suppressed what he had been going to say and she considered him, soberly.

'I'm not unhappily married, Matt. He works too hard and I get cross, but that's not why.'

'Why you're here, you mean?'

'Mm.'

'I've never myself been able to see why being married prevents you from fancying anyone else.'

'It doesn't, of course, but there's an accepted trade-off.' Which you breach at your peril, she thought, suddenly chilled.

'Frannie. Relax. I'm not here to put pressure on you. Just see how it plays. And let me get you something to eat, OK? We can look at the stats at the same time.'

'*That's* why you asked me up, really.'

'Of course. I need the audience.'

And deserved one, she conceded, as they looked together at a set of tables, sitting over coffee after an excellent omelette. Matt had stocked the fridge to some purpose and she was feeling very much better than when she had got up. He was a high quality article, Matt, she thought to herself, smugly; they were not peering at long incomprehensible columns of raw data, but a properly tabulated essay on the women dealt with by the Refuge. Nearly all of them had children, she understood, and she stared at the table which gave their mumbers and sexes, suddenly appreciating the size of the problem. As Matthew's spare prose made clear, all of these children were potential aggressors, or victims, as they grew to man's or woman's estate. And, reading on, it was clear that, given the inevitable second-hand nature of the evidence, the current customers of the Refuge were themselves, or were fleeing from, people who had been battered as children. She rubbed her forehead where the headache still lingered. 'It is the men, isn't it? I mean, women don't go round beating up men.'

'There are some. But yes, the Domestic Violence Act was about men beating women. And as you say, it's odd that you needed to enshrine in a new statute a principle unquestioned if it was men beating up men.'

'So why aren't you – aren't we – working to convert men?' She watched, undaunted, his jaw go tight with impatience.

'If your house was on fire, would you rather have a fire engine or a team of investigators from the Home Office?'

'I'd like both.'

He put an arm round her. 'I'll tell you why I'm a lawyer and not a social worker. Lawyers can do something specific and useful about a particular problem. They don't struggle in a morass.'

'With people feeling free to dump the whole of their lives on your laps,' she agreed. 'That's why I'm a bureaucrat.' She thought on. 'Both of us must want people to keep their distance.' She turned her cheek and he kissed her. 'That can't be right.'

'I want to fix the problem I can see, so people can get on with their lives. Which they're quite good at. Get women away from their blokes, most of them get their heads up and do fine.'

'The Dyno-Rod school of legal advice.'

He grinned, undeflected. 'It works. You wait and see. Take Annabelle. I know she's still messing around with her bloke, but she isn't living with him and he knows he'll be in court if he lifts a finger to her. It'll change, she'll do something different and be a different girl.'

'What about him? Won't he find someone else and batter them?'

Matt looked suddenly tired, and she rubbed her cheek against his apologetically. 'You're probably right. I don't think he's learned anything yet, judging from what Annabelle tells me. But women are going to be less prepared to put up with him, and – well, it's slow work.'

'You think Annabelle is at risk?'

'While she's around him, yes. That's why I keep an eye on her.' The reply was prompt and definitive, and she was disconcerted to find herself jealous.

'Antony's father was a batterer, Annabelle says.'

'Mm. Beat the boys' mother and had a go at the current Mrs Price. We acted – it's all right, the police know.'

'One man can do a lot of damage, can't he? People do kill them, of course – children or wives. I suppose that's why John's not having much luck with this case; he's got a lot of suspects.' Her voice tailed off as she remembered that one of them was destined to be Matt's house guest for a week and she saw him remember it too.

'I'm going to take you for a walk in the park, then we could come back here?' He sounded suddenly uncertain, and she laughed at him, and said demurely that that would be nice, and that they had another four hours before she had to go back.

11

Monday, 25 April

McLeish and Davidson sat in his office, both of them dispirited. It was now the third week after the murder, with little progress made. The day's team meeting had been a useful occasion inasmuch as several unexplained avenues and unconfirmed pieces of evidence had been identified. It had, however, disintegrated at the end into a quarrelsome group speculation as to who might be guilty. It was unusual to be working on a murder case which had five suspects, none of whom had a sustainable alibi, and the conjectures had got wilder and wilder. McLeish had called a halt after twenty minutes, getting, he felt, the worst of both worlds; he had wasted twenty minutes and antagonised the team who would have gone on in exciting speculation for another hour in preference to doing any of the hard grind.

'What *about* Mrs Price then?' McLeish decided he must be tired, but he too could not stop himself speculating. In fairness to himself and the team it had to be said that traditional police investigative work was not getting them much further forward.

'What do *you* think?'

'Well, she was his wife.' Davidson was characteristically not at all flustered by the banality of this statement. 'And most murders are domestic – husbands murdering wives, sons murdering fathers, wives murdering husbands.'

'Less common.'

'Well, he had beaten her, hadn't he? And he was making a hash of the business. He was going to leave her nothing but debts, as Catherine – DI Crane – told us, even if we didn't already know.'

'That's true. Never walk past the obvious suspect. But what about the sons?'

'Well, you know Antony's my nominee for the job.'

'Antony doesn't benefit, that's my problem.' This ground had

143

been covered at the meeting, but McLeish had spoken very little and he wanted now to hear himself think. 'His father seems to have spent his late wife's cash, but Antony knew that that cash was gone. Bill Price was – or had been – a violent husband *and* he was steadily ruining the business, and *that* makes Mrs P, or his partner, Mr Fleming, the better bet.'

'You remember I said I thought Mrs P would be getting it somewhere if not from her old man?'

'Yes.'

'It'll be Mr Fleming. I hadn't seen him before last Friday. Something about the way he watches her.'

McLeish waited, but that appeared to be Davidson's thought for the day. He was, however, likely to be right. He was a sort of sexual Geiger counter; if you wanted to know what was going on and with whom in any group, just point Davidson at it.

'Really?'

'Yes. Yes, I think so.'

'That'd be interesting if it's right. I've got to have a chat with the other bit of the firm. Miles Arnold. Went conveniently off last week on a fact-finding mission to Zimbabwe.'

'What facts would those be, John?'

'Is it really hot there in April?' The rain was sheeting down outside the windows and McLeish had a cold. 'Are all the women beautiful, whether black or white? Is the sea truly warm? Are the beaches golden like it says?'

The beach at Soller was certainly golden, but the sea was only just not very cold on Catherine Crane's bare feet. April was early for Majorca, and at nine in the morning she was none too warm in a cotton sweater, jeans and a jacket. She had been particularly glad of the sweater, and a thermal vest under her nightdress last night in a bare, modern hotel room with light, thin curtains and even lighter, thinner bed coverings. It might all have been delightful in a temperature 20 degrees higher; at the same temperature as an English spring night, it had been a less than cheering experience. The thermal vest she owed to Francesca McLeish who reportedly never journeyed anywhere strange and foreign without one in her case. Catherine had been amused when Francesca's husband had told her this, *en passant*, but she had put one in at the last minute, telling herself it weighed nothing and took up very little space.

But the golden sun was out, higher in the sky than in England, as Catherine turned to trudge back to the line of hotels that fringed the beach. She passed groups of tourists variously attired, square women in cotton frocks and cardigans, several others dressed as she was and a group of hugely tall young men in bathing suits and T-shirts, calling boastfully to each other in Dutch. She walked through the chill hotel reception rooms, tiled and airy against the summer heat, observing fellow guests huddled into sweaters on the hard sofas, and stopped at the reception desk. The squat young man behind the desk blinked, rang for the taxi then detained her with conversation in laboured English, getting round to wondering if she would be interested in going to the island's finest night-club. She said kindly that she was here with friends and turned to greet the taxi driver, who was giving an inoffensively open impression of a man to whom an angel had appeared. It was being blonde, she reminded herself, in a country where most of the women were black-haired, that was making her quite so much of a success. She fended off another invitation, delivered in excellent English this time, to the island's most famous barbecue, and asked if her driver knew of the English company who had been building the apartments to which he was taking her.

'My brother was working for them,' he said, no longer so keen to impress.

'How very interesting. And were they good to work for?'

No, she was unsurprised to learn. Luiz's brother, Paco, who was a skilled carpenter with his own business, had done much of the fitting out – the doors, the cupboards, and so on – for Mr Fleming on two other apartment blocks, over *there* – he nodded towards the sea – but had waited a very long time for his money, which had caused much difficulty at home. Catherine agreed it would have caused problems in anybody's household. Paco, it transpired, had not in the event been paid all he was owed, but he had been promised, absolutely, the fitting-out work on these new apartment blocks. It was as well that, warned by his previous experience, Paco had not depended on this promise but had taken another job when offered, fitting out a villa for a German developer. This, alas, was only a small piece of work and after *that* Paco had nothing else for the summer yet, but the German was a reliable payer. Not, as the Senora would appreciate, that the English were normally perceived as less than trustworthy, it was this one particular representative of the race who had not reached the high standards set by his fellow countrymen. Catherine commiserated, mentally contrasting this courteous recital with the earful she would have received from a London cabbie in the same situation.

'And here are the apartments.' He waved a hand to his right and stopped the cab. They both gazed out at a large site, full of holes and steelwork. She got out of the cab and walked round considering it, Luiz beside her. The foundation work for three blocks looked to be complete, but she appealed to Luiz who was glad to give her an expert tour, regretting only that brother Paco was not here.

'So work could start again quite easily?' Luiz hesitated, drawing back into himself, and she offered him her cover story. 'I work for a bank, and we are considering a loan. It is not my decision, or not mine alone – I am just here to see the work and what the place is like.' She waved an arm, comprehending the pitted dusty road and the silent site. 'We are told that building could be very quick.'

'Paco was going to work with other friends, who are also carpenters, as soon as the walls were up. It was to be a contract for six weeks, for all three. You think it could now be?'

She looked at the clever face, the brown eyes level with her own, the dark head outlined against an acid yellow mimosa bush, dazzling in the sun, and tried to find a formula. 'It is for those senior to me to decide. But people are thinking about this site and after all the foundations are there. Someone should want to build.'

'And that will be good for us here,' he said, straight-backed and dignified, so that she felt ashamed of the whole deception. He hesitated. 'If it were that you found yourself with time to have a drink with us – with Paco also – we should be pleased. But you want now to go back to your hotel?'

'Yes,' she said, regretting that the drink would be impossible, it would be unprofessional to involve herself further with these men. The site was there with the foundations done, as Luke Fleming had said, and she found herself hoping that it would be possible, somehow, to build on them.

'He is in London now. The big boss, Mr Fleming.'

'Yes, so I understand,' she said, cautiously.

'My colleague, Jaime, took him to the airport – he said he had to go and talk to people. We hoped then it would be to get money.'

'Two weeks ago, was it not?'

'Yes, on the Friday. It was a feast day, but Jaime went off with him. You understand that early in the season there is less work so we all take the jobs whatever is happening.'

And late on that Friday Bill Price had dressed himself in ladies' silk knickers and a pair of sheer stockings, climbed on a table and put a thin rope round his neck, leaving himself vulnerable to someone who had pulled the table from under him.

'The Friday?' she said, casually, thinking hard. 'Have you a card? I am with friends but we may need a driver again.'

'It will be a pleasure.' He was disappointed but courteous. 'And I wish you good luck with your bank.'

The route back to the potential witness secured, she rushed up to her room to call the Yard and organise Bruce Davidson into rechecking the flight manifests on the Friday. 'It may be a red herring,' she warned. 'It's not my case so I didn't want to trample all over the ground.'

'Ye're a good lass. And mebbe I'll need to come down and ask a few questions myself in the sunshine. Don't you come back till I've found out a bittie more here.'

It would take him at least a couple of hours, during which she could usefully get on with what she had come to do, which was to talk to her Spanish opposite number. He, like every other male Spaniard she had met, was more than keen to help in any way, and she decided to accept his invitation to lunch, too used to being a living trophy to be much bothered by it.

'Mr Fleming,' her escort, a stocky detective inspector, said, all too obviously ready to spread thinly the three facts that they seemed to have. 'He is here now for five years, working for Wimpey. But before *that* he worked for a small firm which he owned, or he had many shares in. It failed and people here lost money.'

'But he started again in a firm.'

'Yes, but he had worked with Wimpey, for whom we all have respect. And he told people here that this new firm was only in a small way his. That the money was in England and there were big investors and a Member of your Parliament also as part of it.'

'Ah.'

'This was not true?'

'It is true that he owns only twenty per cent of the company and it is true also that an MP is working for them as a consultant.'

'But he is not a director?'

'No.'

By mutual consent they took a break to eat sardines grilled on charcoal, immaculately fresh, washed down with a sharp white wine.

'It would be most unhappy – unfortunate – if Mr Fleming were again to cause people here to lose money,' he said, wiping his mouth.

The man was a colleague and she needed his co-operation, so she told him about the complaints the Squad had received about the uncompleted flats. 'With money they could be quickly finished. He has the foundations.'

The Spaniard nodded and finished his wine.

'But Catherine – I may call you so? – this has happened to us before, many times, with developers from other countries. This is not a big site, it is not like the trouble we have had with hotels which are not finished and no one is paid and tourists make demonstrations. *That* is a great nuisance. This, well . . . it is a small company so we have not paid much attention. I could find out more, I am sure.'

If Luke Fleming were to be arrested for murder the condition of the company's affairs in Spain was probably going to be irrelevant, and she did not want to waste a colleague's time.

'It has always seemed to us that the root problem is in London,' she said. 'You have been most helpful and I would not want you yet to do anything specific.'

'We know also a little of Mr Fleming himself, as well as in his business,' he said, carefully, sipping coffee.

'Please tell me.'

'He has several women friends here. Not of course Spanish but from the many visitors – no, not visitors, that is not quite right – the women who work here for the main season, from the travel agencies. Last year he has been with a German woman – not young – who comes several times a year. She has six villas here, and occupies herself with the lettings.' He paused to order a cigar, courteously asking her whether she minded him smoking. 'She is widow, so we all expected that she would, well, perhaps marry him – he is, you understand married before, but then she is not – not Catholic.' He had, she thought, been going to say 'not Spanish', but had changed it in deference to her. Plainly however a totally different code of conduct was expected of Spanish womanhood.

'But that didn't happen?' she prompted, carefully.

'No. There was also another woman – English – who came often here and *she* was a director of the company for whom he works. He said to one of my colleagues that it was necessary to attend on her and to be very polite because she was married to his boss. She stays, of course, in one of the apartments, but when there is not space, in a hotel. And Mr Fleming is always with her.'

'It might be entirely business.'

'Indeed. But our information is good, and they have been passing the night together.'

A lot to be said, Catherine thought, for a country as heavily policed as Spain, where waiters and chambermaids, no doubt, routinely kept the Garda informed. This, too, needed to be passed back to London as quickly as possible.

They finished lunch with mutual compliments, and she went back to find the phone ringing in her room. It was Bruce Davidson, sounding annoyed.

'Are you sure about Friday, Catherine? He wasn't on any of the scheduled flights.'

'No, I can't be sure. Have you tried the charters? They're not above giving people a ride if they've got a space. He'll be logged as "returning crew" or something like that.'

'I do know and we'll be moving on to that. And the private planes, but I wanted to know how good your evidence was.'

'Risk it,' she advised, and told him about her conversation at lunch. The wine at lunch had left her feeling sleepy and ineffective in the pleasantly warm afternoon, so she put her feet up and went to sleep on the disconcerting thought that Luke Fleming might have been attending a meeting at the airport and not getting a plane at all. The phone woke her with a jerk.

'He came in on an executive jet, with Wimpey people in it. I remembered he'd worked for them, so we got on to it quickly. And I've put someone on to checking Fleming's dealings with his ex-wife, because we know where she is. Well done, Catherine. Soon as the Guv'nor gets back from hobnobbing with Members of Parliament I'll tell him and we'll go and see Mr Fleming.'

'Can't you reach John?'

'Not until he's back in the car. I'll make sure he knows it was you who was so clever, don't you worry.'

*

John McLeish sipped coffee and waited while Miles Arnold MP fussed round the room. It was a rather nasty office, small and cluttered, with mean windows and the inevitable noise of a secretarial office audible through the walls, well below the standards of accommodation at New Scotland Yard and most regional forces.

'Sorry. Just getting rid of this lot.' Miles Arnold, looking too large for the office, brushed past him with a tray of papers, and returned, looking at a couple of messages. 'Good of you to come here, I have to be in the House in an hour.'

'That's all right,' McLeish said, and waited again.

Miles Arnold had rung him that morning, asking if they could meet. McLeish had met Jim Waters, the Private Secretary to the Chief Whip, for the promised drink and aired his problem; an MP who, if not First Suspect in a murder case, was at least on the list, and who had offered a not very credible version of his whereabouts.

'And you don't think he was sitting at home with the constituency post and a dictating machine?' Jim had asked. 'More of them doing that on a Friday night than you might expect, if you read the tabloids.'

'I'm not sure, no. I just got a whisper that, wife and children being absent, he was likely to be doing something more interesting.'

'Or someone more interesting. And you don't want to call him a liar.' Jim Waters had sat nursing his drink which looked like gin and tonic and was, in fact, Perrier water with ice and lemon. McLeish waited too, watching as that experienced shrewd intelligence reviewed the options.

'If there were an explanation which left him in the clear you would be heartily relieved and see no need to make waves. And you would deal with the whole thing yourself.'

'I would, I would.'

'Leave it with me.'

They had talked of other things for the measured forty minutes which was what Jim Waters allowed himself for seeing seekers of help or patronage who were also friends. And eleven days later, the time lag caused by Miles Arnold's absence abroad, McLeish was hoping to put another piece of the jigsaw securely in place. Arnold was having difficulty getting started but the ball was in his court; there was no way of helping him pick it up.

'More coffee?'

McLeish accepted obligingly and took the biscuit pressed on him as the man finally managed to get himself sat down.

'I understand that you weren't happy with my statement.' He wasn't looking at McLeish, who did not attempt an answer. 'I wasn't trying to mislead you. I really was at home – in the flat – from late on Friday night, so I still don't *have* an alibi for the time that I could see you were thinking about.' He managed finally to look at McLeish who made an indeterminate noise of encouragement.

'But to set your – the police's – mind at rest, I will tell you where I was. I am very anxious not to create, well, unnecessary waves, but I understand you do feel you have to know.' He was sounding ill used, and McLeish wondered what made him feel that he ought to be immune from procedures whose application to the rest of the citizenry would have his hearty public support. 'I was with a girl – a woman. At her flat. Until about midnight.' He let out a wholly unconscious sigh of relief and reached for some more coffee.

'On Saturday evening as well?' McLeish asked, and watched the coffee jug jump in Miles Arnold's hand.

'I thought it was *Friday* night you were interested in. Wasn't Bill dead by Saturday night?'

'Yes. But there is some evidence ... some indication that someone may have been in at a later stage. Like Saturday. So we would be glad to know where you were on Saturday evening as well.'

'I was with the same person.'

'Who is?'

'Will you have to talk to her?' He saw the answer in McLeish's face. 'All right, yes you do, I see ... but could you ... well, be careful? And go by yourself? I mean, don't take anyone else.' He looked across the table. 'I suppose it'll all be on a file. Part of the case. Do we *have* to do this? Given that it doesn't even give me an alibi. Or not for Friday. Saturday I spent the whole night there.'

'But you returned home on Friday.'

'Ah. That. Yes.' He looked away. 'The thing is, you see, that I've got an answerphone at the flat. One of the sort you can ring and pick up messages. There was a message from ... from my wife, saying she had rung and would ring again around midnight. Something about the children. I rang her – she was staying with her parents. She was out somewhere with her father and her mother wasn't helpful, so I thought I'd better go back to the flat. To be there when she called.'

'And did she in fact ring you?'

'Yes, just as I told you. At about quarter to one. With some nonsense about music lessons that could perfectly well have waited. But you could check that.'

'Indeed we could.' And that the phone did not have a device which would trip the call on to another phone. Perhaps he should suggest one such for future reference as it were. 'And you didn't go out again after you'd spoken to your wife?'

'Go back, you mean? I only wish I had. Not only would I have had a nicer night but I'd now have an alibi. Or wouldn't I? Depends on how long the whole thing took, I suppose. I didn't go back because . . . well, I dunno, but I thought she – my wife – was a bit suspicious and might just ring again, or pop up first thing. I was feeling paranoid, I suppose. It's the press – we've all got a bit jumpy. I'm not alone, you know.'

'And Saturday?'

'Saturday I took the risk. I checked the phone at midnight. No messages, and I thought if she did ring later, well, I could then say I'd gone to bed and didn't hear the phone. You know. The person – girl – I had left on Friday wanted me to stay.'

He was looking pleased with himself, McLeish observed, and wondered if he himself would manage to cope with a mistress as well as Francesca.

'I shall need to talk to the person in question,' he said, deciding that if he sounded pompous he did not care. 'But by all means ring her yourself and ask her to get in touch with me if that is easier.'

Miles Arnold looked suddenly tired. 'None of this is easy. The whole situation is a bit tense, as you can imagine.' He hesitated, looking at the table, the long fingers clasped round one knee. 'Susie – Susie James, that's her name – is a bit pissed off with me, naturally, for involving her.' He uncrossed his legs, and bounced to his feet, convulsively, discharging tension. 'She's out, I know, for the rest of the day and . . . well . . . it could be embarrassing if you had to see her. She's with clients. But tomorrow morning she'll be at home, I know, if that would suit.'

McLeish indicated that it would, and seeing Arnold glance at the phone offered to wait outside. Any collusion between Miles

Arnold and Miss James had taken place long since, and there was no harm in observing the simple courtesies. He nodded to the secretary who obligingly exchanged a few platitudes with him about the weather without stopping working. It was, they agreed, miserably cold and rainy, particularly for so late in April.

'Mr McLeish.' He smiled encouragingly at Miles Arnold who emerged from the office flushed around the cheekbones. 'She's expecting you – oh, you don't have the address.' He looked helplessly at his secretary who tapped two buttons on the computer and printed out the result without asking whose address was wanted. Jim Waters had always said the House of Commons secretaries knew everything; it appeared to be true. In a small society, more people knew about you than you could bear to think about.

His car was parked just outside the Derby gates and the uniformed constable in the police box saluted him as he passed, drawing curious looks from two men with House of Commons passes round their necks.

'Three messages, sir.'

He discarded two and rang Bruce Davidson. 'Fleming was here on the Friday? Really.' He listened to the rest of the story, and thought, staring unseeing into the door of the Range Rover next to them. 'No. No, I don't want to talk to him until we've got it all. Get on to Records, sort out what he was divorced *for* and so on. He isn't going anywhere.'

Annabelle Brewster looked at the list of patients waiting to see her. Most of the names were familiar even after only four months in the practice, because the partners tended to give her the repeaters, the people who because of age or loneliness haunted the surgery. This was partly in the hope that a fresh, recently trained eye would help and Annabelle had indeed scored a couple of successes, by changing and cutting down the barrage of medicines that three of the older patients had acquired over the years. It was also to provide a new person for the sad, the mad, and the chronically ill to tell their stories to. She longed, nearly all the time now, for the children in hospital who had been really ill but had borne their burdens with such grace and who often could be cured.

'Mr Sutherland,' she called, impersonally, to the crowded room and stared as Matthew Sutherland stood up, grinning, in a pink shirt that shouted at his dark red hair and enlivened the several grey or black layers he wore over it. He had another man in tow.

'Francis?' she said, doubtfully.

Francis Price looked almost unrecognisably less haggard than she remembered him. She pulled the door shut, recalling that he was no longer a patient of the practice, having been delisted after a violent episode in the waiting-room over a year ago.

'We need a doctor and I thought of you.' Matthew was sitting on the edge of her desk, observing her carefully as she sat firmly down on her chair behind the desk to give herself the authority of her position.

'Matt, Francis was delisted here.'

'I know. But he doesn't have a doctor – except Antony – and things have changed. He's off smack, did it cold turkey, but he's got a fucking awful chest. I take it you're not going to pass by on the other side?'

Annabelle had hooked her auscultator round her neck even while Matt was speaking. She got Francis to take off his jacket and sweater and open his shirt – one of Matt's gaudier offerings. Francis was shivering even in the warm room, but he breathed when she told him and managed to cough on demand.

'Bronchitis,' she said, having checked his ears and his throat. 'I'll give you a seven-day course of antibiotics, Francis, and you must stay in an even temperature. Is your room warm enough?'

'I'm staying with Matt.'

'My *room*'s fine,' Matt said, apologetically. 'I took him out for a health-giving walk a couple of days ago. Mistake.'

'You have to be careful coming off drugs,' Annabelle said sternly to Francis, then caught herself up and looked at him properly. He looked very tired and a bit flushed, but ... well, ordinary, human, not far away from the world and its concerns, or fidgeting and sweating as she had always seen him before. 'Do you need anything else, Francis? Painkillers?'

'I'm so full of Anadin I rattle,' he said, smiling at her, and she paused, transfixed because he looked so like Antony when she had first known him.

'They're a bit hard on the stomach. I'll give you something else, but you mustn't take more than eight in twenty-four hours.' She looked sideways at Matt. 'Will that work? Is that enough?'

'Just about. He could do with some more tranks.'

'Valium?'

'Yeah. I won't let him take them too long but it's difficult for him to sleep. It'll help with the cramps.'

'I just need to look up the dose.' She reached for a book and became conscious of a charged silence between the two young men.

'Francis, will you be okay in the waiting-room for ten minutes? I want to talk to Annabelle.'

'About me?'

'No. About her.'

She opened her mouth to speak, but Francis shook his head at her. 'I may be looking like shit, Anna, but you're not looking too good either. See you in ten minutes, Matt. Not more or I'll have finished the last *Woman's Own*.' He got unsteadily to his feet, smiled at her and went, leaving her gaping after him.

'Matthew, he looks quite different.'

'He *acts* quite different, you mean. Being a druggie fucks up all your behaviour.'

'I suppose I've never seen him when he wasn't out of it one way or the other.' She looked across the desk at Matthew, who slid into Francis's chair. 'Well, you've done quite a job there,' she said, rushing into speech. 'How long has he been clean?'

'Ten days.'

'What are you going to do with him next?'

'I've kitted him up with a decent lawyer, who will take his trustees – or rather the surviving one – to court and make a claim on the estate, or rather the executors, one of whom is his step-mother, that's why I couldn't ask Peter to take him on. The bloke I've got – Thomas – is good. He's already put in a statement of claim; prior to a writ if no one takes any notice. Sylvia Price is very upset, I understand. Obviously hoped all hubby's problems died with him.'

'Are you going to send Antony to the same lawyer?'

'No.'

It was definitive and she looked at him enquiringly. He looked back unsmiling, and she felt suddenly utterly exhausted as if her spine was melting. He reached across the table and took her hands in his own.

'You've got enormous hands,' she said, too tired to move, comforted by the warmth.

'Butcher's hands, my mum says. Dad has them too.'

'What does your dad do?' She was talking just to prolong the moment of peace.

'He's a doctor. Specialises in kids.'

She realised that she was going to cry, and tugged her hands free and reached blindly for the Kleenex, so she could snuffle and weep and blow her nose and give in to the awful weariness which she felt all the time. She wanted Matthew to take her in his arms to comfort her, but he did no more than rest a heavy warm hand on her shoulder until she had managed to stem the flow a bit.

'I've got news you're not going to like,' he said.

'What?' She blew her nose, drearily.

'You ever hear Antony talk about a girl called Jane Snow? Francis knew her, he says. The one before you, he says.'

'Yes. They were engaged and he . . . he broke it off when he met me.' It was impossible not to feel something of the glow of triumph she had felt at the time.

'Yeah. They keep records at the Refuge and I've just computerised them. She came in one night about five years ago. Gave his name as the one who'd beaten her. She was advised to go to court but she didn't. Never came back again.'

He fell silent while she struggled to think. 'What date was this? Exactly.'

'December, over five years ago.'

It had been in December five years before, when she was twenty-one, that she and Antony had started their affair.

'I wonder how many more there were,' she said, in an attempt at detachment.

'Dunno. I looked up the other two that Francis could remember and they hadn't been customers.'

'Why are you doing this?'

'You're hanging about with a violent bloke who has beaten up at least one other woman. And he's under pressure himself. He may have killed his father, and I think he had a go at his brother by giving him enough cash for an overdose. Someone did, only Francis has lost that bit of memory so I can't prove it.'

She spread her arms on the desk and put her head on them in utter exhaustion. 'Go away, Matt. You've got Francis to look after. He needs it, I don't.'

'If you could see yourself you wouldn't say that, Annabelle.' She lifted her head to look at him blearily. 'Don't be alone with

Antony. Remember what you learned at the Refuge. Can't you go home to your parents for a bit?'

She thought of her father and brother and the explanations she would have to make. 'No.'

'You could come and live with Francis and me. There's another camp bed – I'd sleep on that and you could have The Bed.'

'No. Thank you.' She managed to get her head off the table and dragged herself over to the wash-basin to restore her face to something that would not frighten the rest of her patients. 'Go and see to Francis, Matt. I will be careful,' she said, hopelessly, to her reflection in the mirror, and when she turned around he had gone, the door swinging behind him.

12

Tuesday, 26 April

The interview next morning with Susie James was proving so sticky that McLeish decided he would have to be content with her grudging confirmation that, yes, Miles Arnold had left her around midnight on the Friday and, yes, he had returned for the whole of Saturday night. Ms James was prowling round her sitting-room – there was no other way of putting it – occasionally swooping on a pile of things and putting them elsewhere. She worked from her flat but, as she explained, she was moving soon to somewhere bigger. The current flat was not indeed designed for visitors, being small and in need of a coat of paint and new windows. Ms James, on the other hand, was superbly maintained, a young woman in her late twenties with dark blonde hair, short-skirted black suit, worn with nothing else but jewellery, and immaculate nails, the whole marred only by the fact that she was formidably angry with him and everything else around her.

'Does this mean the whole of Scotland Yard know about Miles and me?'

'No. Just those of the investigating team who need to.'

'I bet they gossip.'

McLeish was on weak ground here and they both knew it. The *Daily Mirror* had carried a story the week before about a party that had gone wrong complete with prurient detail, courtesy of two members of the Metropolitan police force.

'I mean, Miles is still a suspect, isn't he? I made him tell me. You think the murder was early on Saturday?'

McLeish hesitated to answer, but she was in full spate. 'So you can't just forget about it and say, oh, well, he's in the clear. It was *stupid* to go back, he could easily have told her – Caroline – that he hadn't heard the phone.' She sat down, crossing her legs, giving

158

him an admirable view of well-shaped long thighs. 'And his timing is awful.'

'Why?'

The leg she was swinging checked, and she sat absolutely still for a few seconds, head bent. 'Oh, just everything is happening at once, and I'm moving and half my stuff is packed up.' She took a deep breath and got herself in hand. 'Are we finished? I have to be with a client in an hour and I need to make a couple of calls.'

They were indeed, McLeish confirmed, and got up to go as the bell rang, revealing a courier, motor-cycle helmet in one hand, and in the other a thick envelope with the address of one of the smaller City solicitors on it.

'That's the contract for my new place,' she said, ripping it open. 'It'll be great to be out of here.' She looked at him as if she had suddenly seen him as a man rather than an annoying and worrying interruption. 'Look, sorry I've been in such a temper. It's just that, well, it's my private life.'

'I'm sorry we had to trouble you,' McLeish said, looking into dark brown eyes with long dark eyelashes, and wondering why a beauty like this one was bothering with a married MP fifteen years her senior. The attractions of power, he supposed, not that MPs really had much of that. But they got on the TV. They were instantly recognisable and that conveyed status on anyone associated with them, and that was presumably useful to someone who made their living out of public relations. And possibly she loved him, though that explanation did not sit entirely easily. He went down the shabby stairs which smelled very slightly of drains, and out to his waiting car, turning his mind to the more important matter of Luke Fleming, who had not told him that he was at Gatwick airport on the Friday afternoon, just over an hour from the Price Fleming office.

Not that Fleming was particularly apologetic. A car bearing him, protesting vigorously, and Davidson arrived at the Yard at the same time as McLeish's car, but they let Fleming cool his heels for twenty minutes while they checked their desks and caught up briefly with the team.

'Catherine's back,' Davidson reported. 'Ready to see you when you want.' He waited to see if McLeish was going to want to do that now, then gave him, a touch smugly, a folder with three photocopies inside.

'Mm,' McLeish said, appreciatively. 'Separation order, decree nisi, decree absolute. Adultery. By him, I mean.'

'It would be,' Davidson said, smugly. 'Here's a note of my wee chat with Catherine. He *is* having it off with Mrs P.'

'I never doubted you but it's nice to have it confirmed.'

Luke Fleming was looking calmer when they got to him, collar button done up and tie carefully knotted. McLeish sat down on the other side of the table, waiting while Davidson got the tape recorder into action.

'You were on the manifest of a privately chartered plane which came from Majorca to Gatwick on Friday the 8th,' he said, briskly, when Davidson was ready. 'What were you doing in England?'

'Not murdering Bill. I never went anywhere near the office.' He drew on a cigarette, stubbed it out, and tried the coffee instead, gave that up and clasped both hands together in front of him, the gold cuff-links neatly set against the good blue shirt.

'Where did you go?'

'To see my wife.' They blinked at him. 'My ex-wife, I should have said, Margaret. Maggie. Near Barnsley. I picked up a car at the airport.'

'What time did you get there?'

'About seven thirty.'

'And your wife – your ex-wife – will confirm this?'

'No.' He took a cigarette from the packet and made a perform-ance of lighting it, the big hands unsteady. 'Someone had told me – in Majorca this was – that she'd got a bloke living with her, full-time. Well, I'm paying an arm and a leg in maintenance for her and I'm paying the mortgage, and I didn't see why some other bugger should get it all free. I was offered a ride – friend of mine, who is a pilot – and I thought I'd go over and see what was what.'

'So you didn't see her?'

'Oh, I *saw* her. She came back from somewhere, then she got dolled up and went out. Came back, by herself, dropped off by a woman around midnight. I slept in the car, on and off, hung around on the Saturday just to check no one had got in while I was asleep. There was just her, in and out till about noon. The bloke I came with was going back again at five o'clock, so I went back to Gatwick. I left Barnsley about ... what ... noon. Nothing I could prove there.'

An unattractive recital, McLeish thought with distaste, given the facts recorded in the folder.

'Why didn't you tell us you were in England on Friday and Saturday?'

Fleming, shoulders hunched, was looking at the table. 'Well, I was embarrassed. And, well, scared when I thought about it. I slept in the car, I didn't see anyone who'd remember me. You already know why I didn't contact the wife. Chap in a garage on Saturday morning when I went for petrol. And a pretty girl – a blonde – on the till at the motorway caff at about three in the morning. I could describe her but I dunno if she'd remember me. I could have been anywhere.'

He could indeed, and they pressed him on all the detail, extracting a possible description of a young woman who had been working in the Forte restaurant where he had eaten a full English breakfast at three in the morning. They left him sitting while they repaired for a coffee and a small conference.

'We'll need to talk to the ex-wife,' McLeish said, thoughtfully. 'You'd better go, Bruce. She'll tell you how bad it was with him and what she gets as maintenance. Given what Catherine told us about him and Mrs Price, it gets interesting, doesn't it?' He saw that Bruce was looking doubtful. 'No?'

'Mrs Price wasn't the victim.'

'No. But she's well off and Fleming's probably short of cash. I mean, given what happened with wife number one, wife number two needs to be reasonably well off. Or he needs to catch number one with another man, as he was trying to do.'

Davidson gave him his careful look that had always meant he was missing something.

'What, Bruce?'

'It's no' just the money, do you think? That type of man can't stand the fact that she got away and might have another bloke.'

'Possessive.'

'Aye. Like a child.'

'So he might have done Bill Price in in order to get Sylvia for himself.' It was a more convincing motive, McLeish acknowledged. 'You were of course right about him and Mrs Price.'

'I'm no' infallible, mind, but close. What are we to do with Mr Fleming? Charge him?'

'No, not yet. If we can place him at that service station at 3 a.m. he'd have had difficulty murdering Bill Price.'

'Well, would he?' Davidson asked. 'If Bill Price wanted his jollies, he did'na wait till after the late movie. He had something to eat and a bit to drink, we know *that*, then he fancied a bit of the other. Say he'd trussed himself up by ten o'clock, there's well time for Fleming to have pushed the table over and got himself to Barnsley for three in the morning.'

'It's possible,' McLeish acknowledged. 'But I don't want to arrest him before we've had a go at finding the girl. Let him go. Don't take his passport. We know where he is, and if what Catherine says is right he's got nowhere to go. He needs to rescue the business. If we can place him in Barnsley his alibi is not a lot worse than Mike Arnold's or the Price brothers' right now. At least they were in London.'

Miles Arnold was shown straight up to the flat when he arrived, as Sylvia Price had asked. He looked round the room without pleasure; he had seen it before but had forgotten how cluttered it was. He bent to kiss his hostess formally on the cheek, moved three small silk cushions out of his way and sat down, uneasily conscious of two more cascading off the back of the sofa.

'It is nice to see you, Miles. Thank you for your letter.'

'And very nice to see you too, Sylvia, even though . . . even in the circumstances. I shall be at the funeral, of course.'

'Tea?' She poured him some which he took gratefully, trying to work out how to proceed. He considered her carefully over his cup; she was looking cool and tidy in expensive pale green wool with more jewellery than he liked, but powerfully, containedly feminine.

'Sylvia, I know you have everything to do and it must be very difficult . . . picking up all the reins, as it were, and I'm sorry to add to your burdens, but I am in some difficulty. I do need, urgently, some of the money that Bill was . . . was looking after for me.'

'We are talking of the cash that you say he had in the safe.'

'That he *had* in the safe, Sylvia, I assure you. Not to mention the cheque I wrote him a couple of months ago.'

'Your lawyer has written, yes?' She put her cup down carefully and took a delicate iced biscuit. 'I have given the letter to *my* lawyers who have explained to me that I must not pay money out unless it is part of the business's expenses.'

'But this was a cheque to Bill personally.'

'Indeed, Miles, but he paid it into the business account. *I* do not know for what you have paid or whether I can give money to you. You must see that.' She looked at him, head tipped to one side, eyes wide and earnest, and he felt slightly sick.

'Sylvia, I don't know what's going on but I gave that money to Bill to invest for me. I want either the stock or the money back. It's nothing to do with the business.'

'But that is not now so. Bill – what is it you say? – oversigned the cheque.'

'Endorsed it? To whom?'

'To the business. He never spoke of any of this to me, you understand, and so my lawyer say I must believe that you were investing in the business and we must have more knowledge before we could legally give you money.'

'It's not a question of give, it's *my* money. And I need it.' He stared at her enraged but her hands were folded and she was not looking at him. He took a deep breath and leant forward. 'Look, Sylvia, I know cash is tight and the legal formalities have to be observed, but Bill – or the company – owes me eighty thousand and you've seen the cheque. Just let me have a cheque for twenty grand – which I need now – and we'll sort the rest out as and when.'

She poured them both more tea while he waited, on the edge of his seat, tense with hope. She looked over at him, eyes wide. She paused to blow her nose. 'I am – I have so many people who say that Bill has done wrong things, or taken money, and my lawyer says I must proceed with care. Antony and Francis are both saying that Bill has taken money from a trust for them. I have to say no to them too.' She dabbed at her eyes. 'So, Miles, you must see. I am sorry, I must not use the company's money, I am advised. I am sure that in only a few weeks all will be arranged.'

'That'll be too late.'

'For what, Miles? Surely you can ask your bank? And the insurance company I know are considering our claim – your claim – that there was £20,000 in the safe.'

He tried again, several times, tense with exasperation, but although she wept prettily, she never came close to yielding. All his increasingly desperate proposals were met with suggestions that he should go and see the insurance company, or that his lawyer should see her lawyer and discuss what was to be done.

Finally he understood that he was not going to get any money that day or in the months to come without a monumentally awkward public fight.

'You're just like Bill, aren't you?' he said bitterly, slamming the teacup down. 'Couple of crooks, the pair of you. Deserved each other. Fuck you and your bloody husband. I hope you end up in an even worse way than he did. I'll see you in court, don't think I'm going to give up.' He tripped over a small footstool on his way out, and narrowly avoided cannoning into one of the over-done gilded mirrors on his way to bang the door and stamp down the elegant winding staircase, sick with rage.

'Catherine. Welcome back.' McLeish got up from his desk to greet her, truly pleased to see her. She was looking tired but beautiful. 'Great work – I know you weren't doing it for us exactly, but it was enormously helpful. I've just seen Fleming.'

'Arrested him?'

'No. He's got – well, not exactly an alibi, but an explanation and it'll need checking. Have you just got back?'

'No. I came back last night. I came to look for you this morning but you were out.'

'I was having an interesting time there and all. Another alibi that doesn't quite work.' He caught himself up; Catherine was not even in C Division, much less one of his team, and he must resist the temptation to confer with her as if it were the old days. He looked at her with affection and realised that she was not in the same mood as him at all; the long hands were clenched in her lap and she was very pale.

'What *was* Fleming doing here?'

'Ah.' She was owed this piece of gossip; but for her they would not have known about Fleming's marital track record. Or not at this stage – sooner or later, if this case wore on, everything would be checked. 'He was spying on his ex-wife. He admitted it perfectly freely. He didn't try and contact her, so he doesn't have an alibi.'

'Just watched. What was he looking for? Another man, I suppose.'

'Yes.'

'Trying to control her behaviour after she threw him out.'

McLeish hesitated. 'What he said was that if he found her, well, cohabiting, he would use that in any application to reduce payments to her.'

'What the bastard meant was he couldn't take her having walked out and found someone else.' She wasn't looking at him but to his left, out of the window.

'I suppose that may be true as well,' he said, lamely, resting his eyes on the clear profile, desperately sorry for her and unable to think of anything to say that would stop her looking quite so grim.

She drew in a deep breath and unclasped her hands and made a visible effort to return from wherever she had been, and turned her head to look at him before he had got his expression in order. For a long moment they just looked at each other and he felt himself blush.

'You've heard the gossip too, then,' she said, pulling her back straight. She looked ravishingly pretty and as if she was about to explode, and he tried to find the words.

'The story I heard made it clear you'd had a bad time.'

She did not speak and he decided to go on, both feet in it if need be, anything rather than this tense, angry estrangement. 'I'm very sorry, Cath, you deserve better.'

'And I could have had better, too, you must think.' She was, he saw, bitterly angry and he dared not go near her.

'Me, you mean,' he said, flatly. 'You could, yes. You did, after all,' he added daringly, and to his relief saw the edge of her mouth quiver. 'But it's not what I was thinking. You could have had lots of other blokes, but they weren't what you wanted, or not at the time.'

'But Francesca has always been what you wanted?'

'By no means. I was thirty-three when I met her. And I wobbled as you have cause to know.' He considered his statement. 'But she suits me, yes, and I love her, and I hope she feels the same.'

She looked past him again, out of the window. 'There's no escape in our business. When I . . . when Dave . . . well, I ended up with a WPC telling me it wasn't my fault and I must be brave and take him to court. She'd worked with Dave when he was at Mile End. You should have seen her face when she realised who the lads had arrested. I could have laughed. Except that when her partner on the shift arrived I'd trained *her*. I wrote a report on her, saying she was unsuitable for CID, better put her with juveniles, or women's issues. So they did.'

'Oh Jesus, Cath.' He wanted to touch her but everything about the way she was holding herself suggested he would get bitten, if not worse.

'Yeah. And I could see it would be round everywhere by the morning.' She was holding herself ramrod straight, but she looked as if she was still being beaten. 'I think it was *that* more than anything which made me give him up. While no one knew, it was between *us*, sort of, then it was different, but once everyone knew and was, oh, not quite sorry for me, you know, wide-eyed but couldn't wait to get out of the room and tell their mates.'

'That must have been very hard.' And she must, he understood, have been badly hurt or in danger of her life, or both, to have invoked police help. He drew in a breath, carefully. 'Did you have to go to court?'

'They didn't tell you? The lads, I mean?' She looked away from the window, to his face, then studied his desk, shoulders rigid. 'He's in hospital. Dave, I mean. Complete breakdown. This was six months ago.'

'The bastard.' The words were impelled out of him, her head jerked back convulsively and they stared at each other. 'Couldn't even face the responsibility for what he'd done, so he ducks out and hides in a bin. Cath, what were you *doing*?'

'I thought it was me. I thought it was my fault.'

He sat speechless, looking into her small pale face.

She stared back at him, sniffed convulsively, and drew in a huge breath through her mouth like a child, and he felt an appalling rush of tenderness. It is true, he thought, as he got up clumsily, banging his knee on the coffee table, and bent over, weight on the table, to enfold her in a cuddle, it does feel as if the heart is melting; it isn't a literary statement.

'Sorry, sorry, sorry,' he heard himself saying, as he rubbed her back comfortingly while she wept and snuffled on his shoulder. 'I have to get off this table,' he said, when he felt able. 'It'll break and I'll never be able to explain to anyone.' He was relieved to feel her ribs convulse, and managed to get himself arranged on a chair alongside her, so that he could go on holding her.

'I can't believe anyone would choose that table for a spot of light relief,' she said, in his ear, and he kissed her. She pushed him away, gently, and he watched while she found a handkerchief and a mirror and a comb and put herself to rights. She looked, even with eyes gone small with weeping and a red nose, powerfully attractive, and he rearranged his jacket self-consciously.

'Cath,' he said, telling himself he could not possibly leave her in this state, 'I'll buy you supper and take you home.'

She gave him a watery smile and shook her head. 'You'll be expected, surely.'

'No. Frannie is . . . well, she's out.'

This was not true, but he was righteously cross with Francesca. She had told him that morning she was spending much of the day with Matthew Sutherland, sorting out the Refuge data for the article he was writing on the Domestic Violence Act. He had objected on the basis that she was already overloaded and over-tried, and what about playing with William instead, only to be reminded that Susannah was, by long prearrangement, taking William home with her to show her mother in Durham. Well, if she was going to wear herself out doing wholly unnecessary Good Works with young Sutherland there was no reason for him to struggle to get back. In any case he was not going to leave Catherine in such distress.

'Matt. It's six o'clock; I haven't done anything about food and John said he would be back. Well, he hasn't been back any time in the last week, but he may be.'

'It's all right. I have to collect Francis.' He kissed her neck and rolled over, putting his feet on the floor with a thump. 'Want a shower?'

'Please.' She scooped her watch off the floor – niceties like bedside tables were not in Matt's furnishing canon – and made for the bathroom, suppressing the wish for her own towel and soap. This was only the second time they had managed to get back into bed together since the first time, just over a week ago. Her house was full of nanny and child and window cleaner and man come to repair the boiler, and his flat was full of Francis, or had been, until he had recovered enough to be posted to a library, under the supervision of another friend. Francesca, water drumming on her back, remembered suddenly and precisely a time when she had been just older than Matt, in a flat in Washington, having an affair with a married American politician. There had been a great deal more planning, telephoning, and promises than action, because of the difficulties of finding somewhere out of sight of flat-mates, wives and gossip columnists. Her present situation was uncomfortably familiar; instead of the press it was necessary to avoid any members of the Metropolitan police force, among whom gossip raged as freely as in any girls' school. She stepped out of the bath and stared anxiously into the dulled mirror while she combed her hair.

Matt met her at the door with a cup of tea and she took it gratefully. He was very good at small attentions like this for all his ferocity. She had understood from the first time in his bed that he knew exactly what he was doing and that any perception of herself as experienced Older Woman gently educating a younger man was wide of the mark. Someone – or several someones – had been there before her. He had admitted, matter-of-factly, that he had started at fourteen and accumulated a lot of valuable experience by the time he left New Zealand, never mind whatever else he had managed in three years in London. It was all of a piece with the rest of him, she thought, wryly; a high-quality well-trained article in any field.

'You want the bathroom?'

'In a minute. I need my cup of tea. You look good.'

She did, she did, she acknowledged guiltily. This affair had removed her usefully from what she was beginning to see as an endless slog of motherhood, mortgage and struggles to maintain a career. No joy in it, all the effort going into just keeping all the balls in the air at once, as if the whole desired panoply of husband, child, home and career had been some particularly dreary examination course.

'What are you going to do with Francis?' she asked.

'I have to keep him another six days; he's on antibiotics and shouldn't travel. And I've got something to do for Peter – yeah, he's decided I may as well work since I'm being paid.'

She put her arm round him protectively. 'Your boss is doing his best, Matt. And I *have* reminded my . . . reminded John to have a word with Notting Dale, to see what's what. I know it's difficult.'

'Impossible. I need to work. It's what I know how to do. If not as a solicitor then somewhere.'

'I'd feel the same, Matt,' she said, acknowledging very clearly the subtext, knowing that she too had always set more store by the work than the lovers.

'I didn't mean . . .'

'Yes, you did. Don't look like that. Anyone I've ever been involved with – or would fancy – puts the work first. It just makes living a bit difficult sometimes.'

'Hey.' He leant over and kissed her, gently, then with some urgency and she relaxed against him, laughing.

'You're showing off.'

'Wanna bet?'

'No, Matt. I must go home. I don't want to run into Francis.' She stood up and he wrapped his arms round her waist, and she bent to kiss the dark red hair. 'Ring me?'

An ambulance was pulling away from the big house in Kensington Church Street as McLeish and Davidson arrived and half the neighbours were in the street, or hanging out of windows to watch the show. It had finally stopped raining but it was a dark evening with promise of a further downpour. They headed through the small crowd up the steps, and two young constables fell back to let them through.

'We had to get her away, sir.' It was a CID sergeant from Notting Dale. 'We got the call and as soon as I saw where we were I called the Yard but we couldn't wait to get the lady away. She'd fallen down the stairs and got a dunt to her head, or I'd have waited. Maybe a broken arm, maybe some ribs as well. I couldn't wait.'

McLeish opened his mouth to snap at the man to stop bloody apologising, then got a grip on himself. He had just eaten the first two courses in an Italian restaurant near where Catherine lived, had seen her relax and the colour come back to her face. When the call came, they had just agreed that he would drive her home and have a cup of coffee, and he had been in a state between overwhelming desire for her and sheer terror at the thought of the consequences.

Davidson had found him; he had left the number of the restaurant with the team, thinking it better to do that than have them ring Francesca and worry her by assuming he was already home. He had offered to send a car, but McLeish had refused and dropped Catherine on the doorstep collecting a chaste and sisterly kiss for his trouble. He was feeling sick from disappointment and was having trouble concentrating on the problem in hand.

'What stairs? Oh, from the flat above? She fell?'

The sergeant closed a half-open door into the hall firmly. 'She said she'd been pushed, sir, or rather thrown down the stairs. By someone she couldn't see, who was behind her when she was leaving the flat. She kept on saying it.'

They looked up the stairs, silently. There was a little landing outside the flat off which the door opened and there was no cover at all, nothing anyone could shelter behind.

'The light has gone, sir. No bulb.'

Now *that* changed the situation radically. With no light overhead someone could have stood outside the flat door in the shadows, waiting.

'No bulb?'

'That's right, sir, you can see.' The sergeant shone a powerful flashlight on the shade.

It might be of course that someone had taken the bulb out and realised they didn't have a spare, but it was so dark on the stairs that it was unlikely anyone would have tolerated the situation for more than the time it took to get to the shops.

'Who found her? Or did she ring you?'

'No, sir. Her son – no, sorry, stepson, Dr Antony Price. He's in the little office place; I knew you'd want to see him.'

'Anyone else here?'

'There's myself and one of my lads, and two uniformed.'

'Thank you very much. You're new, I think, since I was at Notting Dale? Sorry you had the trouble.'

The sergeant, young and keen, hesitated. 'Sir, could it have been just some chancer who knew the house was upset? Nothing to do with . . . well, your case.'

'Any sign of robbery?'

'No. No, but I wondered was he hoping to steal her keys and do the flat?'

It was not impossible but it was unlikely. McLeish, always reluctant to discourage, said he thought it would be better to assume the attack was connected to his case and dismissed the man, noting his name. He turned back to Bruce Davidson who had summoned a scene-of-crime squad on his mobile and was standing stock still in the hall, looking at the darkened stairs.

'He could have followed her down the stairs and finished her off, John.'

'I thought the same.'

'I frightened him off, I think.'

McLeish turned, the hairs on his neck prickling, to see Antony

Price in the doorway from the office. It was a bad light but the man looked ill, thinner, and very tired.

'When I got here I saw the lights flash in the hall. I rang the bell and nothing happened. Then I heard someone calling so I used my key and when I got in there was Sylvia – on the floor.'

'What did you do then?'

'Took a quick look at her; she was conscious but bleeding from the head and her eyes were a bit crossed. So I called an ambulance. *Then* I thought about where I was and what, well, what's been happening, and I called the police. I rang 999 again. I've got your number somewhere but I didn't think of you.'

'Did she say anything?'

'Yes. That someone threw her downstairs.'

'Using those words?'

'Yes. You'll find that her injuries are what you'd get if you came down a long flight like that. Possibly a cracked skull, broken arm, ribs I think.'

The front door bell rang and Davidson admitted a doctor and half a scene-of-crime squad. He could be heard explaining what the problem was. McLeish saw that two of his team at the Yard had got there and set them to finding Luke Fleming, Miles Arnold and Francis Price, as being the injured Mrs Price's closest family and associates, and the most likely candidates to have pushed her downstairs. And Margaret Howard, who would be invaluable.

He installed Antony Price with Bruce Davidson in the room near the office which was used as a waiting-room and turned the office into the headquarters for the scene-of-crime squad who were clattering about, changing and observing how unusual it was to find yourself in the same place again two weeks later.

'It's not a death this time,' McLeish observed, more sharply than he had meant to, achieving a disciplined, reproachful silence which left him no option but to retreat. He decided he would catch a breath of air and work out what to do with Antony Price.

People were still loitering in the damp evening, drawn by the presence of three police cars, but they moved on under his disapproving stare. Except one, who stepped forward, so that his hair showed a rich dark red under the street lights.

'Chief Superintendent.'

'Mr Sutherland.' McLeish walked down the steps.

'What are you doing here?' The young man was very pale and

the big hands were clenched. 'Do you have Antony Price?. . . Have you arrested him?'

'Why would we have done that?'

Matt Sutherland cast a hunted glance at the uniformed constable hovering well within earshot.

'Have you something to tell me, Matt?' McLeish had meant to continue as formally as he had started, but it was too like dealing with one of Francesca's younger brothers in one of their many and varied spots of bother.

'Yes, I do. I must. She wasn't dead, was she?'

'Matthew.'

'Right. Sorry. I'd rather not run into him. Antony Price, I mean. But I must talk to you.'

McLeish took him downstairs, into the kitchen, now immaculately clean and obviously unused.

'Is this where . . .?'

'Yes. It is also the only room not occupied. Now, what is it you have to say?'

Matthew's colour had come back; he was still tense but he was determined and had his mind ordered. 'I'd been to try and find Antony Price – I wanted to talk to him.'

'What about?'

'He'd given his brother *cash*. This morning. When Francis had been off drugs for eleven days and Antony well knew that. Francis is a good lad, he walked round for a bit, then he gave the cash to a mate who is helping me look after him. The mate bought foodie things – recovering druggies eat all the time – and stuck the rest in the Post Office. But *that* was deliberate, Antony knows better, he's a doctor. So I wanted to know what the fuck he thought he was doing. So when I got back from . . . from where I was I went to look for him.'

'But you didn't find him?'

'Not where he lives. So I came on here – it's more or less on the way home. And I saw him go in and I was deciding whether I'd wait half an hour, see if he came out, or I'd barge in. Then the ambulance came and this stretcher was carried out, and I couldn't see who was on it. Then I heard the policeman say "she" to the ambulance men, so I knew it wasn't him. Antony.'

'Why didn't you come in straightaway when the police arrived?'

'I was going to, but . . . well . . . I didn't want to talk to one of the Notting Dale CID.'

172

'I'm going to take you to the Yard and get all this in due form, Matt. But just tell me, did you see anyone come out of the house after Antony Price went in? Remember there is a side entrance through into the garden.'

'No one. I thought of that . . . I watched. No one at all.'

13

Wednesday, 27 April

'How is she this morning?' John McLeish decided to ignore Davidson's barely concealed dissent and disapproval.

'Nae bad, considering. Broken arm, bruising, but they're going to let her home today.' Davidson was looking tired – well, they all were. He himself had got to bed at 2 a.m., sneaking in hopefully beside Francesca who had turned away in her sleep, snarling in protest. It was to be hoped that Davidson had fared better wherever he had been.

'I've asked for a meeting at nine.'

'So I hear.' Davidson finished his coffee and looked into his empty cup. 'I take it we've somebody watching out for Dr Price?'

'He's operating this morning. He's safe.'

Davidson looked up, meeting his eyes for the first time that morning. 'Ye're giving him rope to hang himself?'

'He didn't push Mrs Price downstairs.'

Bruce Davidson's expression did not change. 'He called the ambulance.'

'Yes. And he didn't need to do that. He could have left her. Or finished her off if he thought she'd identified him. He had no reason to suppose anyone else knew he was there. Matt Sutherland's presence was entirely fortuitous. But he called an ambulance and made sure she could breathe.'

'He said Mrs Price had asked him to come round. He would have assumed, surely, that she'd told someone.'

It was the argument of the night before, replayed, and John McLeish wished he had maintained a stern chief superintendent-like silence. He was relieved to hear the footsteps in the corridor which heralded the arrival of his meeting. He rose to greet Catherine Crane and saw Bruce Davidson's wooden disapproval change to sheer surprise.

'I've asked DI Crane from the Fraud Squad to join us at these meetings,' McLeish said generally, when they were all sitting down. 'They have an active interest in the affairs of Price Fleming Limited.' And since no murderer had emerged from two weeks of investigation by C Division, all sources of assistance must be brought in if only as a necessary preliminary to dropping the case. 'Catherine, would you tell us what your people are doing?'

'Certainly.' She was wearing a navy suit with a short skirt, four inches above her knees, and more when she sat down, with a V-neck silk blouse and long collar-less jacket, and every man at the meeting was watching her. 'I have a meeting today with the accountants, who are going over the company's business.'

'Who instructed them?' McLeish asked, for clarification.

'Mr Fleming and Mrs Price, as executors.'

'What information would we get from these accountants, Catherine?' Bruce Davidson was going to make it clear to all at this meeting that she and he were old friends.

'Whether the company is solvent. Whether it can go on trading.'

'And does that do anything for us?'

'It tells you how much trouble the late Mr Price was in – we were already investigating, remember – and therefore how much grief his fellow directors, Mrs Price and Mr Fleming, had coming. And, of course, the MP, Mr Arnold.'

'Would any of them have lost money personally?' McLeish asked, for general elucidation.

'They'd have lost any money they had lent to the company.'

'But the sons were not in the company?' McLeish was making sure the meeting was up to speed.

'True, but they might have lost money too. Dr Price – and his brother – are alleging that their father took money from the trust left by his first wife and converted it for the use of the company. If all this is true – and it looks as if it is – they have a claim on the company's funds, which could not be paid if the company were insolvent.'

'They all lost if the company couldn't pay up, but some lost more than others. Who had most to lose? Who would have gone to jail, for instance?' McLeish asked.

Catherine Crane sighed. 'Assuming the company was insolvent, we would have been able to prosecute Bill Price as MD, and Luke Fleming as an active director. Whether either of them would have got a custodial sentence I wouldn't like to say. We probably wouldn't have prosecuted Mrs Price. And we couldn't prosecute a consultant, like Mr Arnold, unless he had been drawing unauthorised monies from the company and there's no sign of that.'

McLeish left a pause for further comment, then asked the chairman's question. 'What do you expect the accountants to say, DI Crane?'

'That while the company may well have been insolvent while Mr Price was alive it isn't now, provided always the expected £2m insurance payment on the life of William Price is received. As is expected.'

'In that case you would not be able to prosecute?'

'Not under the Act. We would, of course, have a case against the directors of the company if an individual had been defrauded. And we thought we did. But I don't doubt that the man who complained to us will take the money if it's offered and withdraw his complaint.'

Two of the team started to speak when McLeish lifted a hand for silence. 'Are there any more questions for DI Crane? No? Thank you very much, Catherine.'

She nodded to him and rose, picking up her papers in one contained movement, and got herself out of the room, every man's eye following her regretfully. Comment and questions rose the minute the door closed behind her until McLeish silenced them.

'That makes Fleming the one with most to lose.' It was Roberts, a newly promoted detective sergeant, who was pink with excitement. 'He'd have been prosecuted as well as losing his job. And, if the info from Spain is right, he wanted Mrs P too and he wouldn't have got her.'

'What about Mr Arnold, the MP? Being in with a bunch of crooks wouldn't have been good for him.'

McLeish pulled the meeting to order. 'Right. Let us just briefly consider the assault on Mrs Price last night. We know that she had a row with Mr Arnold – or rather we have Miss Howard's word for that. Mr Arnold has given me an account of where he was at the time of the assault and I have no reason to suppose that won't be confirmed.' His team looked at him hungrily, but he was not going to say more until he had talked to Miss James in whose company Miles Arnold had been whiling away a couple of hours between votes. 'We know from Miss Howard that Mrs Price also

176

had an argument with Mr Fleming and we haven't been able to interview him yet.'

'What about Francis Price?' Roberts asked.

'Has an alibi. Matt Sutherland left him with a friend. And Antony Price, you all know about. He says he found Mrs Price and he certainly called an ambulance and I find it difficult to believe he assaulted her.' He saw that Jenny Martin, the only woman on his team, who had done such good work on finding the trust file, was trying to catch his eye. 'Jenny?'

'We did a general check on everyone involved with Mr Price, with his family as well. Dr Price – Antony Price that is – owes Ladbroke's £7,000. He's paying it off but he's had an account with them a long time, and I wondered . . . I mean, if he's a betting man he'd have other bills or debts somewhere else.' She reddened under the appalled attention she was getting from the whole table. 'I'm sorry, sir, we only just got the information this morning, just before I came to the meeting, and Chris – Sergeant Stewart – said I should tell you. He's out, looking for Luke Fleming.'

'Yes,' McLeish said, heavily, managing not to look at Davidson. 'I'd have been glad to know that before. *That* was why he was so fussed about his mother's trust. He was furious with his father but he really needed the money, did he?'

'Sorry, sir.'

'Lesson to us all.' McLeish wasted no time on public recrimination; he would have words with Sergeant Stewart who should have made sure that this sort of information was in his hands in less than sixteen days after a murder.

The group looked at him hopefully, but he had nothing useful to say; they knew a lot more than they did sixteen days ago, but they still had the same five suspects in the frame. He suppressed a sense of discomfort at the thought of Antony Price.

'What about the assault on Mrs Price though, sir?' Roberts asked. 'Doesn't that put her out of the running? As well as the MP and Francis Price?'

'Not necessarily. That may have been about something else entirely. We haven't been able to interview Mr Fleming yet. Might have been a lovers' quarrel.'

'Dr Price must be favourite.' It was, inevitably, Davidson. 'And if, as Jenny here says, he's a betting man, he'd have known what to do with the cash that was in the safe the night Bill Price died.'

That was a sound point, McLeish conceded silently, as his secretary came in and laid a note before him. 'Ah, right. Sergeant Stewart has found Fleming. I'll see him. Thank you all. Jenny, will you make sure all the personal stuff on our suspects is in and checked, and get it round all of us. Bruce. A word.'

Davidson waited stolidly while the team filed out.

'Go and pick up Antony Price, will you? Wait till he finishes operating, but bring him then.'

'And if he doesn't want to come?'

'Charge him with assault on Mrs Price.'

Davidson rose without comment but it was unfair to leave it like that.

'It's the gambling element that has rattled me. Gamblers can also dispose of cash without going near a bank.'

'Rather than his record of violence?' Davidson could be a grudging sod and this was one of the occasions.

'I still don't think he assaulted her and I don't quite believe he murdered his father. But you're right, there's enough against him. Better safe than sorry.'

A sidelong look reminded him that this had not been the basis of his argument, but having carried his point Davidson wasn't going to argue. Or complain that he was not going to sit in on the Fleming interview.

'Can I sort my desk, just?'

'Oh yes. Price is safe enough. He's started his operating list – and he'll be there till one o'clock at least.'

Luke Fleming, it transpired, had turned up at the Price Fleming offices at the usual hour for the commencement of business and had expressed forcibly a preference to stay where he was. He had pointed out that he was the only principal in Price Fleming still on his feet, one being dead and another in hospital. If the company was to have any chance of carrying out its commitments to its customers, someone had to mind the shop with the assistance if necessary of the two detectives on the premises. McLeish, acknowledging the justice of his comments, agreed to meet at Kensington Church Street.

The driver got him there in fifteen minutes, during which he slept; he had arrived home at 2 a.m. to find Francesca awake and miserable, having been sick twice. He had left her uneasily asleep that morning.

He opened his eyes, blinking in the bright April sun as the car stopped outside the house in Kensington Church Street, and waited a minute to gather himself. Stewart came down the steps and slid into the front passenger seat, craning round to speak.

'Sir, Mr Fleming is here.'

'What's he doing?'

'He's in a meeting with the accountants, I understand.'

'I'd have been glad to know what they were saying to him.'

'Oh.' Stewart looked disconcerted.

'No matter. He might not have asked the same questions with you there. How is he behaving? In a rage?'

'No, sir. Not at all. Like . . . well, like anyone who wants to get on with the day's work. We told him about Mrs Price.'

'And? What did you think?'

'That he was really surprised. He asked what time it had all happened, but I played stupid.'

'Thanks. I'll see him – if, that is, I can detach him from the accountants. Come and take the note.'

'Sir? I'm really sorry we didn't get the stuff about Dr Price and the gambling. We didn't look for it because the financial check on him was slow coming in. But there were credit card debts and all sorts when it did.'

'Mm. The point is, Stewart, you need a routine so you know if something hasn't arrived.'

'Sorry, sir.'

They went up the stairs, stopping in the outer office to greet Margaret Howard. McLeish realised from her response that he must be looking more approachable than usual. It was, he reflected, natural relief at meeting the only person in the Price Fleming *équipe* who could not have murdered William Price, or pushed Sylvia Price downstairs. Margaret Howard's attendance upon an aged aunt over the night of William's death had been confirmed by two irreproachable witnesses apart from the aunt herself. And last night she had chosen to attend one of the Lloyd Webber musicals in the company of a woman friend, being half-way through Act 1 at the point where Sylvia Price was measuring her length on the stairs. He gave her the latest news of her employer.

179

'She'll be back today? Oh, I am glad.' She looked anxiously at the closed door to the inner office from which the noise of raised voices could be heard. 'Mr Fleming dictated lots of letters today and he has signed them but I thought ... well, that Mrs Price would want to see them before they went ...'

She was holding a large leather-covered signature book, letters visibly interleaved between the blotting paper pages, and McLeish's fingers itched.

'Well,' he said, judiciously. 'I'll be talking to Mr Fleming myself in a minute, and I could have a word if you'd like to give me them.' She put the book into his hands with the speed of relief and he understood that she was going to back away from any goings-on that threatened to involve her. Anyone who had worked for five years for the deceased would have needed to preserve some detachment from the inner reality of the Price Fleming business. He expressed, wistfully, the hope of coffee. She hesitated and explained that she had been making coffee in the little kitchen in the flat, which Mrs Price had kindly said she could use, but the stairs had been roped off by the police. She was, she knew, being silly, but she had not yet managed to use the kitchen downstairs. She would most willingly go down to the corner for them.

McLeish apologised for his thoughtlessness, and accepted promptly, instructing the young constable on the door to go with her, and as the door closed after her he and Stewart fell on the correspondence file, hunched over it shoulder to shoulder.

It was a very businesslike set of letters, and McLeish understood that he had not fully appreciated Luke Fleming's qualities. Twenty of the letters were the same, to different addressees; all explained that despite Price Fleming's best efforts it was not now realistic to assume that three apartment blocks in Spain would be ready by the end of June. No reference to the death of William Price was made. The tone was apologetic but there was careful reference to the terms of the contract which stopped short of a full guarantee. Nineteen of the customers were offered alternatives and the twentieth, whom McLeish recognised as the young man who had gone to the Fraud Squad, was also offered, *ex gratia*, the option of full reimbursement of the capital sum he had paid if this was his preference. Of the remaining three letters one was to a Spanish firm of solicitors with workmanlike instructions for a six-month lease on a substantial apartment block in Majorca, one to the National Westminster Bank in Brompton Road, confirming that what was proposed had been discussed with them, and asking for monies to be transferred to cover the deposit on the lease and expenditure on refurbishment. Another letter directed a firm of Spanish contractors to prepare themselves to quote for creating three apartment buildings described as 'being built to foundation level', the job to be complete for end September.

A change of tone, and the scrape of chairs from the inner room, made them shut the book and arrange themselves in waiting posture. The door was flung open and Luke Fleming emerged in a vile temper, flushed on the cheekbones, eyes narrowed, the big hands clenched round a substantial bound volume of paper, on which only the word 'DRAFT' stamped top and bottom of the cover was visible. He nodded to McLeish, took a paper cup of coffee without thanks from the hands of the returning Margaret Howard, then put it down to snatch up the correspondence book.

'I'll take that. When did you say Mrs Price would be back? Right. Let me know the minute she gets here. I'll be in the waiting-room if that will suit you,' he added to McLeish.

They followed him across the corridor, Stewart carrying his coffee for him, and settled themselves while he banged about putting down papers.

'You would *not* believe I was a director of this company,' he said, surveying the pile of papers and books. 'And I'll tell that popsy from your lot the same. I'm the one who has been keeping the place going in Majorca; Sylvia had *had* that accountants' report for twenty-four hours, would you believe? And I was in this office most of yesterday.' He spread his hands in furious appeal.

'Mr Fleming, as you know, Mrs Price was injured in a fall last night. She claims that she was pushed down the stairs.'

'Pushed? Your man said she fell.' He glared at Stewart, who gazed fixedly at his notepad. 'I didn't push her downstairs. I never even went up to the flat yesterday, Sylvia was down here when I was. What time was all this?'

'What time did you leave here yesterday, Mr Fleming?'

Luke Fleming stared at him. 'Right. I see. Another person keeping their cards so close to their chest that some of us don't even know what game we're playing.' He took a deep breath, clenched both hands together and sat back. 'I left about five thirty. Then I went to my flat, had a drink and a shower and watched the telly – the Channel 4 news till whenever it finishes. Then I had another drink or so and I went at about . . . what . . . nine o'clock.

Had dinner at Café Pelican – big place in St Martin's Lane. When was Sylvia attacked?'

'Did you see anyone at your flat or on your way out?'

'No. It's supposed to be a serviced block but you never see any service.' He hesitated. 'I met someone at Café Pelican, though. There's always a few people there to talk to. I've got her phone number. And no, I didn't bring her home, I thought I'd got enough on my plate. But she could be asked, I suppose.'

Sylvia Price had been attacked at seven thirty the night before, and Fleming's flat was not more than twenty minutes away.

Fleming tried his question again. 'So what time was the attack?'

'Seven thirty, or just before.' Someone was going to tell him that in the course of the day.

'So I was alone with the TV.'

'What are your immediate plans, Mr Fleming?'

'Talk to Sylvia. Mrs Price. Doesn't she *know* who did it, for heaven's sake? It wasn't me.'

McLeish concluded the interview after a few more questions destined to elicit any detail of Fleming's journeyings the night before, and let the man go back into his office. He told himself that Fleming was hardly going to assault Sylvia Price, in the presence of Margaret Howard and at least two accountants.

He suppressed an urge to ring Davidson and tell him to go *now* and wait outside the operating theatre for Antony Price – it would be an inefficient use of time, of course it would. He would wait until Stewart got the statement typed up for signature and meanwhile try to find Susie James on the telephone. By Miles Arnold's own statement she would not be providing him with anything approaching a secure alibi, but whatever she had to say ought to be recorded, and he had undertaken to deal with her himself.

He thought for a moment he must have got the wrong number because it was a man, unctuously smooth-spoken, who replied. No, Miss James was not available but a message could be passed to her, and would be, if he liked to leave his own name, an indication of whom he represented and a number where he could be reached. McLeish left his name, shorn of its rank, and the number at New Scotland Yard, but he was puzzled. Nothing about Ms James, or her business surroundings, had suggested that she could afford assistance of the calibre suggested by the man's voice. Still, he had been saved a wasted journey and the call had only taken five minutes.

And a very useful delay too, he realised, as he looked out of the window for his car. It was there but so was a taxi and another unmarked police car from which Catherine Crane was emerging. She stopped, the fair hair shining in the sun, to wait by the taxi which Sylvia Price was paying off, left arm in a sling, a large plaster on her left temple, her eyes hidden by dark glasses. Despite the sling and the bandage she did not look dishevelled; her blonde streaked hair was immaculate and her beige mackintosh swung fashionably clear of the injured arm. Nor was she in a hurry; she had stopped to greet Catherine Crane in a leisurely way, and the two women sauntered up the steps together chatting in the sun, Catherine carrying Sylvia Price's bag. If he played it right, he could take Sylvia Price through her statement of last night again, and get a look at the accountants' report or, at the worst, a digest of its contents from Catherine. And it would be interesting to see how Luke Fleming would receive Mrs Price.

Like a valued associate, it turned out. Fleming appeared on the doorstep carrying his copy of the accontants' report to embrace her in a comradely way, to commiserate on her injuries and to welcome her to a meeting with the accountants. Catherine was greeted in much the same spirit, and McLeish almost hesitated to destroy the general accord by emerging from the waiting-room. Luke Fleming simply wanted him to go away, and Sylvia Price was not altogether pleased to see him. Catherine, however, just before she got her professional mask back in place, looked as if her prayers had been answered.

'I'm so glad you're here, sir,' she said, in her super-efficient personal assistant persona, he noted, appreciatively. 'I'm carrying some papers DI Davidson wanted you to see. Look at the back in the notes first, he says.' She excused herself prettily to the others and sifted papers rapidly, so that he received, unblinking, a note on the Metropolitan Police Pension Fund and a photocopy of the accountants' report tucked into a copy of the *Police Gazette*.

'If I may,' he said, generally, 'I'll stay here and wait until Mr Fleming's statement is ready and until Mrs Price is free for another word.'

All assured him with varying sincerity that it would be no problem, and Margaret Howard offered him more coffee. He closed the door and fell on the report, starting from the back as he had been directed. The conclusions, he was unsurprised to find, were that, provided the £2m proceeds of the insurance policy on Bill Price's life were received within the next month, the company was solvent, in the Companies Act sense of being able to pay its creditors as they fell due. The accountants had been thorough; in the list of creditors appeared the names of people who had hoped to holiday in the unfurnished apartments and the cost of the alternatives being offered to them. The total list came to £700,000 odd. The unwritten corollary was clear; without that £2m the company would have had to find some £500,000 odd in cash in the next two months to pacify non-bank creditors. They could not have looked to their own bankers; the agreed £1.5m facility had already been exceeded. Had Bill Price not died, thus handsomely insured, the comapny must have failed with serious legal consequences to its two surviving directors, Luke Fleming and Sylvia Price, and serious reputational cost to Miles Arnold MP. And none of its unsecured creditors would have been paid; the bank had all the security there was. So both Price brothers would have been unable to recover any of the money they were expecting from their mother's trust. If ever there was a timely death this was it, the classic case of a man worth a great deal more dead than alive to his family and associates. This could not be regarded as a quirk of modern insurance practice, or bad luck on Bill Price since it was also clear at whose door the insolvency of Price Fleming should be laid. Bill Price had paid himself £300,000 a year and drawn expenses of the same again, between holidays, cars, the upkeep of three racehorses and a yacht which appeared, conservatively valued, among the assets of Price Fleming Ltd.

But Catherine had already told him much of this. There must be something else, some new fact or facts which she had wanted him to get hold of immediately, presumably involving some of the people currently present in the building. At the back, she had said, and he started to flip through the appendices. Francesca, who had taught him to read accounts, had said that you always looked at the Notes, that's where all the bodies were buried. And there it was at Note 19. There was £43,219 less cash in the bank in Majorca than in the books of the Majorca subsidiary. Various explanations had been offered by Local Management, but the note made it clear that it had not found them convincing. And Local Management was Luke Fleming.

He sat back to think about Luke Fleming. With Bill Price alive he might not have been worried about being found out abstracting cash from the company. Bill Price had after all done a great deal in that line. Nor were Sylvia Price's hands clean; she had taken a salary of £40,000 a year and shared, presumably, in all the goodies her husband had looted from the company. But somehow, even if Luke Fleming was her lover, McLeish could not see her receiving with understanding his attempts to secure rainy-day money by stealing from the company. Catherine, sound detective that she was, had wanted him to understand that Luke Fleming had a reason for incapacitating Sylvia Price. It should have given him a chance to get the money out of wherever he had put it, assuming he still had it, and, as Local Management, triumphantly restore it to the accountants, but for the fact that Sylvia Price had got hold of their report first.

He shifted uneasily, but recalled he had a few hours yet to make any decisions; Luke Fleming was in a room with three accountants as well as Sylvia Price. He read on through the notes, just to make sure there was nothing else that Catherine had wanted him to see. Another pencilled cross caught his eye and he read the entry twice to be sure. A cheque for £30,000 and another for £50,000 to William Price signed by Miles Arnold had been countersigned in favour of the company. So Miles Arnold was a shareholder – no, the note said the purpose of the payment was unknown, but there was no record of any share issue. Time and beyond to talk to Miles Arnold again, but he would check his alibi – such as it was – with Miss James before he did that.

'You look tired.'

'I am a bit. I was sick in the night. I don't know why. It's nice to see you, Matt. I'm not sure I can make you anything to eat but please help yourself. There are some more biscuits in the cupboard. Or have an egg.'

'It's just that I missed breakfast. Francis has to eat all the time so he had the rest of the cereal.'

Francesca, still feeling very peculiar, had woken finally at eleven o'clock much relieved that William was still away and opened the door to Matthew Sutherland, who was fidgeting with anxiety.

'Is he all right? I hear you've been "Helping with Enquiries".'

'He's doing bloody well, no thanks to his brother. Sit down,

Wonderwoman, I'll make you something to eat. What made you sick? Where's your fridge?'

'To what do I owe the honour, Matt?' she asked, watching him boil milk. 'I didn't think I was going to see you today.'

'I can't find Annabelle.'

Francesca accepted a mug of hot milk and sipped it carefully, her stomach heaving uneasily. Matthew was on his knees, going through her refrigerator, sniffing suspiciously at everything.

'Should you be able to?'

'Yes. Francis and I had a late supper with her last night. *She* was sick too. I went through *her* fridge but it wasn't food – Francesca, this chicken is *off*, you'll poison everyone – it was old-fashioned stress. As I told her.'

'And you a qualified doctor too.' Francesca was conscious of pure jealousy.

'So she said she'd consider taking the morning off. She rang in sick, but she isn't at home.'

'She decided to go shopping to cheer herself up.'

Matthew shot her a look of mixed indulgence and scorn. 'She isn't like that.'

'Get off. We're *all* like that if push comes to shove.'

'Antony Price is unstable, in the literal meaning of the word. *He* doesn't know what he's going to do. He isn't safe.' He rooted out another two plates from the fridge and scraped their contents into the bin, rinsing his long hands under the tap, his back to her. 'He's operating this morning however, which ought to keep him out of mischief.'

Francesca, wanting his attention herself but conscientious, considered the point. 'If she's not at home, and not in the surgery, where else do you think she is? His flat?'

'We saw her back to her place last night. And he *was* operating first thing this morning. I rang up disguised as a worried GP.'

'Then she's out somewhere.' She watched his back as he washed up, very tall in her kitchen.

'Yes.' He swung round, long jacket flapping. 'It's usually a cock-up not a conspiracy, isn't it?' He did not sound at all convincing.

'Why don't you just check her flat and the surgery again and then go up to Antony Price's flat, see what you can see. It's better than standing here mucking out my fridge, I mean, don't think I'm not grateful, but . . .'

He stood, irresolute. 'Am I being an idiot, Fran?'

Francesca, queasy and tired, in a torn dressing-gown, gazed at him. 'Better make a nonsense than waste your day.'

He nodded, took her cup away from her and bent and gave her a brisk kiss on the cheek, standing back to look at her. 'You look a bit better.' He rose to go and she remembered a conversation in the early hours of the morning and clasped at his jacket.

'Matt, I forgot. John told me last night or rather early this morning. The drugs case against you is being withdrawn.'

He looked down at her blankly, then suddenly sat down on the nearest chair. 'What?'

'You've gone green now.' She gave him the rest of the milk, anxiously. 'You're not to tell anyone, but the two who arrested you are both being suspended. Nothing to do with you, they're thought to have been doing awful things with other cases. So you won't be prosecuted.'

He was still pale, the eyes unnaturally wide, and she hooked an arm round him. 'It doesn't mean you'll get your stash back, I'm afraid,' she said, deliberately watching his head jerk back. She saw he was unable to speak and got up shakily to boil a kettle, and give him time to regain his composure. 'Isn't that good, though – John was pleased,' she said, her back to him. She heard him draw a long painful breath.

'He must be one of the fuzz who thinks it's a nuisance prosecuting for marijuana.'

'Quite the contrary. He believes that hash is often a step on the way to Class A substances.' She reached for the tea-bags. 'We have not discussed your case, Matt, or not in words, there have to be some limits. But he approves of you, he admires how you've stuck to Francis, and thinks you'll make a good solicitor.' She turned, cautiously, and sneaked a glance at him; his head was bent and he was scrubbing at his face. 'And so do I, and I'm sure you can manage on some less contentious, recreational drug, like booze. Tea?'

'Yes, please. And about half a packet of sugar.' He rose to stand with his arm round her and reached for a handful of kitchen towels, so that he could blow his nose, noisily. 'Now I know what it's like not to be hung,' he said, soberly. 'Thanks, Fran.'

'Didn't do anything as it turns out. I had a few ideas, and one or other would have worked.'

He wrapped her in a bear hug. 'Can I tell Peter?'

'Why not? It is OK, though you may need to wait another ten

days while the warning order expires. But someone at Notting Dale will confirm. Now go and see if you can find Annabelle, since you're worrying, then you will be a totally happy bunny.'

He kissed her on the lips and thumped up the stairs, leaving her to wash up his cup in a state somewhere between misery and relief.

In Kensington Church Street, John McLeish was trying to arrive at a rational view on whether to arrest Luke Fleming and sweat him. Several facts pointed to Fleming as a murderer and as Sylvia Price's attacker. The murder had been opportunistic and Fleming was a chancer. There had been £20,000 in cash in the safe and Fleming knew exactly where to find a home for *that* in Spain. He had no real alibi either for the murder or the attack. But the trouble was, none of it quite jelled; the evidence was highly circumstantial and would not do for the percentage players of the Crown Prosecution service.

The phone rang, and as he picked it up, he heard Bruce Davidson shouting at the other end, and the anxiety that had haunted him all morning clenched his stomach.

'John? Sorry, just getting the lads out. Antony Price isn't here. He walked out after the first operation this morning, said he wasn't well. His number two carried on, with everyone saying how wise to stop if ye weren't feeling quite the thing.' Davidson was sounding savage, 'I should have gone down there right away.'

'I should have charged him.'

'Ah. Aye, well. Perhaps, but it didnna look cast iron, did it? And he *may* just be ill, John.'

'No. Something's gone wrong. Get someone to his flat – you have? Good. I've got a driver here, I'll meet you.'

He scribbled a note for Catherine, gathering up the papers she had given him, observing distractedly that the sum payable on the death in-service of a detective chief superintendent was now five times his annual salary. Perhaps, like the late Bill Price, he was more valuable dead than alive, particularly if he was going to let dangerous suspects roam free.

14

Wednesday, 27 April

The flat looked dusty and smaller than Annabelle had remembered it and somehow dated like an old photograph. Nothing had been changed in the three weeks since she had moved out, but the solid mahogany furniture Antony inherited from his mother looked heavier and seemed to take up more space. The place *was* grubby; well, she herself had always spent time cleaning up and without her Antony's Spanish cleaner must have been losing the battle.

'Sorry I'm a bit untidy,' Antony said, behind her, 'but I thought it was better than the caff. I'll get the coffee, you sit down, Anna.'

She did not want to sit down, indeed she did not want to be here at all. Antony had appeared at her tiny flat at ten thirty that morning, just as she had finally got out of bed and dressed. He was unkempt and not coherent, and it had been she who had suggested a walk through the park to his flat as something that would do both of them good. Antony was a bit calmer but he was ill, not managing to finish sentences, and changing subjects at random. And he had abandoned his operating list, that much he had managed to tell her, without seeming to know why. The kitchen suddenly seemed very small and airless. She propped open the flat door to ventilate the whole place and bustled about, putting things into the sour-smelling dishwasher, in which several flies were also trapped.

She made the coffee, gave Antony a cup and slipped into the bathroom to give herself a minute alone. It was dirty too, a tideline of several days' stubble in the basin, and the towels were damp and musty. Antony, like any surgeon, had always been fastidious, and she looked around with increasing anxiety. But she had determined not to be afraid of him and she was not going to go back on that.

She went through into the living-room where Antony was sitting, slumped on the sofa, and removed six cups and five glasses from the coffee table and took them through into the kitchen.

'Annabelle.' He had come up behind her. 'Do stop tidying. We have to talk.'

She turned to face him, stepping back because he was crowding her, and noticing that he had shaved but that his shirt was at least two days dirty. 'Let's sit down,' she suggested, as calmly as she could, and waited a long moment while he turned and went to the living-room. She followed, placing herself the other side of the coffee table on the other little sofa.

'I've been a complete bloody idiot,' he said, finally, not looking at her. 'And I'm in real trouble.'

'At the hospital?'

'No. Though *that's* only a matter of time. I walked out this morning because I couldn't remember what I was doing.'

'Was the patient all right?'

'I expect so. Gall bladder. Bill was there, he could finish up.' He got to his feet, cautiously, in one disjointed movement and went to the window. 'I've . . . I'm . . . I owe money.'

'Who to? What for?'

'I've been going to the clubs, since you went away.'

She let this pass; she knew he had always made occasional visits to the London casinos. She had thought it glamorous five years ago, and although disillusioned, had been too terrorised by him in the last eighteen months to argue. The memory of that fear made her angry.

'How much did you lose?' she asked his back.

'Don't *sound* like that. A lot. I owe about £20,000.'

He swung to face her and she quaked. She knew that expression, a sort of blind, inturned look which meant he was going to lash out. She was awkwardly placed, her knees too close to the coffee table to get up and run.

'Oh dear,' she said, as flatly as she could. 'I am sorry. I'll get some more coffee.' She got up slowly, holding her breath.

'Don't fidget about,' he shouted and she froze. 'Ladbroke's are going to sue me. The other people I owe came round to Wigmore Street, as if I wasn't already in enough trouble with the clinic. I'm being screwed.' He was scarlet and shaking, and she measured up the distance to the door. He saw her eyes shift and moved between her and it. 'Sit down and bloody listen,' he shouted, but heart hammering, she stood her ground.

'Not if you're going to scream at me. I've had enough of that. *You* sit down. Over there.' It worked, she saw, sick with relief. He moved to the other side of the table and sat down heavily, so she sat too, making sure she could get up, fast. 'Now. You're £20,000 in debt and they're pressing you. What about your bank?'

'I'm over the limit there. What I need is my money, that Mum left. And that bitch Sylvia won't give it to me, though my bloody father put it into the company. She's got all the insurance money, she can afford it. I could kill her.' He looked into her face. 'Oh, you needn't look so bloody shocked. I would have if I'd thought I'd get away with it.'

'What shocks me is the state you're in, Antony,' she said.

'Annabelle, I'm in a state because I'm in a mess, and because I don't have you. Come back. Please come back. I'll do anything.' He was crying, looking about sixteen, and she felt only the need to get out of the room. He saw it and was across the intervening space and on his knees in front of her, holding her arms so she was pinned to the sofa. 'You must. You have to.' He was rocking her back and forth, teeth set, hands clenching painfully round her upper arms.

'I can't. Let me go,' she said, frightened, and understood she had made a fatal mistake. He slapped her so hard her whole head snapped sideways before she could react. 'You're not going anywhere,' she heard him say, and then his hands were on her throat and she was fighting to breathe and the light was going and she thought as she blacked out sadly of her mother and of Matthew Sutherland . . .

She choked and tasted dirt and the light came back. Someone was pressing on her chest and she croaked, hoarsely, in protest. A face loomed above her, dark red hair, bright in the sunlight, and she felt her head being lifted and something soft put under it. She could hear groaning coming from somewhere, but she couldn't move.

'I'll be back.' She lay, eyes half shut against the light, concentrating on getting breath past the painful swelling in her throat.

'I would not give a flying fuck if you snuffed it, here and now.' That was Matthew Sutherland, but why was he here?' 'But it could be awkward, so just you stay there where you can breathe.' There was a scuffling noise. 'Try *that* again and I'll put the sofa on top of you.' Then he was by her side again, moving her head to get another pillow under it. 'Better? No, OK, I'll take it out again. I'm *here*, Annabelle, I'm just getting an ambulance, hold on.'

She heard the tinkle of the phone, then the sound of trampling feet, somewhere across the room. 'Matt.' It was an inhuman croak, but he was there, holding her hand.

'It's the fucking cavalry, isn't it? About fifteen minutes too late.' He lifted her tenderly, cradling her in his arms so that she could see several sets of knees, in navy and grey.

'Is the lass all right?' She knew the voice, but could not focus her eyes on the man kneeling beside them.

'Only just. I was getting an ambulance.'

'We'll do that.' She could see black hair now as the man turned to shout orders. 'Two ambulances. What's with Dr Price?'

'You mean why is he lying on the floor? When I arrived he was strangling Annabelle, so I did my best to kill him.'

'You shouldna say those things, lad, causes nothing but grief.' She flinched from the gentle touch on her throat. 'We'll need a statement.'

'You can bloody wait till I've got her into competent hands. Why did your lot let that bugger loose?' It was clear from the way the other man's knee jerked that Matt had scored a point.

'Aye, well, there's a story to that, but we can't arrest people just because we've got our doubts.'

'That's not my experience.'

'Ye're speaking of yourself?' Annabelle could see a bright blue eye now, edged by long dark lashes. 'Less said the better there, I would have thought. Ye're a lucky lad. Ah. The medical help is here. No, not the lass, take the young man over there, he's worse off.'

'Something accomplished then,' she heard Matthew mutter, and realised he was shuddering and the hand she was holding was suddenly cold.

'You'd better take the lad as well in the second ambulance,' the Scots voice said, with resignation. 'I'll mebbe get my statement later.'

Thank God for the car telephone, John McLeish thought, without impiety. He had been on his way to Antony Price's flat, siren going, his sweating driver cursing his way through traffic so thick that even the most co-operative members of the public could not physically find space to give them passage, when he got the call. He had told the driver to turn around and make for the Yard; he did not have to face Bruce Davidson's reproaches just this minute. They had been lucky, Annabelle was not seriously hurt, and this wretched case might finally be cracking open. He walked into his office with a sense of reaching sanctuary, called in Detective Sergeant Roberts to tell him the latest developments and waved away questions on the basis that Davidson would be back soon to do a full report. He called for coffee and stared at the wall, reminding himself that he was one of the youngest detective chief superintendents in the country, and that he had a long and largely successful track record. The assault on Annabelle Brewster that morning ought not to have happened, he ought to have kept surveillance on Antony Price, and he and everyone else owed the dogged Matthew Sutherland one. All he had to do was to think as he was paid to. He sat, coffee cooling disregarded, concentrating, occasionally making a note, just conscious of his secretary deflecting phone calls and visitors.

He came out of this process, shaking himself, an hour and a half later, and called his secretary to consider his resources. Davidson was at St Mary's, and Stewart at Price Fleming's offices, so he sent Roberts off to get the answer to his question, and dispatched another sergeant to get Francis Price.

Then he rang Susie James, but found himself talking again to the over-smooth, over-compliant male voice which changed to something rougher and sharper when he gave his rank and demanded to know Ms James's whereabouts forthwith.

'I've got a number, yes, but I do know she's not there. Will you leave it with me and I'll ring round and make sure she gets in touch. No, there's only me here, I wouldn't tell you a lie.'

McLeish put the phone down and rang Miles Arnold; he had no time to waste and not causing embarrassment to Members of Parliament had got to the bottom of his priority list. 'I must speak to him,' he said, briskly, to the secretary. 'Where is he?'

'In his constituency, Detective Chief Superintendent. I can find him for you in five minutes and he will ring you.'

'Give me the number.' There was a pause and he looked at the phone incredulously.

'This is going to sound rather strange, but I am afraid he may not come to the phone except for me. May I try first and then give you all the numbers if I can't get through? In the next ten minutes.'

Thoroughly taken aback, McLeish agreed, eyed his cold coffee and asked for fresh, drank it and was just about to snatch up the phone when it rang.

'Miles Arnold.'

'Sorry to trouble you. I cannot find Miss James at the number you gave me.'

There was a short, smarting laugh. 'Not surprised. We think that she's with the *News of the World* people.'

'Oh.'

'I'm sorry I can't help. I'm sure she'll talk to you sooner or later, once she's finished with the paying customers. Doesn't really matter though, does it? I could see from your face I hadn't been there at the right time.'

'We need to talk to you about another matter.'

'What other matter? I'm bloody *not* coming into town today. We've got the press parked three deep outside here and I'm not putting my nose out until I've got a statement released. So you'll have to come here if you want to talk. *What*? No, I didn't beat up Sylvia Price, though I cannot imagine why not. We were taught not to hit girls, but as far as I can see I'd have done better to lay about her with a bat. Where *was* I? At what time? Well, I left the office about ... what ... six o'clock, and I went for a drink. I needed one. Where? At the House, where else? *Then* my secretary found me and told me the solid matter had hit the air-conditioning and I came back here. I left the House about seven thirty – Jim Waters suggested I take a lawyer with me, so I did.'

'You were having a drink with Jim Waters?'

'Did I not say? Yes.'

Well, that settled that. Whatever else his involvement with the death of Bill Price, Miles Arnold had not thrown Sylvia Price down the stairs last night. McLeish gritted his teeth and asked without further preamble about the £80,000 Arnold had apparently invested in the company.

'I'm suing,' the telephone informed him. 'I don't know how you know but I gave that money to Bill Price to invest for me on the stock market, not to put into the company. *He* was going to give it back. I'd told him I'd sue otherwise, and the twenty grand that may or may not have been in the safe – no way of knowing if Bill was telling the truth – was the first instalment. Sylvia Price wouldn't do anything, so I've told my solicitor to put a writ in to wind up the company. Not that it'll do me a lot of good, but I'm probably going to need the money. Yes, I could make time to talk tomorrow, but I don't know where I'll be. Read your papers, I'm afraid.'

McLeish, seeking for a silver lining, hoped that the issue of a writ might hurry matters on at Price Fleming. Or, with the way this case was going, cause another of the participants to try and dispose of one of their associates. He went into the day's team meeting to report Arnold's phone call.

'Does that put him in the clear, sir?' Roberts asked hopefully.

'For the attack on Mrs Price, yes. Leaves him as a murder suspect. He had urgent need of the £20,000 in the safe. How urgent we're all going to see tomorrow.'

He was relieved to be called out to speak to Bruce Davidson, who told him Annabelle Brewster was being kept in hospital till the swelling on her throat went down, but was all right. Antony Price had a minor skull fracture – Matt Sutherland had hit him with a chair, apparently – but had been *compos mentis* enough to be charged with assault, and left where he was under guard. And Matt Sutherland himself, rapidly restored with the aid of nothing more medically advanced than sweet tea and biscuits, was demanding to make a statement.

'Bring him here, if he's got the time.'

Davidson indicated that Matt was prepared to go a good deal further than SW1 to ensure that Antony Price was put away where he could do no further damage, so all McLeish had to do was to eat a belated lunch at his desk and get down to an interview room to meet Davidson and his witness as they arrived. Matt Sutherland was looking pale, and had a bandage over one eye. He scowled unwelcomingly at McLeish and behind him Davidson shook his head to indicate, unnecessarily, that no break in ranks had taken place.

'We're all grateful to you, Mr Sutherland,' McLeish said, bluntly. 'But for you we'd be in a very nasty situation.'

'He'd have killed her.'

'I hope you're not right. Can we take your statement? You'll have to appear whatever he pleads, of course.'

They took his statement and McLeish understood they had been even luckier than he had realised.

'I don't know if I could have got through a closed door in time.' Matt, who had been answering questions in a bleak and unyielding manner, suddenly looked very young. 'But it was open – Annabelle said she'd been airing the place.'

'Ye'd likely have distracted him enough just by breaking down the door,' Davidson said, soothingly, but no one in the room was convinced, and Matt finished his statement on a very subdued note. Davidson went off with the tape to get the typing done, leaving McLeish and Matt Sutherland together in a difficult silence.

'You let him away after he'd assaulted Mrs Price.'

'I "let him away", as you put it, because I didn't have the evidence to charge him. You're a lawyer, or you soon will be, now you're not being prosecuted.' It was a low blow and the scarlet flush on Matthew's cheekbones, clashing unbecomingly with the dark red hair, told him he had got home.

'You need to disentangle me in your mind from Francesca's siblings,' Matt said, surprising him.

'Yes, yes, all right, fair point. I don't dislike them, you know.'

'You don't take them seriously either.'

'All right, I'll take you seriously.' First *you* have to distinguish in your mind between Antony Price's behaviour to Annabelle and the question of whether he murdered his father and attacked his stepmother.'

'And gave his brother enough cash to kill himself with, knowing that he would buy drugs.'

'Did Francis ever tell you himself that Antony gave him cash?'

Matthew's head went back, and he tipped his chair in thought. When he came back to the vertical he was looking quite different. 'No, as a matter of fact he didn't. Quite the reverse. When he came round in hospital he said Antony hadn't, but I assumed he was either lying or confused – druggies tend to be – because he'd been up to see Antony.'

McLeish nodded. 'So what about a touch of the Oliver Cromwells, could you consider the possibility that Antony Price may have been telling the truth throughout about his dealings with his father and his stepmother?'

'No need to patronise. I'm capable of considering a hypothesis put to me straight. And I know about Cromwell. "Consider if you will, I beseech you, in the blood and bowels of Christ whether you

196

might not be mistaken." I even know who he said it to ...' He cocked a challenging eye at McLeish.

'Who? To whom, rather?'

'The gentlemen of the Covenant, in Edinburgh. They were, as usual in the Scots Church, about to divide brother against brother on tenuous religious grounds.'

'Thank you so much, Mr Sutherland. I had forgotten that. So. Try it my way and assume Antony Price was telling the truth. This is not a proper discussion to be having but you know it all from Annabelle. You know that he told us he went to the offices on the Saturday around nine thirty and found his father hanging dead and the safe empty. And he, being a doctor, thought his father had been dead for twelve hours. If all this is true then he was with Annabelle when his father died.'

'I thought it too pat to be true.'

'Remember that the murderer cleared out the safe with £20,000 in it. If it had been Antony Price who had got to the safe he would have been able to pay his debts. And he couldn't.'

'Or he meant to pay his debts but gambled the cash over the weekend? You can lose £20,000 pretty quickly.'

'Indeed, but he didn't. Or not anywhere in the UK. And all these people would have accepted cash. And remember, he was desperate to get some money from Sylvia Price.'

Matt gazed at him. 'So he *did* push her down the stairs?'

'He says he didn't, try believing him. It's no good constructing a case wrongly; not only do you come unstuck trying to make a face fit, but the bloke who really did it is on his way past you.'

'Who do you think? Ah. You're not going to tell me.'

'I can't yet,' McLeish said, soberly.

'Fair enough. Unless you have Francis in mind in which case you need to take your own prescription. *He's* telling the truth and you should believe it.'

'Where is he now?'

'I'm glad you understand that I didn't leave him alone. He's with a mate of mine, in a library.'

'In a library?'

'The degree he didn't finish is in Maths. We reckon – this mate and I – a quick go of computer science and he's off into the job market.'

McLeish considered him, deciding that he could easily be one of Francesca's siblings, improvers all. 'Is Francis Price going to stay off drugs?'

'Won't be for want of trying.'

Davidson came in, carrying pages of typescript, and McLeish rose to go. 'I'll leave you to it – sorry, but I need to get something checked. I've asked to see Francis, but the man I sent won't find him if he's in a library. It'll do tomorrow. Get him to ring me, or any of the team, will you? No, he can bring his solicitor with him if he likes, I just want a couple of answers.'

At the Kensington Church Street house, Luke Fleming and Sylvia Price sat opposite each other at the small round table in the front room office. It was a fine evening, the sun still high in the sky and warm, and the lime tree outside the window had put on the piercing clear green of new leaves. They had, jointly, seen the accountants and Catherine Crane off the premises; and Margaret Howard was still finishing up in the outer office. The conversation had started awkwardly and was proceeding in fits and starts.

'So, you're planning to come to Majorca, Sylvia. Why now when we've decided what to do about everything there?'

'I must see our bank manager out there, and I must also talk to the people in the office.'

'You mean Constancia, or Pedro? They don't know anything I don't.'

Sylvia Price uncrossed her legs, recrossed them and glanced towards the door. 'They also do not know why there is this difference? Where the extra money is?'

'I told you. I'll get all that sorted when I get out there. The police can't stop me, the company's solvent and they can't prove I had anything to do with Bill's death.'

She was plainly not listening, the corners of her mouth tight, frowning impatiently, and he reached over to take her hand. 'Sylvia, love, do listen. You've got nothing to worry about in Majorca. The accountants didn't understand one entry and it's wrong, and I know where the rest of the balance is. I just wasn't going to tell them.' He ran his thumb over the back of the hand that lay passive in his own. 'You knew Bill – I mean, you were married to him, you knew he was a bugger about money, so I just kept a little cash somewhere else to pay the bills. I didn't tell you

198

because I thought you'd be better off not knowing. It'll all be fixed as soon as I get there.'

'I do not like this . . . this way of going on with money. I hated it with Bill.'

'Yeah, well, you weren't going to change him, were you? But I'm not the same. *I* don't like ducking and weaving every time there's a bill to pay which is why I kept an account he didn't know about.'

In the outer office, Margaret Howard heard his voice go up and hurried to finish what she was doing. She would be late for dinner and for the seven o'clock news. She listened for a minute; she could not distinguish any of the words but she could hear Sylvia Price's cool, even, accented tones. She hesitated and decided it would be more tactful to go home without saying goodnight to her employer. She would bang the door as she left as a signal that she had gone, and also an indication that she had been kept twenty minutes beyond her normal time of leaving.

In the big office, Luke Fleming was angry and uneasy. 'What do you want me to *do*, Sylvia? I'm the only person who can draw out the cash. Why don't you wait for a few days and we'll have a bit of a holiday. I mean, we know there's some cash there. And you're looking washed out – well, no wonder. The police might even find out who's being doing all this while you're away for a few days.'

'Excuse me, Luke.' She got up and opened the door to hear the definitive slam of the heavy front door to the house. She stood, poised, by the door. 'Luke, I do not wish . . . I have not yet thought . . . but I believe I have not understood how much shock I have over Bill's death.'

His shoulders relaxed, and the hands spread expansively. 'Well, of course it was a shock. You didn't get on that badly . . . well, I mean in spite of us.'

'So what I am saying is that I am not wanting yet to decide what is to come. What I must do is put the company in order and get in all the money I can.' She paused. 'John Pope – you know, the company solicitor, he tell me that if you write a letter to the bank in Spain asking them to give the money to the company they will do that, you do not need to be there yourself.'

'When did you ask him?'

'Ask him what? Oh, about the account. When I saw the report.'

'Let me get this right.' He got up and moved towards her. 'You

199

saw the accountants' report yesterday, right? It says there's a bit missing. And you assumed at once that it was me and I'd got it hidden somewhere.'

She shook her head. 'Luke, I assume that it was exactly how you have told me. I was married with Bill, I too have a little account of my own. So I ask John if this is so, how we should make it right.'

He felt himself going scarlet. 'If I signed something like that I'd be letting myself in for a right pile of shit, wouldn't I? I'd be admitting taking money from the company. *As* your solicitor friend well knows. He must think I'm stupid.'

'Luke . . .'

There were tears in the round eyes and he relaxed and reached over to take the uninjured hand. 'Look, Sylvie, stop worrying about it all, eh? We've got the insurance money, the company's solvent, we're OK for ready cash for the first time in bloody years. We'll both go to Majorca and sort things out there, get you away from all this. Yes?' He peered into her face while she took her hand away to find an immaculate, embroidered handkerchief. 'That's better. I'll get us on to the three thirty flight tomorrow. Come on, you need to get out of here – we'll have a drink and some dinner.'

'John?'

'Catherine. Where are you?'

'In a call box, opposite the office in Kensington Church Street. Look, I've just seen Sylvia Price and Luke Fleming leave. She looked awful and worried, and he had a tight hold on her.'

'Mm. What were you doing there, by the way?'

'Having a drink with one of the accountants – you saw the point of the report?'

'Yes. Thanks for that. It must be Fleming who was on the take. I'm seeing him tomorrow.'

'John. What I'm asking you is whether that is soon enough. I'm worried about *her*. She told me in the taxi that she found him – Fleming – frightening.'

'Did she say it was him attacked her?'

'No.' The denial was reluctant, and McLeish sighed inwardly. 'No, she didn't. She said she really didn't know.'

'Cath, I don't think he's going to do anything to her under our very eye. I mean, he must feel he's under a microscope right now. Did he ... did they see you? Where you were, I mean, with your admirer.'

'*She* did. She waved. And he's married, the chap I was having a drink with.'

'She ought to be safe enough.' In the silence that greeted this effort, McLeish remembered the last time he had made that judgement about a woman and her lover, and reminded himself doggedly that Luke Fleming had no record of violence with women or anyone else. 'But Cath, thanks ...' he said, not wanting her to go away, or feel that he was treating her contribution with less than due respect.

'So you want to see if he banks anything in Spain,' she said, thoughtfully. 'Is he due to go there?'

'He's trying to go as soon as possible, he told me. The business needs him there.'

'So you can't afford to stop him.'

'Something like that. Shall I see you tomorrow?'

'Tonight if you're still there in half an hour.'

15

Thursday, 28 April

'Poor sod.'

'Indeed,' McLeish said, sedately, gazing at the *Sun* headlines. 'But he had made promises he was not in a position to keep.'

'So she says,' Davidson agreed. 'Silly bitch to believe him, mind – married blokes don't usually leave their wives whatever they say.'

It had been the broken pledge of cash rather than of marriage that had caused Ms James to seek her thirty pieces of silver from the tabloid press. McLeish had talked again to Miles Arnold late the night before, when they had both seen the morning papers, and got the rest of the story. Ms James, Miles Arnold had said, wearily, had, on the basis of a promised cash subvention from him, entered into a contract to buy a bigger and better flat. When he had been unable to deliver the cash – which he said was in Bill Price's safe – she had refused to believe his explanation, alleging him to be using Price's death as an excuse for reneging on his offer. He had sought delay, but she was under pressure to produce the ten per cent deposit required on exchange of contracts. So she had found the shortest line between two points and taken her photogenic self and her highly saleable story to the best, or worst – depending on where you stood in the story – agent in London. He had sold the package for a rumoured £30,000, a good price but, as Miles Arnold observed, nothing to what could have been achieved if she had waited till he was a minister. McLeish had confined himself to sympathetic noises, but had found himself reflecting that it would take a long time to save £30,000 out of the pay of even a detective chief superintendent. At all events Miles Arnold had gone out in the betting as a suspect. He had needed money urgently, yes, but the prima facie evidence was that Bill Price had intended to give it to him, and had indeed gone to the bank and drawn out £20,000 for that purpose. And further in Arnold's favour, it was clear that if it *had* been he who had robbed the safe he would have given the cash to his mistress; as he said, it would have been well worth £20,000 not to have to have the acutely embarrassing conversation with his constituency chairman which had just taken place. He would be very lucky indeed, he said bitterly, if he kept his place as an MP with that sour-faced old bat in the chair. And, as he did not need to say, his substantial income from various consultancies depended on his still being an MP with access to the seats of power.

'Does all this blow his alibi away?' Davidson asked.

'It was never solid, but it hasn't got any worse. She confirmed that he was with her when he said he was.'

'But you don't fancy him for it?'

'No. Never did.'

'Well, that way we don't have to bother about the politics.'

'The publicity is a nuisance. We'll get a lot of calls.' He stared gloomily at a column headed baldly SEX DEATH LINK which described, inaccurately, the death of Bill Price, and Miles Arnold's relationship with Price Fleming. A photograph of Miles, looking furtive, Ms James, legs showing to knicker-level, and the late Bill Price (taken from the Price Fleming brochure), smiling reassuringly with rather too many teeth, illustrated the page.

The phone interrupted their reading and Bruce Davidson answered it. 'They're both booked on the three thirty, John. What made you ask? They doing a runner?'

'It's a bit easier than that. Mrs Price rang this morning, when I was just in, and said she needed to go to Majorca, was there any objection? If not she was getting the three thirty plane. I rather thought Fleming would be on it too. I have no good cause to keep either of them back and I want to see what they do.' He looked to see if Bruce was going to remind him of what happened the last time he released a suspect he had no good reason to hold, but discipline had prevailed. He decided to explain further. 'They got a writ this morning, or rather the office did. From Miles Arnold's solicitor, asking for his money back, or alternatively seeking that the company be wound up. Catherine says it's what you do when you're *really* desperate as a creditor. I thought it would put a bit of pressure on, so I encouraged Arnold to get on with it.'

Bruce Davidson's expression shifted marginally, and McLeish

spread his hands. 'I know what I *think*, but I can't get anywhere near proving it.'

'Who *do* you fancy?'

The phone rang and McLeish grabbed it. 'Yes, put him on. Matthew. What? I do not believe it. No, no, I don't mean it like that. Bring Francis in. Quick as you like. And his jacket. Don't touch anything else. No, wait, I'll send a car.' He put the phone down and looked across at Davidson. 'I need the original statements made by Fleming, Mrs Price and Antony Price. Quick. You can take the note when Francis gets here.'

Ten minutes later he was clattering downstairs, Bruce Davidson at his heels carrying a pile of files, with a young DC barely able to see over the heap of papers bringing up the rear. 'Give it to me, Matt,' he said, reverently, eyes on the envelope Matthew was carrying.

'I'm afraid I did touch it. I didn't think . . . I was just so pleased with myself. You'll need my prints.' Matthew was trying to maintain his customary cool. Francis Price, pale and anxious, was standing behind his right shoulder, keeping as much of him as possible between him and the policemen.

McLeish slid the plastic-covered packet out of the envelope and peered through the film. 'Get this printed now. Take prints from Mr Sutherland as well.'

The young DC, infected by the general atmosphere of urgency, rushed from the room, carrying the envelope and falling over his feet. Bruce was working down a list, lips moving.

'Here.'

'All right, all right, let's get this done properly. Get the tape on. Mr Price, you sit in the middle, will you? Yes, all right, Matthew, you can stay. Now, Mr Price. How did these notes come into your possession?'

'I was given it, plus about another £400, by Sylvia. My father's wife.'

'Why?'

'I begged them off her, and she's always been quite nice to me, I mean reasonably human. Soft, I suppose. I spent the rest – gave it to a dealer. I didn't know this was here, or I'd have spent it too.'

'When was this? Take your time.'

'A few days after my father's death. The Wednesday. The day I collapsed in the pub and Matthew picked me up.'

'And you are quite sure these notes were given to you by Mrs Price?'

'I am, yes. And I'm sorry not to have told you before. I told Matt when I remembered but I couldn't prove it. Then Matt had an idea and we went through all my clothes.'

McLeish glanced across at Matthew to indicate that he might speak.

'You suggested I try assuming Antony Price was telling the truth. He *said* he didn't give Francis cash when he was on drugs, and Francis himself said the same, but I never believe druggies. So I started again and asked Francis who did, and he managed to remember. *Then* I thought, well ... what if, and we searched everything. I mean, *I* stuff things into pockets and lose them. So we looked. Me, Francis and this mate of mine, so we had a witness.'

McLeish considered the two young men in front of him, wondering if they had grasped all the implications, and saw that Francis Price at least had thought his way through.

'I knew you might think that I'd stolen the money, or that Antony had, and given me some of it. But that isn't what happened.'

McLeish, following a train of thought, did not reply and Matthew sat bolt upright, red hair bristling up. 'I wouldn't have brought him here if I thought that's the way your minds worked.'

'And it wasn't the first time, you see,' Francis Price said earnestly, ignoring Matthew. 'I mean, this is the bit you really aren't going to believe, but I don't care, it happened. It came back to me. She gave me some cash the evening my father was murdered, only I spent that straightaway.'

McLeish saw that Matthew was doubtful about this part of the story. 'What time was this?'

'I'm sorry, I've thought, but I'd been sleeping on and off all day. It had got dark but not for long.'

Bruce Davidson had Sylvia Price's statement out and was flipping through. 'Mrs Price says she left for the country at 4 p.m.'

'Couldn't have been dark,' McLeish said, doubtfully, watching Francis Price.

The young man looked defeated. 'I'm sorry. Perhaps I haven't got it right. But it was dark, I'm sure. I know it was because she's blonde, or rather she isn't but the white bits on top shone in the lights. So the street lights were on.'

Both policemen stared at him, and McLeish found his tongue. 'Where was this exactly? I mean, where were you both?'

'Oh, in Kensington Church Street, near the house. I needed cash, you see, and my father ... well, he sometimes gave me some. To get rid of me.'

'Francis, are you *sure*?' Matthew Sutherland said.

'Shut *up*,' Davidson and McLeish said as one man.

Matthew Sutherland, blushing scarlet to his hair-line, made himself as small as he could the other side of the table and McLeish returned to Francis Price.

'I told you I was in the street, I think,' he protested.

'Ye did.' Bruce Davidson had found the relevant bit of the statement. 'But ye didna tell us ye'd met Mrs Price.'

'I forgot. Drugs do that, but when Matt and I were talking about it last night, I remembered. She'd given me cash before. It all came back.'

McLeish looked at the young, pale face. 'And the other day? Just recently, someone gave you cash, didn't they?'

'Oh, that *was* Antony.' The young man frowned. 'Yes, I see what you mean, he never used to give me any cash. I suppose he thought I was all right, you know, cured.' He looked at their expressions. 'Anyway, it was only £100, you can't buy enough to kill yourself with that, and Antony wouldn't want to kill me.'

McLeish, Davidson and Matthew Sutherland, who all thought this confidence misplaced, looked woodenly back, but it was Matthew who spoke.

'I guess, that time, he just wanted Francis out of the way. He was desperate to catch Annabelle. Didn't care what Francis did with the cash, provided he buggered off.'

McLeish decided he badly needed to confer, called for coffee, and took Davidson out of the room with him.

'John, if Francis took the cash out of the safe himself, this is a bloody good cover story.'

'Only one way to find out. Let's just hope there's some of that cash left. Put those two lads somewhere quiet, give them a good book each, whatever ... I have to see the AC.'

*

Twelve members of the team was probably overkill, McLeish thought, as he looked out over the two long lines of passengers, waiting to get through Passport Control. He was in one of the small first-floor rooms overlooking the area, and they had the door open not just for air but so that the party could get out and down the stairs and into the security area to join the two members of the team already there as soon as Sylvia Price and Luke Fleming came through. He looked to the left; the Home Office had left nothing to chance, or perhaps the senior man had made the same decision he had and was sharing the excitement around his team. A second man in a suit had been posted at the right-hand side of both the usual executive officers on checking-duty, to watch the faces. He saw Luke Fleming's black hair. He was looking ruffled, encumbered by three small flight bags. Sylvia Price was just behind him, looking tired and pale and anxious, her right arm in a sling, her left holding a large handbag. The buzzer went off at the same time, triggering a stampede, and McLeish and Davidson followed sedately on the heels of the team. They marched towards the group which looked, McLeish thought, like a tableau vivant portraying 'Misunderstanding at an Airport'. Sylvia Price and Luke Fleming had been moved out of the line and were both protesting; Fleming, red with exasperation, towering over Sylvia Price, who was dabbing at her eyes, complaining in the high clear accented voice. They both saw McLeish at the same time; Fleming started towards him, hands moving, but Sylvia Price stood absolutely still. Then her eyes rolled up and she fell sideways on to the WPC standing beside her, who only just managed to support her before she hit the floor.

Fleming exclaimed and turned to help and remonstrate, and both lines of entering passengers spread untidily sideways as people, jerked out of their trance, stopped to stare, dropping bags and documents as they peered over for a closer look. McLeish went to help the young WPC with Sylvia Price while Davidson, cursing in best Glasgow, got the rest of the group into one of the interview rooms hidden by an unmarked door, barely visible in the smooth yellow-grey walls. Davidson came back to help but McLeish had scooped Sylvia Price bodily from the floor; much smaller than either Francesca or Catherine, she was nonetheless surprisingly heavy; a plumper body than she had appeared, and, to his momentary amusement, much more armoured and corseted than the women he was used to. Her eyes were rolling and she was fighting back to consciousness, so he lowered her carefully into the chair produced by several sets of willing hands and stationed the two WPCs to prevent her falling out again, while Davidson shouted crossly at a BAA uniform to produce a glass of water. The room, though containing only two chairs and a trestle table, was markedly overcrowded with eight people.

'What the hell is this?' Luke Fleming was scarlet with rage. 'You told Sylvia yesterday we could go. What the fuck are you playing at? We'll miss the plane.'

McLeish was looking at the neat line-up on the table. Three flight bags and Sylvia Price's handbag. 'Do sit down, Mr Fleming. I have a search warrant and I intend to search these bags. And your hold baggage.' He nodded to the young man who had put his head doubtfully into the room; he withdrew and appeared with two suitcases.

Luke Fleming gaped at him. 'You got our bags taken off the plane? Where've you been the last ten years? You can't do a runner to Spain. And we've got a business there.'

'Which are your bags, Mr Fleming?'

'Oh *Christ*. The next flight is two hours on and it's Iberia. Well, I wish you joy of them.' He indicated one suitcase and two of the flight bags, and turned to talk to Sylvia Price, white-faced but sitting up and sipping at a glass of water.

'We'd like you to come to the table, please.' Luke Fleming stared at him, fists clenched, but John McLeish was gazing reflectively at the nearest wall and Davidson contemplating the table while the rest of the team stared at their boots.

Fleming opened his mouth to discharge rage, and McLeish turned to look at him in polite, bored enquiry. Luke Fleming met his eye and thought better of whatever he had been going to do, or say. He stood back on his heels, a big man in the small, crowded room, and visibly thought about where he was and what was happening. He looked sidelong at Sylvia Price, but she was staring stonily ahead, the glass of water clutched in her uninjured left hand.

'Right,' he said, on an indrawn breath, and walked over to the table. 'None of them are locked.' He stood stolidly while two detectives neatly unpacked his expensive case, quick hands moving carefully over all the pockets, patting the lid. 'What are you looking for? I don't do or carry drugs.'

No one replied but they put the suitcase aside and proceeded to open the small flight bag, sorting carefully through the pile of papers. The searchers handed McLeish wordlessly a bulging unmarked envelope, and he weighed it in his hand, raising his eyebrows at Fleming.

'Cash. Open it, do, don't mind me. It's not illegal, is it, taking cash out?'

McLeish pulled on plastic gloves and opened the envelope, glancing at the serial numbers with Davidson, also gloved, craning at his shoulder.

'Got it out of the bank this morning,' Fleming volunteered. A small movement behind him caught his attention and they watched as he slowly reddened. 'There's ten thou there – I thought we'd need some cash.' He turned towards Sylvia Price who was sitting up straight, colour in her cheeks. 'You weren't up to it, Sylvie, so I got it out for us.'

'I have not signed a cheque.'

'No, well ... the bank let me have it. I explained about your hand.'

There was a quiet knock on the door and a BAA man put his head round, eyes wide with interest, and waved an envelope at the room generally. Davidson took it, motioned the man out, read it and passed it to McLeish; it was from Catherine Crane to tell them that Fleming Price's bank manager, who had cashed a cheque two hours before for £10,000, had had another look at the second signature and had got cold feet, deciding that it could not be Sylvia Price's signature, even with a broken arm.

'Thank you, Mr Fleming,' he said, neutrally, folding the note away.

'Mrs Price, do you feel able to come to the table?'

Sylvia Price indicated that she could make the effort and was assisted to the table and the chair replaced for her while the process was repeated. McLeish watched impassively; she was carrying several credit cards and a little cash, but nothing else of any interest, except a lot of embroidered silk underwear, substantial enough but nothing that suggested any real support. Mrs Price watched, equally impassively, and turned and said something confidential to one of the WPCs.

'Sir?' The girl appeared by McLeish and he tried to relax. 'Mrs Price says she must go to the toilet.'

'Yes, OK. Go with her,' he said impatiently, grimly staring at the pile of clothes being packed back into the suitcase. 'No,' he said, 'wait.' The WPC turned enquiringly, her arm tucked for support under Sylvia Price's. He took a deep breath and strode over to them. 'You may of course visit a lavatory but the WPC will have to accompany you into the cubicle. Unless you can wait until after you have been searched.'

It was right, he wasn't out of his mind, she knew what he was talking about, he saw, as the colour flooded up under the skin and she started to breathe very fast, and turn up her eyes. 'Stop that,' he snapped, holding her shoulders, and her eyes flew open in surprise, like an animal, like a cat.

'Sylvia! What's happening? What are you doing to her?' Luke Fleming came up at his side, ready to be angry all over again, but she gave him a look of rage which stopped him in his tracks. She shrugged off McLeish's hands and went out of the door with both WPCs in attendance, and Bruce Davidson right behind them. Detective Sergeant Black, the senior of the two, was experienced but Jenny Martin was frightened and unsteady.

'What are you looking for, for God's sake?' It was Fleming, who had sat down on the edge of the table, looking older and heavier. 'You can search *me*,' he volunteered, with a flicker of bravado, rapidly extinguished by McLeish, who warned him that he could be charged with uttering a false document assuming that Mrs Price would maintain her statement that she had not signed the cheque.

'Sir.' It was Davidson. 'In her stays, £50 notes.'

'What about the numbers?'

'They're right. They check. About £800 light and the one we've got already is in the sequence. Congratulations.'

'Thanks, Bruce. Bring her back in a couple of minutes, will you?'

'But what has she done? What have you found?' It was Fleming, suddenly very white. He stared at McLeish then sank into a chair. 'You've found the *cash. Christ*. She killed him. I didn't know, I didn't know, she didn't tell me.'

McLeish charged him, formally, with uttering a forged document and as an accessory after the fact of William Price's murder, and sent him, shaking with shock and protesting, off in a police car with Roberts and two of the squad. He went through to where Sylvia Price was sitting between the two WPCs, attended now by Davidson as well, and charged her with murder. The brown eyes had no light in them, he realised as he recited the familiar lengthy words of caution, and the rest of the face was expressionless. She spoke only to demand her solicitor, and McLeish put her into another car with a telephone. He went back with the remaining three of the team, too much in awe of him to rejoice aloud, but very pleased with themselves, and he was in his office working through the formalities of consigning Sylvia Price to a police cell when Peter Graebner arrived. McLeish took him to the interview room where his client was sitting and offered him coffee and, as he turned from concluding these civilities, saw Davidson and Jenny, all but jumping up and down with excitement, give him the thumbs-up sign.

'Tell me.'

'The prints match. The notes were given out by the bank on the cheque Mr Price wrote. Mr Price's prints are on the bands or somewhere on nine of the bundles. Mrs Price's are on three or four of the notes on the eighth and on the band.' Davidson had decently let Jenny give him the news. 'She must have opened up one to use for expenses, like giving Francis Price cash.'

'And Fleming's?'

'On none of them. You didn't think he'd done it, did you, John?'

'No. I thought, and I think now, it was she alone.'

'We can check any shop she might have been in.'

'No, anything like that will be lost in the system by now. We were just incredibly lucky that Francis Price had a hole in the inner pocket of his jacket.'

'Weren't we just,' Davidson said, soberly. He hesitated.

'Spit it out, Bruce.'

'If she's the sense to confess to taking the cash but not touching Mr Price, we've got a problem.'

'Oh, she'll plead that more than likely. Peter Graebner will point her that way.' He looked down at Jenny, who was looking appalled. 'I told the AC that this morning. It'll depend a good deal on how Francis copes in the box. His is the only evidence that places her on the spot at the right time. And he was a druggie then and may be again.'

'Can't we find something else?' It was Jenny, and both men regarded her kindly.

'Oh, we'll try. That's the next two weeks' work,' McLeish said. 'Save it for the meeting.'

They had the team assembled within thirty seconds of their arrival on the fourth floor, and McLeish explained where they had got to. 'Now starts the leg work,' he advised. 'She left the office at four o'clock and she went to Bosham; we know that, she was placed there by the garage at 6.45 p.m. But she came back.'

'She used her own key to get into the house?' Roberts suggested.

'I think not through the front door. Lots of people in the street who might have seen her. She knew her husband, she knew how he was likely to entertain himself with her gone and nothing else to do but worry about the company. So she waited somewhere until he drew the curtains in the basement. Then she watched, or counted to twenty, or something, till he was well away, let herself in via the garden door, wearing gloves, pulled the table away from under him, went upstairs and emptied the safe, and went out again through the garden door.'

'At what time, sir?'

'Just before Francis Price met her, whenever that was. About nine thirty, I think. It would have been dark for half an hour or so. And Antony Price, next morning, thought his father had been dead for twelve hours.' He looked round his team: their expressions ranged from openly sceptical to downcast and unhappy.

'We know she was there, but I'd be glad to have more proof,' he said. 'Once she'd got to Spain, we'd never have seen the cash again. So we had to take her and we'll just have to find another way of placing her at the scene. We're starting now from knowing she was there.'

'But someone attacked her two days ago,' Roberts protested.

'I don't think so, and I didn't at the time. She did it herself.' He did not look at Bruce Davidson but saw him nod in acknowledgement. 'It was too pat; she said she didn't know who had attacked her, but she had Antony Price, known to be violent, on the spot, she knew Miles Arnold had flung out, and she knew that Fleming would be in his flat by himself. Good way of deflecting attention on to the three men in her immediate circle. And rather bad luck on her that Miles Arnold – who had every cause to wish her ill – was drinking with the Private Secretary to the Chief Whip at the time.'

'So what happened?'

'She took out the light bulb and threw herself down the stairs. Took resolution but she's not short of that. We'll never prove it, of course, and it's just another loose end for the defence to make hay with, as it were. I'm going to wait for Mrs P's solicitor, but the rest of you need to start the hard graft. We need to place that car in the area on Friday night.'

Epilogue

Tuesday, 3 May

'Catherine. Come in. How are you?'

'Frustrated.'

'I *am* sorry to hear that.' McLeish smiled at her; she had been avoiding him and he had not known how to ease the situation without putting himself in a false position.

'All I've got, after a lot of work, is Luke Fleming pleading guilty to attempted fraudulent conversion of the £10,000 he tried to take to Majorca. The £20,000 odd he took out in Spain he paid back, explaining it was in another company account all the time. We *could* have done something there, except it all happened in Majorca and it had come back. It just wasn't worth the bother, not now the company is being sold. But how are you doing, John?'

He passed her the coffee his secretary had just brought in. 'You've not heard?' She blushed, and he grinned. 'Nice to see you anyway. Well, we placed the car here for Friday night. We must have had every copper in West London on house-to-house, but we got lucky. She'd left it so a woman in Portland Road – you know it? – had a struggle getting into her patch of off-street parking, and noted the number in order to ring up if the car was still there in the morning.'

'Not quite enough.'

'Enough to get her to change her story. We'd caught her with the cash and even if her brief had managed to rubbish Francis Price as a witness, we'd placed the car exactly where it shouldn't have been. So she's saying now she came back from Bosham, having forgotten something, walked in on a dead husband, hanging from the ceiling, realised someone had moved the table and rushed out again, panicked.'

'Pausing only to take the cash from the safe.'

'A weak point, thank God.'

213

'Will it play?' Catherine asked, carefully.

'The CPS are still thinking about it. There are two other possible suspects which the defence can play with unfortunately, particularly if they don't put her in the box. I've got people trying to place Fleming in Barnsley to get *him* out of the way. The defence can muddy the waters by suggesting either Francis or Luke Fleming did it. The AC thinks Fleming must have been in it, but Mrs Price isn't saying if he was. My own feeling is that he wasn't, and that he is truly staggered by the whole thing.'

'He'd been thinking of her as a little woman.'

'Yes. As it turns out she had all her buttons on, kept clear of the business and did her old man in when it looked as if he was going to get both of them into trouble.'

'Was she going to marry Fleming?' Catherine asked. 'I mean, before.'

'Not sure. If it looked like the best way of having a comfortable life, well then, yes. But she might have decided against him when she found he was on the take.'

'Or done him in too.'

'Yes,' McLeish agreed, thoughtfully. 'And done it somewhere outside the jurisdiction so she didn't meet us again.'

They considered the prospect in silence and McLeish collected himself. 'My best bet is that the CPS will agree to go ahead, but who knows?'

'You seem fairly relaxed about it.'

'No, I'm not, but I've three active cases ... well, two. We've got a result in Neasden and it's the eighty per cent rule, isn't it? Put the effort where you can get a result.' He studied her. She was drinking coffee, calmly, showing no signs of getting up to leave. 'Cath?'

'Yes?'

'I hear that Dave is going to come up in court after all.'

'He's decided he's recovered and he's pleading guilty to assault. He realised he could be in a bin for ever if he just went on having a breakdown.'

'You're over him?'

'Yes. Yes, I didn't know I was, but I am. I have to appear of course, and go through the story, and it'll be all over the Met again, but that'll be it finished.'

'So you'll go on here?'

'Yes. Fraud's my bag, I've found what I want to do.' She considered him under her eyelashes. 'What about you?'

'I'm here for two or three years.' He hesitated. 'Cath . . .'

'Don't say it, John. I need to find a bloke of my own. And not a policeman for preference.' She looked into his face. 'Or isn't that what you were going to say?'

'It's what I ought to have been going to say.'

She looked away finally. 'I need to get back.' She put her cup down and waited as he struggled to his feet, banging a knee on the coffee table, then stretched up and kissed him lightly on the cheek and was gone, leaving the smell of primroses behind her.

Francesca hesitated at the ward door, taking in the group on the balcony. It was a cold spring day and Annabelle Brewster, her face very pale, was sitting in a chair wrapped in a blanket. Matthew was sitting on the balcony rail, perilously close to overbalancing, looking like a bird of prey in his long black coat, and Francis Price was also present, shivering in a denim jacket. She took a deep breath and sneezed as she inhaled the scent of the bunch of daffodils she was clutching.

'Bless you.' Matthew had slid off the balcony and was coming towards her to kiss her and she sneezed against his shoulder.

'Sorry about that,' she said, disengaging herself, and presented the daffodils to Annabelle. 'How are you?' she asked, and wished she hadn't, as tears came to Annabelle's eyes.

'A lot better. I feel feeble sitting here.'

'You just bloody stay there until you're right,' Matt said, brusquely. 'Everything's under control.'

Francesca considered him. She had only spoken to him on the phone once in the last week, and she was both delighted to see him and apprehensive. She knew from John that Peter Graebner, acting for Sylvia Price, and his lawyer friend, acting for Francis, and Antony's solicitor had jointly applied to the court to appoint an administrator to Bill Price's estate. Matt had rung her up between meetings and had observed that there was a marked shortage of suitable executors in the late Bill Price's immediate circle: his widow was on bail, charged with his murder, his partner was on bail, charged with theft from the company, his eldest son was in custody, charged with attempting to murder Annabelle, and his second son, even if currently reformed, had two recent convictions for drug abuse. Bit like the last act of *Macbeth* or *Titus Andronicus*, she had suggested, and as if all that were not difficult enough, no one of the survivors was prepared to agree that any other should be appointed. It made you understand, they had agreed, what the law and the whole system for administering it was *for*, to cut through these Gordian entanglements. And no sooner had the administrator – a partner in a firm of accountants – been appointed, than he had received an offer for the business which, while not generous, was good enough, and it seemed likely that all parties would manage to agree to accept. The only point of debate was whether a much chastened Luke Fleming would succeed in getting himself taken on by the new owners, on the basis that, provided they never let him sign a cheque, he did at least know where all the buildings, the bank accounts, and people were. The administrator had also let it be known that he was not going to attempt to defend claims from Antony and Francis Price for the return of trust funds invested in the company in defiance of the Trustee Investments Act, or from Miles Arnold for monies wrongly diverted. So, as Matt had observed, Francis would have enough to buy a flat, Miles Arnold could finance a new career if his constituency association could offer no more than the very lukewarm support they had managed so far, and Antony Price could pay his own legal fees.

She understood, as the atmosphere of the room settled, that she had interrupted an argument, and looked enquiringly at Matt. He looked back, in a moment of swift and complete communication.

'Antony Price's brief is negotiating for a charge of assault rather than attempted murder.'

'Mm,' she said, glancing at Annabelle's white, miserable face. 'And what do we think the truth is?'

The other three gazed at her.

'Always a good place to start,' she pointed out.

'Yes,' Matt said appreciatively. 'Well, I *know* that I had to hit him over the head to get his fingers off her neck – I couldn't get him away. No, for fuck's sake, Anna, shut up.'

'She's not interrupting you, only weeping, you thug,' Francesca protested.

'Well, she can stop doing that and all,' he said furiously. 'Personally and professionally I object. There's no way I'm going to lie in court.'

'Matt,' Annabelle had managed to get her voice under control,

216

'I don't want him – well, destroyed. In jail for years. How do you think I'm going to feel?'

'How do you think the next girl he takes up with is going to feel? Or are you planning to go back to him?' He stared at her furiously, and Francesca, watching, felt a swift cold pang of misery, succeeded, disconcertingly, by relief.

'Irrespective of Annabelle's future plans, this is an ethical problem,' she pointed out to the combatants. 'And the answer to it is well established. *Fiat justitia, ruat caelum.* Though the heavens fall, let justice be done. No other way of running society.'

'I think that's what I was trying to say, Wonderwoman,' Matt said, straightening up and patting her shoulder as he returned to his seat on the balcony railings. 'Sorry, guys,' he said to the other two. 'I'm sorry if I can't persuade you, but I can do no other.'

'I don't want him in the nick either,' Francis said. 'He's my brother. He's always been decent to me. He needs treatment and support, like I've had. I mean, he was under strain.'

'That he can plead in mitigation,' Francesca pointed out, to stop Matt reminding the group that on that basis the strain would have had to have been endured for at least six years, given Antony's history of beating up his women. Apart from her own need to be alone with Matt, the group should be prevented from continuing this discussion further today. 'You're looking worn out, Annabelle, I only came by for a minute. You need to get some rest if you're going to see Great Ormond Street next week. Are you sure about that?'

'Oh yes.' Her face gained colour. 'Not about much else, but that, yes, I must.'

Francesca bent to kiss her and looked to Matt.

'I'll see you to your car. Wait for me here, Francis, will you?'

They marched silently to the car-park and she thought for a moment they were not going to be able to speak in anything but commonplaces. She willed herself to silence and they stood and looked at each other.

'You've got your hands full,' she heard herself say suddenly. 'What with Annabelle and Francis.'

He went on looking at her carefully. 'You wishing we hadn't done that?'

She felt herself blush scarlet. 'No. Yes. I'm no good at all at the casual affair, and I should know that by now. I'm happily married too, dammit, most of the time, and I shouldn't be risking that. But I don't want to lose you.'

'Don't agonise, Wonderwoman. I'm not sorry we did, but I agree, we'd better stop. I don't want to lose you either, not for ever.'

'No,' she said, in a flash of revelation. 'We may have had it as lovers but I can see us now, me as a Senior Administrator and you as London's toughest criminal solicitor, probably on a committee together.'

He put his arms round her and held her to him, and she patted his shoulder.

'I must go.'

'Drive carefully.' He shut the car door for her and when she looked in the rear mirror she could see him waving, the black coat flying in the wind, and she wept.

Wednesday, 4 May

'John?'

McLeish opened his eyes cautiously to see his wife, with William perched on her hip.

'Don't carry him,' he said automatically. 'He can walk. Can't you, Will?'

'No,' his son said, firmly, and flung both arms round Francesca's neck. She subsided on to the bed, holding him.

'It's eight thirty and I thought I'd better get you up. I've fended off Bruce, a chap called Roberts, and just now the Commander. I said you were in the loo. Here, as a treat, is the *Mail*. We went down the road in our pyjamas, didn't we, Will?'

'When did he wake?' McLeish asked, struggling to sit.

'Seven o'clock, the good boy. I feel like a new woman.'

Will crawled out of her arms, placing himself firmly on his father's chest between him and the newspaper. McLeish rested his chin on Will's head and spread the paper out at the full stretch of his arms. A picture of Luke Fleming greeted him and he read with interest an interview with the erstwhile Mrs Fleming. 'Kicking the poor bloke when he's down.'

'He's not a poor bloke, he'd been trying not to pay any more maintenance. Matt Sutherland told me; one of his chums acts for the wife.'

218

McLeish considered his wife; something – perhaps a decent night's sleep – had cheered her, and he decided to tackle his worries directly. 'Have you and Matthew finished that essay for the Refuge?'

'I was never really doing it, just being Admiring Audience. He's finished it.'

'Good. Are you ... do you feel you have to go on doing things for the Refuge? I know you miss your brothers very much and you're fond of Matthew, but it tires you.'

She gazed out of the window, colour coming up in her cheeks. 'I don't need Matt as a substitute for the boys, no, if that's what you're saying. And he's got Annabelle to look after. What we need, I decided yesterday, is a little treat.'

She was heavy in his arms, but not relaxed, and he felt her draw breath carefully. 'The thing *is*, you see, I wondered about the weekend after next. We leave Will with Susannah and fly to Budapest.'

'Budapest?'

'Tristram's lot are touring *Tosca*, you see, and ...'

'Let me guess. Perry is coming over too, since it's Tristram's first lead part. And Charlie? And Jeremy?'

'No,' she said, pink, but resolute. 'Just Perry and Mum.'

He wrapped his arms round her to protests from William, who had been peacefully engaged in picking a hole in the duvet. 'Of course we can. And I'll try and cut down the hours a bit. I'm getting the job under control.'

She kissed him and they lay together against the pillows, watching their son until the telephone rang again.

READ MORE IN PENGUIN

In every corner of the world, on every subject under the sun, Penguin represents quality and variety – the very best in publishing today.

For complete information about books available from Penguin – including Puffins, Penguin Classics and Arkana – and how to order them, write to us at the appropriate address below. Please note that for copyright reasons the selection of books varies from country to country.

In the United Kingdom: Please write to *Dept. EP, Penguin Books Ltd, Bath Road, Harmondsworth, West Drayton, Middlesex UB7 0DA*

In the United States: Please write to *Consumer Sales, Penguin USA, P.O. Box 999, Dept. 17109, Bergenfield, New Jersey 07621-0120*. VISA and MasterCard holders call 1-800-253-6476 to order Penguin titles

In Canada: Please write to *Penguin Books Canada Ltd, 10 Alcorn Avenue, Suite 300, Toronto, Ontario M4V 3B2*

In Australia: Please write to *Penguin Books Australia Ltd, P.O. Box 257, Ringwood, Victoria 3134*

In New Zealand: Please write to *Penguin Books (NZ) Ltd, Private Bag 102902, North Shore Mail Centre, Auckland 10*

In India: Please write to *Penguin Books India Pvt Ltd, 706 Eros Apartments, 56 Nehru Place, New Delhi 110 019*

In the Netherlands: Please write to *Penguin Books Netherlands bv, Postbus 3507, NL-1001 AH Amsterdam*

In Germany: Please write to *Penguin Books Deutschland GmbH, Metzlerstrasse 26, 60594 Frankfurt am Main*

In Spain: Please write to *Penguin Books S. A., Bravo Murillo 19, 1° B, 28015 Madrid*

In Italy: Please write to *Penguin Italia s.r.l., Via Felice Casati 20, I–20124 Milano*

In France: Please write to *Penguin France S. A., 17 rue Lejeune, F–31000 Toulouse*

In Japan: Please write to *Penguin Books Japan, Ishikiribashi Building, 2–5–4, Suido, Bunkyo-ku, Tokyo 112*

In South Africa: Please write to *Longman Penguin Southern Africa (Pty) Ltd, Private Bag X08, Bertsham 2013*

BY THE SAME AUTHOR

Death's Bright Angel
Winner of the 1988 John Creasey Award for the Best First Crime Novel

At Britex Fabrics, Francesca Wilson's economic investigation and John McLeish's murder inquiry are getting inextricably confused – with an American senator, a pop star and the Bach Choir as well as each other.

'Sharp, intelligent and amusing' – *Independent*

'An excellent first book' – *Daily Telegraph*

'A rattling good read-on-the-beach yarn' – *The Times*

Death On Site

Why does experienced climber Alan Fraser – mountaineer and scaffolder – fall from the Highland rock face?

Chief Inspector John McLeish, on holiday with high-flying Francesca Wilson, sees the near-fatal accident. Gathered in the same village are many of the powerful Vernon family, who employ Fraser and his partner on their vast building sites. When the group return to work in London, suppressed emotions explode and there is another fall. But this time it is definitely murder . . .

'Janet Neel writes with sprightly humour, a genuine talent to bemuse, and a forthright heroine in Francesca' – *Sunday Times*

'A worthy successor to this author's prize-winning first novel' – *Mail on Sunday*

'Janet Neel brings the rivalries and suspicions to a nice bubbling head' – *Observer*

BY THE SAME AUTHOR

Death of a Partner

His relationship with wilful Francesca on the rocks, a harassed Detective Chief Inspector John McLeish is assigned to the case of missing Angela Morgan.

An attractive, wealthy lobbyist, and fiancée to a high-ranking government minister, Angela courted success – and the envy of her detractors. When her badly decomposed body is found a week later, the shock waves ripple through Whitehall, and only the murderer knows why.

Temporarily distracted by Sergeant Catherine Crane, the newest addition to the team and a stunning blonde who adds her own delicate touch to the case, McLeish gradually uncovers a labyrinthian network of lies, jealousy, fraud and revenge . . .

'A gripping novel of Whitehall intrigue' – *Daily Express*

'Neel's insider feel for the subtle undercurrents of Whitehall and the boardroom combines with precise plotting and believable characters . . . a winner' – *The Times*

'She writes with admirable crispness . . . top marks' – *Sunday Times*

Death among the Dons

When the Warden of Gladstone College dies of a lethal combination of pills and booze a mystery remains – was it accidental death or suicide?

As new Warden, Civil Service grandee Dame Sarah Murchieson soon understands the pressures that drove her predecessor over the brink; the college finances are in chaos, a long-running internal battle over Gladstone's future still rages and the sexual meanderings of a charismatic Fellow are causing a stir. Even with allies like the redoubtable Francesca Wilson, seconded from the DTI, and her husband Superintendent John McLeish, setting the college back on its feet is a formidable challenge.

'Janet Neel sets her nerve-tingling plot in a wonderfully alive and intelligent collegiate milieu' – *Sunday Times*